THROUGH THE CLOUDS

by Erin Aslin

ISBN 978-0-9890097-1-3

Acknowledgements

Thanks go first to my son, Jerry Galinsky, for his never-ending support and input, and all his help with the storyline. This book would not have happened without him.

To my daughter-in-law, Virginia Galinsky, for her undying enthusiasm for editing.

To the early reader, my longtime friend, Joan Gehron, for the tireless reads and her support of a new novelist.

To Kathleen A. Fleming, another writer, for her input and inspiration.

To Dana Lang, my New York friend, for believing in my novel.

To the memory of my dearest dog Chicka, who has always been there for me with support and comfort.

"Be like the bird that, passing on her flight awhile on boughs too slight, feels them give way beneath her, and yet sings, knowing that she hath wings."

-Victor Hugo-

Part One

CHAPTER ONE

The plane glided through silvery clouds, offering its passengers a glimpse here and there of the patchwork landscape below. Divided by tiny threads of roads and serpentine rivers, the flat rectangles of cities, small towns and fields crawled by despite the plane's high speed.

Lisa Trubin's twelve-year-old son, Irving, focused on the view. It was his first flight, and he was amazed by the entire experience. The panorama that sprawled beneath him captured his whole attention, and it seemed that nothing could distract him. Lisa smiled and stroked his soft hair. Then she plugged her earphones into the outlet and lay back in her seat. The plane's engines droned, lulling her into a dreamlike state. She reclined her seat farther back and closed her eyes. Soft music filled her ears, and she didn't notice when she began to envision scenes from her life.

When did it all start? The darkness, the infinite stress, and the pain? Had it started when she met him, her only love, hope, and dream? How could that be? Everything she had with him promised her a great future...

***

Sunlight had filled the apartment with light, washing over the fresh flowers in vases at the windows. The flowers had looked beautiful and alive, nourishing the living room. Beyond the windows, the trees were showing off their colorful late-September leaves, tossing in a playful breeze. Fluffy light clouds hovered over the landscape in a blue, almost transparent sky. It was 75 degrees—perfect weather in every way for Chicago. Lisa thought it would be a sin to stay inside on a beautiful Saturday afternoon like this.

The phone rang. Her friend Sonya sounded excited. "Isn't it a great day? I'm having a picnic for a few friends today. Can you come?"

"Of course I'll come!" Lisa said. "I'd be thrilled to." Her seven-year-old son, Irving, was spending the night at a friend's house, and being home alone, especially on such a beautiful day, didn't appeal to Lisa.

"When, where, and what should I bring?" she asked happily.

Sonya laughed. "Just bring yourself. We'll pick you up in an hour, and I have a surprise for you," she added in a mysterious voice.

"What's the surprise?" Lisa asked, intrigued. "What are you talking about?"

Sonya laughed again. "Don't even ask. It's a secret. Bye now, and see you soon."

An hour later, a white SUV pulled up in front of Lisa's building. The horn blew. Lisa grabbed her linen purse—a Liz Claiborne that she had packed earlier with a small blanket and a makeup kit containing lipstick and a mirrored compact—and ran downstairs. Within seconds she was outside, looking at the faces of the people in the SUV who waved to her through the open windows.

"Come on in," Sonya invited.

Lisa got into the SUV and sat next to Sonya. There were ten people inside, most of whom Lisa had met before.

"Okay," Sonya said loudly, "I think everybody knows everybody, but if you see any unfamiliar faces, please raise your hand." One hand at the back of the van went up. A tall man in his late thirties, wearing designer glasses, asked with a smile, "Who's this pretty lady you've been hiding from me, Sonya?"

"That's my little surprise," Sonya whispered in Lisa's ear before she said, "Mark, meet Lisa. Lisa, this is Mark."

Lisa couldn't say a word. She couldn't explain what was happening. It was as though a bolt of lightning had shot through her, taking her breath away. She managed to smile back at Mark and murmur something indistinct. He kept looking at her. He was poised and confident. Waves of attraction washed over her. A miracle was taking place. It was something that couldn't be explained rationally. She had never experienced this before. It was as if an unspoken message had passed into her subconscious, giving her understanding. Lisa couldn't see straight. She knew in her heart that he was the ONE. He was the man she was meant to be with. She also knew that the feeling was mutual. That was how she met Mark Wally and how her new life began...

"Mom, Mom, are you sleeping?" Irving tugged at her shoulders. "Look, we're inside the clouds."

Bending into Irving's seat, Lisa peered out the window. Their big plane was suspended in a milky-white powder puff.

"Are we stuck, Mom?"

The plane's engines were working with all of their might, pulling them above the clouds.

"Don't worry, Irving," Lisa said softly. "We'll make it out. See how strong the plane is!"

True to her word, the plane carried them out into the bright sunlight and blue sky, leaving the clouds far behind.

"It's awesome," Irving exclaimed, pressing his nose against the window again.

Lisa smiled at him. She thought again, as she had so often, how blessed she was to have this boy as her son. He was her own blood, a part of her soul. He was the only one in the world who gave her a reason to live, to struggle, and to win.

Lisa lay back in her seat and closed her eyes, drifting deeper into her memories again. She envisioned the events that happened after her meeting with Mark.

***

He called her the next morning. He sounded a little nervous and less confident.

"Do you mind having dinner tonight?" he asked with barely disguised hope. His voice was deep and soft at the same time.

"Yes, I'd like to," Lisa replied. "Just let me see if I can find a baby-sitter on such short notice."

"Yes, of course," Mark said promptly. "Would it be all right if I call you back later?"

"Sure, you can call me around three. I'll know for sure by then." Lisa hung up the phone and smiled. He'd called her! She knew he would!

She dashed to the kitchen, pulled her address book from a cabinet and opened the page that had the babysitter's phone number. She was an older woman who occasionally helped Lisa by watching Irving. *Oh, please God, let Mary not have any plans for tonight!* Lisa prayed as she picked up the phone and dialed. Her prayer was answered—Mary was home and was happy to babysit Irving. Lisa was very excited. Everything was just going perfectly for her. Mark called five minutes past three and they set a time for the date.

At seven o'clock, he was standing at the corner across from Lisa's apartment with a big bouquet of white and red roses. Lisa looked at him as she approached from behind. Mark had broad, strong shoulders, which she hadn't noticed yesterday. He looked very elegant in his midnight blue suit. He was carefully holding the flowers out in front of him. There was something in his pose; something in the way he held those flowers, that mesmerized Lisa for a moment. She felt an indefinable closeness to him, as if she hadn't just met him yesterday but had known him all her life. Lisa's heart started to beat a bit faster, and she stopped walking for a moment to allow it to slow down. Suddenly, Mark turned around and saw her. He smiled.

"Hi, Lisa. I'm so glad you could make it." He held the flowers out to her. "These are for you."

The flowers were fresh, vibrant and beautiful. There was no doubt that he hadn't simply bought them at the grocery store but had carefully chosen them one by one, at a flower shop. It was very sweet of him.

3

They spent a lovely time at a fabulous restaurant that evening. Lisa remembered that night now as if it were yesterday. They left the car with valet parking, and Mark opened the heavy glass door into the lobby. The classic, old-fashioned style of the restaurant pleasantly surprised Lisa. There was an antique cherry wood desk in the right-hand corner, a large crystal chandelier overhead and red linen curtains on the windows, all creating a fashionable atmosphere. The gray-haired host welcomed them and escorted them to their table through the main hallway, which was covered in a handmade brown carpet. Their table was in a cozy corner across from a pianist who was playing a light, romantic piece. The ceiling lights were dimmed. Two gorgeous candles in crystal candelabras glimmered on the table, casting merry shadows.

"Do you mind if I smoke?" Mark asked, putting his cigarette pack on the table.

"No, I don't mind," Lisa said, smiling. "I smoke sometimes."

A tall, shorthaired waiter with a thin, curly tipped mustache appeared to take their order. Mark suggested that Lisa try the White Zinfandel with fried calamari for an appetizer and filet mignon for the entree. Then he chose Merlot and Absolute steak for himself. While their dishes were being prepared, they drank wine and listened to the soft music. Mark gazed passionately at Lisa through his designer glasses as he smoked. There was something very sexy about him—the way he looked at her, the way he held his cigarette.

"How about dancing?" he asked, putting his cigarette down.

Lisa smiled at him and didn't have a chance to answer. Mark held his hand out to her and gently pulled her up, guiding her from the table. They proceeded onto the hardwood dance floor where a few other couples were dancing. Pulling Lisa close, Mark placed her arms on his shoulders so her right cheek was buried in his chest. They moved to the sounds of the music. Lisa felt his strong body pressed against hers and his strong arms wrapped around her. He smelled like cigarette smoke, which affected Lisa like a strong sedative, making her pleasantly light-headed. It was strange, because usually she couldn't stand other people's cigarette smoke unless she was smoking too. She managed to raise her head to look at Mark and smiled. "I can feel your heart beating," she said.

He didn't say anything, just bent toward her and lightly touched her temple with his chin. Then his cheek gently tapped hers, softly tickling it with its stubble. Lisa shut her eyes. Mark held her tightly in his arms. His lips moved to the side of her neck, burning her skin with his breath. They moved into her hair, softly caressing it, and then brushed over her eyelids. Lisa felt herself shiver. She felt giddy. She couldn't resist anymore. Her lips opened toward his. Mark gently kissed her and then slightly relaxed his embrace, still holding her in his arms.

"I see our food is already on the table," he said. "Let's sit down."

"Yes, I'm starving," Lisa said awkwardly, trying to compose herself. Holding her hand, Mark led her back to their table. Then he pulled the chair back for Lisa to sit down. He filled the glasses with wine and they started eating. The calamari, covered in a creamy white sauce, looked very appetizing and, upon Lisa's first bite, proved to be very tasty. Her filet mignon was tender and delicious. Mark asked her to try his steak, and it was so tasty and juicy that it melted in her mouth. Undoubtedly, Mark had a sense for good food. From that moment, she always trusted him to order for her when they were dining out. He'd often encourage her to try different foods at different restaurants, and she was never disappointed with his choices. It was very comforting not having to go through the list of fancy menu items but just letting Mark order for her.

Mark drove her home around midnight and walked her to the door.

"Last kiss?" He smiled, opening his arms and hugging her. He sounded so eager and acted so skillfully that Lisa couldn't help but welcome his hot lips on her eyes, then on her cheeks, and finally his hard and hot kiss on her lips.

Then he moved a little aside. There was guilt and discomfort in his look. His look told her that he wasn't sure if he crossed the line by rushing things, and he was offering a heartfelt apology.

There was a mixture of male confidence on the one hand and gentle hesitation on the other that Lisa found very appealing.

"Do you want some coffee?" she asked.

"Yes. I'm desperate for some strong, black coffee and a cigarette."

They went up the stairs to the second floor, where Lisa's apartment was. When she opened the door, the small hallway that led to the living room was lit, but the rest of the apartment was dark. Mary was a very economical person, and she always turned the lights off when there was no one in a room. She kept the hallway light on though, as she didn't want Lisa to come home to a dark apartment. It was one of the sweetest things that she did for Lisa, and Lisa always appreciated it.

Putting her finger to her lips, Lisa showed Mark to the kitchen. Then she went into Irving's room and found him asleep in his bed. Mary was sleeping on the couch to the right of Irving's bed. Lisa smiled, quietly closed the door, and went back to the kitchen.

The kitchen window was open, letting in a warm breeze. Mark was sitting in the dark; the only light in the kitchen was coming from the tip of his cigarette. Waves of attraction washed over her.

She quickly turned on the light and started to make coffee. She was so glad that she had good-quality coffee and a small porcelain coffee set.

"Why are you alone?" Mark asked suddenly. "Are you divorced?"

Lisa held her breath. Her heartbeat increased. It had been around six years since her husband, Irving's father, had died, but even after all those years, talking about it was hard for her.

"My husband died in a car accident," she said slowly.

"I'm sorry. I didn't know," Mark added, and silence filled the room.

"Well, it's not your fault," Lisa said. "It happened six years ago. Irving was about a year old," she added and tried to change the subject. "Tell me more about yourself."

Mark drew on his cigarette and paused, pensively looking at the tiny stream of bluish smoke drifting off the tip of the cigarette. "I've been divorced for two years now; have two kids—a girl who's ten and a boy who's eight," he finally answered. "They aren't here. They live in New York with their mom." He drew on his cigarette.

"Do you miss them?" Lisa asked quietly, turning away to watch the coffee maker.

"Yes," Mark said. "I miss them, and I hate that judges automatically favor giving children to the mother. It's unfair and it discriminates against fathers' rights. I dream of the day when I'll gain full custody of my children." Suddenly, he rose and hugged Lisa from behind as she stood at the kitchen counter. "How's the coffee coming?" he whispered in her ear.

It was ready, but Mark didn't let her answer. His lips slid to her neck as he turned her around and pressed against him, burning her skin with his hot kisses.

"No, Mark, no." Lisa softly pushed him away.

Mark stepped a little aside. "Let me help you with the coffee," he said. Lisa poured it into her beautiful porcelain cups, and then placed them on the saucers. Mark carried them over to the table. They sat down and ended the night by talking and drinking coffee. There was a lot of kissing and touching that night, but Lisa believed that it would be inappropriate to have sex on their first date, so they didn't.

After a while, Mark started getting ready to leave. The next day was a workday, and he was apologetic for staying so late. He gave her a goodbye kiss—one that made Lisa always remember that moment. Standing at the open door, ready to go, Mark bent and gently touched her lips, his eyes intent on her. There was a mixture of passion, confidence, and softness in his look and in his demeanor, and there was something else too, something indefinable that made her heart melt. That was the image of Mark that Lisa carried throughout their life together. Visualizing that moment would help restore her love for him later in their lives. It always worked.

CHAPTER TWO

After Mark left that first night, Lisa locked the door and leaned against it, smiling. She wanted to laugh out loud, dance, talk to someone, and share her happiness. She thought of calling Sonya to tell her about her wonderful day, but Sonya was probably asleep at this hour. Lisa stood leaning on the door for some time and then stretched her arms upward. It was really late, and she had to go to bed so she would be able to wake up early the next day. On her way to the bedroom she looked in Irving's room. He was sleeping on his stomach with his cheek buried in the pillow and his arms spread wide. His blanket was almost on the floor. Lisa quietly readjusted the blanket, softly kissed her son, and then left the room.

She went to her bedroom and dove under her bed sheets, but she couldn't fall asleep. Her thoughts were full of Mark and the wonderful time they spent together. Closing her eyes, Lisa recalled their dance at the restaurant. She felt again his hot lips touching her skin and felt the strength of his arms around her. Those images rolled over and over in her memory.

Lisa didn't know when she fell asleep, but the next thing she heard was her alarm buzzing at 6:30 a.m. The blinds were drawn so it was still dark in her apartment. *Should've opened the blinds just a bit before going to bed last night so the room would be brighter now,* Lisa thought as she struggled to wake up. She stretched her body under the sheets and closed her eyes. She didn't want to get up. All she wanted to do was stay in her warm, comfortable bed, dreaming about Mark, but she couldn't allow herself such a luxury. She had things to do. Lisa opened her eyes and forced herself to jump out of bed. She hurried into the bathroom, took a quick shower, put on some makeup, then threw on her soft white robe and went into the kitchen.

Mary was already preparing coffee and waiting for the bagels to pop out of the toaster.

"Good morning!" she said, turning toward Lisa with a smile on her face. She then set some fresh, steaming coffee and bagels on the table. Lisa was very appreciative of Mary. It wasn't often that there was breakfast or dinner or any sort of meal on the table for Lisa unless she put it there herself. This morning promised to be the beginning of a beautiful day and possibly a beautiful life ahead.

Soon after breakfast, Mary left and Lisa went to Irving's room to wake him up. Irving considered himself very grown up so he didn't allow Lisa to help him with his morning routine. He went to the bathroom and closed the door. Lisa had asked him not to lock the door so she would be able to come in and help him in case something happened, so Irving always double-checked that his mom knew he was in the bathroom and wouldn't walk in. "Mom, Mom, I'm in the bathroom!" he yelled.

"Okay, son. I'm waiting for you in the kitchen. Please don't be late," Lisa called back.

She grabbed two new cereal boxes and put them on the table. She knew that Irving didn't eat just any cereal, and she always tried to have a couple of his favorites for him to choose from. Then she sliced a banana into a bowl and took the milk out of the refrigerator. Breakfast for Irving was ready. He walked into the kitchen ten minutes later, dressed in his khaki pants and dark blue shirt. Lisa pulled out a chair for him and watched with a smile as he sat examining the cereal boxes, checking each one carefully, and finally opening the Honeycombs cereal box with obvious satisfaction. She stroked his hair and smiled. Her little son was precious, and her heart was filled with motherly love.

After breakfast, Lisa changed quickly into her white uniform, walked Irving to the school bus stop, and rushed to her car to get to work on time.

A massage therapist, she arrived at the salon about fifteen minutes before her first client arrived. She liked to have some extra time to prepare the room, the products, and the equipment before the session began. First, she headed to the front desk to get her schedule.

"You have a busy day today," the receptionist, Laura, said as she handed Lisa her appointment tickets.

Lisa smiled. She was never bored at work waiting for walk-in clients. Indeed, people had to book their appointments with her at least two weeks in advance if they wanted to find a spot. Some of her regular clients even reserved their weekly appointments several months in advance.

She looked at the tickets. She had three one-hour relaxation massages, one deep tissue massage, and two seaweed body wraps. She went to her room, pulled the massage cream from the upper cabinet, and set it on the counter. She tucked a fitted bed sheet over the massage table, making sure that there were no wrinkles. Then she laid a blanket on top of the sheet and covered the headrest. Once everything was in place, Lisa dimmed the light and lit the candles that were located at intervals around the room. She looked around and smiled. This room wasn't just her place of work; it was her life and her passion. She couldn't imagine herself being without this massage room, her clients, and her lovely coworkers, who had become her friends. She gave the room one last careful look, then left the door open invitingly and walked to the waiting room to greet her first client.

Her regular client, Shannon, was already sitting in an armchair, sipping water from a cup. The salon always had water, juice, and coffee laid out on a wooden table for their clients.

As soon as Lisa entered, Shannon exclaimed, "Lisa, dear, I've been waiting for you. I'm so looking forward to this massage." She rose and hugged Lisa.

Shannon was a tall, full-figured woman; Lisa was almost buried under Shannon's armpits. She gently pushed against the large woman, setting herself free, then asked, "How are you, Shannon?"

"You know how I am. Busy with my three kids and a house and everything, with no time for myself." Shannon sighed loudly. "But this time of the week, I dedicate to myself. Myself and only myself. Even if there's a fire or aliens attack, I'm here with you, and nothing can deprive me of my massage."

They both laughed. Lisa liked this woman. Shannon was a fun person and an excellent client. Lisa really appreciated clients like Shannon, who gave her respect and trust. The sense of comfort that developed between her and her regular clients positively energized her and allowed her to give her clients her best work in return.

They approached the door, and Shannon eagerly entered the room. She knew the routine, and started to take off her shoes right away. Lisa closed the door, allowing Shannon time to prepare for the session. In a few minutes she knocked on the door, and entered the room after hearing Shannon's, "Ready." She locked the door so nobody would accidentally disturb them and began the session.

She positioned herself at the top right side of the table, putting her hands on the right side of Shannon's shoulder, which was covered with a blanket. She started by slowly pressing down Shannon's back, moving her hands from the top to the bottom right, then gradually to the left side of her back, moving them in an upward direction. That combination was specially designed to warm up the muscles, relax the clients, and familiarize them with Lisa's touch. She then grasped both ends of the blanket and pulled them down, exposing Shannon's back. Quickly coating her hands with massage cream, Lisa rubbed her hands together so that the cream would become warmer. She applied her hands to the tops of Shannon's shoulders, and slowly moved them along the spine, pressing and stretching the muscles on her way down.

The candles flickered in a dim light, weaving mysterious shadows on the ceiling and walls. Soft music filled the room with gentle sounds of bird songs and waves breaking on the shore. Lisa's hands massaged Shannon's neck, enfolding and stretching it. They slipped downward along the side of the neck, enfolding the shoulder muscles and working over the shoulder blades. Lisa's technique had been perfected through a lot of experience. Her body bent side to side, falling into the rhythm of routine as her mind wandered off into daydreams.

She thought about Mark. She visualized their evening together, recalling it from the moment they entered the restaurant. She could see them sitting at the table in the dimness of the dining room. The soft music created a relaxing, cozy atmosphere. Mark was sitting across from her, thoughtfully dragging on his cigarette. He gazed at her. The sensation of his stare rolled over and over in her memory. She recalled how it pierced through the bluish, hazy smoke, penetrating her somehow. She felt his obvious interest in her. He was curious, yet there was something stronger than that. Although warm, his look expressed both strength and domination. Lisa couldn't find the words to explain that stare; she just remembered feeling a little tremor coming from the upper half of her shoulders and slowly moving down to her lower back. His eyes hypnotized her in some primal way. She'd lowered her head under his direct, powerful stare.

It wasn't like her to act that way. She had always been a strong, independent woman who didn't accept any hint of patronization. Nevertheless, she had to admit that, for a moment, she enjoyed the sensation of being overpowered by his apparently innate male supremacy—somehow it felt very natural and comforting. Lisa wondered whether there were inherent submissive genes present in all women that went back to when males dominated. This idea raised sudden, controversial questions in her mind. Still, the feeling was intriguing, new, and worth thinking over.

The squealing and squawking of the recorded sea gulls interrupted Lisa's daydreams. She looked at the table clock, which showed that half of the session was complete. She asked Shannon to turn over on her back.

Stretching enjoyably, Shannon followed the instructions. "How do you feel so far?" Lisa asked, already predicting the answer.

"Oh, I'm in heaven. It's so great. I feel as weightless as a bird, soaring freely in the clouds," Shannon said melodically.

She sounds so poetic, Lisa thought, surprised. Shannon didn't usually express herself with such emotion. *If it's a side effect of the massage, then it's great!* Lisa smiled. She should probably do a study on how massage therapy can evoke people's hidden talents, and then publish her research. It would be a great scientific work. Lisa smiled again to herself as she carefully pulled each of Shannon's arms over her head for a nice muscle stretch. Then she sat on a small chair that she kept underneath the massage table and softly rubbed the cream into Shannon's left foot. The last half of the session continued with reflexology, which was the most enjoyable part of the session for all of her customers.

As Lisa's fingers routinely and skillfully worked at gliding, pressing, and stretching Shannon's foot, her mind escaped again to a place far from the room. For the second time, she saw herself at the restaurant with Mark. Now they were dancing on the hardwood floor, slowly circling to the sound of the music. Mark was holding her in his strong embrace. She was wrapped up in the soft, comfortable feeling of his presence. His lips touched her eyes. His breath burned her skin. His arms secured and supported her. They were the only people in the whole world...

As much as she enjoyed her memories, Lisa started to worry about escaping too frequently to the "other world." She shook her head, trying to return to earth, and glanced at the table clock. Ten minutes still remained until the end of the session. For the first time, Lisa regretted that her client was not much of a talker. She would rather talk with Shannon about anything than perform this routine in such great silence. Trying to compose herself so she wouldn't fall into her persistent daydreams again, Lisa started forming a list of things that she had to do after work today.

Usually, she did her shopping over the weekend. However, under the circumstances, she hadn't found the time to shop for the last two days. What was she going to prepare for dinner tonight? Lisa did a fast mental examination of what she had left in the fridge. *Not much*, she thought, except for the milk she bought on Friday, some bagels, cereal, and a few potatoes and carrots. Although she could survive by herself on the food she had, it definitely wasn't good enough for Irving. It wouldn't be a dinner for him without some meat on his plate. She ought to buy some steaks or some chicken and prepare them on their indoor grill. She also needed to buy some vegetables and fruit.

Vegetables weren't Irving's favorite part of dinner. Lisa grinned, remembering Irving's arguments about vegetables. "The body knows better," he announced. "Our teacher said that we have to listen to our body about what it likes and what it doesn't. And my body doesn't like any veggies!" It had taken all of Lisa's patience and skills at persuasion to convince her son that veggies were a necessity for a proper diet. They had finally reached an agreement. Lisa would make veggies in any way that Irving found most palatable, either fresh, steamed, fried, or in any combination. They also agreed that she wouldn't object if once in a while only one small tomato represented vegetables on his plate.

As long as that tomato wasn't being thrown into the garbage behind her back, it worked fine for her. Irving even learned how to make grilled vegetables and sometimes experimented, making them with different sauces. Lisa thought most of them were delicious, and she was proud of her son.

The last ten minutes of the massage passed by very quickly.

"I don't believe that an hour has passed by already," Shannon said with regret in her voice. "If it were possible, I would ask you to start it all over again."

Those words pleased Lisa. It was always rewarding to have her clients enjoy and benefit from her sessions. However, she had to hurry. The salon rules didn't schedule any breaks between sessions, so her next appointment was going to start in eight minutes. She left the room, giving Shannon some time to dress, and went to the back room where they kept fresh bed sheets, towels, and laundry bags. This room also doubled as a small kitchen: it had a coffee machine, refrigerator, spring water cooler, and microwave. It was very convenient since Lisa didn't like eating out every day at fast food places or expensive restaurants, and with these facilities, she could bring her own lunch and sit with the other girls at lunchtime. They would talk and enjoy homemade food. Sometimes, employees would go there between clients to drink some coffee and gossip. Lisa liked those rare moments when she was able to join them and relax with a cup of fresh coffee or tea.

Lisa's next client, John, was a young man in his mid-twenties. He appeared a little awkward, keeping his eyes down and stumbling on his way to the massage room.

"Have you had a massage before?" Lisa asked.

"No, never," John said, nodding. "It's a woman's thing to have creams, lotions, and massages," he murmured. "If this gift certificate wasn't a present from my wife for our one year wedding anniversary, I wouldn't be here under any circumstances, to tell the truth."

"Well, massage is a therapeutic procedure rather than a skin care treatment. It heals the body and mind in a way that benefits people from all walks of life," Lisa responded with a smile as she opened the door. She explained the routine and left the room so John could undress and lie down on the table.

When John was ready, Lisa entered the room, locked the door, and washed her hands. She began the session with her usual stroke, pressing the muscles along each side of John's spine through the blanket. Even without touching his muscles directly yet, she could tell how tight and stiff they were. She decided to give him a longer warm-up before moving on to the deep tissue massage.

"How are you doing?" she asked at the end of the session when John opened his eyes and stretched.

"It was amazing," he said.

Coming from such a skeptical client as John, Lisa considered this a great compliment. Pleased to hear that, Lisa left the room for John to dress, and then walked him back to the waiting room where he could relax before leaving the salon.

Laura informed Lisa that her next client, Rebecca, had already arrived. Rebecca usually came for the soft tissue massage, but today she signed up for the mud body wrap. Lisa quickly prepared the mud mask and set it aside. She took a body brush and with gentle strokes brushed Rebecca's back then the back of her legs and arms. Body brushing was a wonderful procedure that assisted in skin exfoliation and blood circulation. Finishing the last couple of strokes, Lisa put the brush on the counter and quickly spread the mask over the back of Rebecca's body, and then she instructed Rebecca to turn over and repeated the routine on her front. She wrapped Rebecca's body first in a plastic sheet, then a linen sheet, an aluminum sheet, and finally a blue thermal blanket. When Lisa had finished, Rebecca lay on the table looking like a big, blue cocoon. Lisa dipped a towel in some cold water and put it on Rebecca's forehead to prevent overheating, and silently left the room to give Rebecca some time to relax.

She went into the kitchen and found the manicurist, Margaret, helping herself to a cup of coffee. "How's it going?" Lisa asked.

"Very busy; extremely busy. It seems like all the women in the world decided to get their mani/pedi today. My old client called demanding an appointment since she's having an important party tonight, and I don't have any spot to squeeze her in. What was she thinking, waiting for the last minute! It's a crazy day. I barely had time to squeeze in this coffee break and now I have to stay late to fit her in," she complained.

"Well, it's still better than the slow days," Lisa said, smiling.

"Yes, I guess you're right," said Margaret as she sipped her coffee.

Lisa poured some coffee for herself, which she drank while talking with Margaret and periodically checking on Rebecca. When Margaret left for her client, Lisa pulled out magazines to skim. When the mask time had expired, she went back to her room to unwrap Rebecca and showed her to the adjacent shower. When Rebecca came back into the room, Lisa let her rest on the table while she applied some light lotion to the young woman's body.

"Ooh, my skin feels so smooth and soft!" Rebecca exclaimed.

"Isn't it amazing?" Lisa said, smiling.

"Definitely. I can hardly believe that such a magical transformation is possible." They both laughed.

The rest of the day was filled with two more relaxation massages and one body wrap. Lisa was preparing her room for the next day when Laura stepped in to hand Lisa her gratitude envelopes.

"I'm sorry I didn't wait for you to pick them up," she apologized. "I'm in a big hurry. I'm already fifteen minutes late for my date."

"I think Margaret will be working late today, so she can turn the lights off and lock the door," Lisa said.

"Yes, I already confirmed it with her." Laura rushed to the front. "Good night, girls. Have a great evening," she called.

Lisa stretched, inhaled deeply, and smiled. Although a little tired, she felt very satisfied with how her day had gone. She couldn't imagine what life would be like without her job. She started opening the envelopes and pulling out her tips. As much as a sign of appreciation of her work, this money was also a great addition to her budget. She put it in her wallet, threw her coat on, hung her purse over her shoulder, and left the room. On her way out, she wished Margaret a good night and then turned on her cell phone to check her messages. There was one from Irving and another from Sonya. There was no message from Mark.

CHAPTER THREE

At her favorite grocery store Lisa quickly filled her shopping cart with the products on her list and headed to the checkout. There was a small line where an elderly lady was arguing with the cashier about her coupons. The cashier was a young girl who indifferently explained to the lady that her coupons were not valid for the products she was buying. The lady insisted otherwise. The conversation seemed to be endless, and to Lisa's disappointment, there was no other cashier available. She glanced at her watch, berating herself for not doing her shopping over the weekend so Irving wouldn't be starving and worrying while waiting for his unorganized mother to come home.

Well, starving sounded a little harsh. Lisa shook her head trying to interrupt her self-recrimination. Irving wasn't starving; neither was he worrying. She had plenty of snacks for him at home and had just called him from the car to say that she was on her way to the store. Still, it wasn't good for him to spoil his appetite before dinner by eating his beloved cookies.

Lisa found herself getting upset again. The elderly lady now searched her purse, pulling everything out onto the counter. The young cashier remained calm and indifferent. Not being able to wait anymore in this infinite line, Lisa asked as kindly as she could, "I'm sorry, is there any other cashier open?"

The girl gave Lisa a hard stare. Her expression showed disdain for rude people who couldn't wait patiently. She opened her mouth, but Lisa spoke first. "It would be such a help," she said sweetly, offering up a pleasant smile.

The girl studied Lisa for a moment and then picked up the phone. Her voice blared over the intercom.

"Please open register number two; please open register number two."

Hanging up the phone, she stared into space, ignoring the elderly lady who stood shaking her coupons, trying to get her attention. *It must be a blessing to have such strong nerves*, Lisa thought wryly.

"Register number two is now open," the girl finally announced. Lisa promptly pulled her cart into the other checkout, and in a few minutes she was on her way driving home.

She opened the door to her apartment, holding some shopping bags in her left arm and leaving the rest of the bags in the hall.

"Mom's home!" Irving jumped to the door toward her and hung onto her shoulders. "Hi, Mom, what took you so long?"

"Sorry, Irving, I tried to come as fast as I could," she said as she kissed him on the cheek. "I missed you very much, kitten."

"What did you buy?" Irving asked, helping her with the bags. "Any ice cream?"

"Of course I bought you ice cream—your favorite strawberry-vanilla bars. But you have to eat dinner first." She took off her coat, put her slippers on, and carried the bags to the kitchen.

"How was your day?" she asked while she unpacked the groceries.

"Everything was all right," Irving answered, looking suspiciously at the items on the table. "What are you making?"

Lisa grinned. "How about chicken steaks with mashed potatoes and some salad?"

"Sounds good!" Irving said.

"Can you turn on the grill so it will warm up while I'm preparing the chicken?" Lisa asked as she washed the meat and put it on the cutting board.

Irving was happy to help with the grill and even offered to make the chicken himself. Lisa didn't object. She washed and peeled the potatoes, putting them in the boiling water. Then she made the salad and transferred it into a large ceramic bowl. She set the table for two, arranging the napkins and placing two water glasses near the plates. She liked to have dinner at a nicely set table, even if it was only for herself and her son. Sonya always made fun of her "just-right set-up," as she called it. "Wouldn't it be easier to use plastic plates and cups that you can throw away after dinner? Don't you have other things to do besides washing dishes?" She would tease while sipping her coffee from a delicate porcelain cup.

Lisa just smiled, knowing that Sonya was joking. "I consider you a very important guest. I wouldn't dream of serving you coffee in some cheap plastic cup," she usually retorted. "You deserve better!"

While the potatoes were boiling and Irving was taking charge of the chicken, Lisa stepped into the living room to check her answering machine. There was no message from Mark on this phone either. Lisa skipped through the numbers on her Caller ID, hoping that Mark had called but didn't leave a message. To her disappointment, she didn't find his number there, even though she checked it twice.

Dinner was ready in about thirty minutes. Lisa transferred the chicken that Irving had made to a serving plate and decorated it with a few cilantro leaves. The golden-brown, tender pieces were mixed with grilled onions and glistening in their juices. It looked delicious.

"Let's get started," Lisa said, pouring the grape juice in the glasses and serving the food. "My saliva's already on the go," she added, laughing.

"You're telling me," Irving mumbled, through a mouthful. They ate for a while, enjoying the food.

"So, any grades today from the tests or pop quizzes you had?" Lisa asked.

"No, our teacher hasn't graded the tests yet. We had a pop quiz in math, though," Irving said. "It was easy. I'm sure I got an A," he bragged.

"I hope that's what you'll get," Lisa said with a smile.

"Oh, Mom! I forgot to tell you a story," Irving said, as he stopped eating and looked at her, his eyes wide with excitement. "You know what happened today in the cafeteria? It was awesome!"

"What's that, Irving? I hope it wasn't another cockroach." She grimaced, remembering the story of the kid who found a cockroach in his food and the great panic that had caused among the parents. "So, what happened today?"

"I was eating my lunch with Bob and Derek." Irving picked up his fork and waved it around. "Then the noise in the cafeteria got louder. I turned around and saw these kids flicking peas at each other from their plastic spoons. Soon everyone started flicking peas." Irving illustrated his story by throwing imaginary peas with his fork and making whistling noises.

"Irving, put your fork down," Lisa said.

"It was so cool," Irving continued, now helping the story along with his hands. "Peas were flying across the whole cafeteria. I didn't get to flick too many peas, though, because the lunch lady ran in and yelled at everyone," he added with regret.

Lisa raised her eyebrows. "What's so funny about throwing food at each other?"

"I don't know. It was just fun." Irving shrugged.

"You've got to be kidding me," Lisa said, disappointed. She set her fork on the table. "I can't believe that my son was part of such Three Stooges antics."

Irving made a little laugh but simultaneously ducked his head, sensing something was wrong.

"Do you know how hard the cafeteria lady, the cook, and the other kitchen personnel are working to put that food on your plate, and then to clean everything up after you're done?" she asked. "You see your mother working every day, you help me cook and clean, and you know how hard it is! Would it seem fair to you if a friend you invited to dinner threw food in our kitchen?" she pressed. "Do you have any idea how disrespectful and offensive that was to the lunch lady?"

"Yes, I guess you're right. I saw her cleaning everything up when the kids left the cafeteria. She seemed sad," Irving said thoughtfully. "I won't do it again, Mom. I promise."

"That's good, son. I know you won't." She smiled at him. "Have you done your homework?"

"Sure I have. I had plenty of time before you came home today, remember?" he looked at her with a trace of reproach in his eyes.

"I'm sorry, Irving." Lisa patted his head. "I'm terribly, terribly sorry. I won't disappoint you again. Forgiven?"

"Yep, sure, I forgive you. I actually wasn't very angry with you. I know you have a job."

Lisa pulled Irving to her and hugged him. "I love you so much sonny. You're the best, the cutest, and the smartest boy in the whole world. Do you know that?"

"Yeah, yeah, I know that," he grumbled, trying to break free of her arms. "Mom, let me go, I'm not a little girl." He finally managed to escape. He was blushing, but even though he seemed embarrassed, he looked very proud of the compliment. How many times had Lisa thought how wonderful and gracious God was to have given her this boy as a son. This boy was a ray of sunlight that brightened her life, gave her warmth, and filled her with a sense of existence. She was so grateful to God for this child!

"Want to play some checkers?" she asked as she packed the leftovers into the refrigerator and cleaned the table. She put the dishes in the sink, intending to wash them later.

They played checkers and talked. Irving was much better than Lisa in this game, and he always won. "Mom, you have a lot of learning to do in playing checkers to be able to compete with me," he said after a few games.

Lisa smiled. "Okay, son. You have twenty minutes to play your computer games if you want. Then you have to brush your teeth and go to bed."

Irving went to his room, and Lisa started to wash dishes. It was around nine. Mark still hadn't called.

At 9:30 p.m., Lisa sent Irving into the bathroom to brush his teeth and get ready for bed. In the meantime, she spread his bed sheets and gathered up dirty clothes from the floor. Lisa never stopped marveling at how sloppy her lovely son could be sometimes. Hundreds of times she asked him to put his clothes in the laundry basket when he took them off, but he was still leaving them on the floor. "Oh, yes Mom, I just forgot," he would always respond innocently and then promptly pick up his clothes. Even though she was disappointed, Lisa could never get angry with him and smiled at his "short memory." Still, she wanted to teach him neatness, so, even with irregular success, she persistently reminded him to clean his room.

Irving came from the bathroom and jumped into his bed, diving straight under the covers. Lisa sat by him and adjusted the blanket.

"Time to go to sleep, sonny."

"Mom, tell me a story?" he asked.

"Okay. Once upon a time, one little boy...," Lisa began.

"Mom," Irving interrupted impatiently. "I know you're going to make up a story about me."

Lisa laughed. "Well, let me sing you a song instead," and started, "Itsy bitsy spider—" She sang only one verse when Irving interrupted her again.

"Mom, please stop singing. You aren't Celine Dion. You can't sing."

Lisa laughed again. "You loved my singing when you were a baby," she objected. "Remember this song I used to sing for you every night? Oh how fun it is to—"

"When I was a baby, I couldn't talk yet to ask you to stop," Irving said, making his point clearly. Lisa smiled. She bent over and kissed him on the cheek.

"Good night. I love you son."

"Good night, Mom. I love you, too." Irving sighed sweetly, stretching on the pillow.

Lisa turned off the light, closed the door, and went into her own bedroom. It was almost 10 p.m., probably too late to expect Mark to call.

She turned on her nightstand lamp, slipped into her pajamas, and lifted her covers. Then she adjusted the pillow and settled into bed with book. Skipping through the pages for a while, Lisa found herself unable to concentrate on the story. She slid into her slippers and went to the kitchen for a glass of water. Back in the bedroom, she climbed into bed and turned off her lamp. Suddenly, the telephone rang. Lisa scrambled from the bed, found one slipper with her left foot but missed the other one, and rushed to the phone jumping on one foot.

"Hello," she said, trying not to sound out of breath. Her heart was pumping blood into her temples.

"Lisa, hi. It's Mark." His deep voice spread warmth through her body. "Sorry I'm calling so late. I just got home from work. Did I wake you?"

"No, not at all," Lisa assured him, resting her bare foot on top of the one in the slipper. "I was just reading," she said to sound truthful.

"I already miss you. I couldn't go to sleep without saying good night to you," Mark said, making Lisa fall into a happy smile. "Sleep well and think about me," he added softly.

"Good night, Mark. I'm glad you called." Lisa hung up the phone and stayed there for a moment, feeling elated. *I'll certainly think about you, Mark. I can hardly stop*, she thought.

She went back to bed and closed her eyes. Life was beautiful. Everything was just beautiful.

CHAPTER FOUR

The rest of the week dragged by. Tuesday, Wednesday, Thursday... and Thursday... and still Thursday. Lisa began to think Friday would never come. It would be a never-ending Thursday for the rest of her life. Mary had already agreed to watch Irving Friday night so she would be able to go out on a date with Mark. Today Irving had asked her if he could sleep over at his friend's house. Lisa didn't want to say yes, since she had already asked Mary to watch him, and she hated changing the plans at the last minute. But Irving had begged and begged, using every excuse he could think of—like needing to do a school project together, and his friend's father promising to take them fishing. Lisa finally gave in and called Mary, apologizing for the cancellation.

Finally, Friday came around. It was about seven when a dark blue Acura flashed its lights in front of Lisa's apartment. Mark got out of the car and greeted Lisa with open arms as soon as he saw her coming. He pulled her into his embrace and kissed her on the cheek. Their meeting felt so natural, as if they'd been together for years and had never been apart. He opened the passenger side door, helped her in, and then went around and stepped into the car as well.

"I'm so happy to see you, Lisa," he said, squeezing her in one of his many tight hugs.

"Me too," Lisa said, smiling. "Where are we going?" she asked, softly easing herself from his arms.

"Hmm...it's a surprise." Mark paused, turning the car around. They moved to the exit of her apartment complex and then turned onto the main road. Mark drove with a calm, steady confidence. Lisa recalled Margaret's semi-serious words, "Always look at how the guy drives his car, because his driving habits reflect his personality." Lisa grinned, recalling Margaret's serious expression when she shared her life lessons and thoughts.

"What? Why are you smiling?" Mark turned to his right, pulling out a CD from the case and glanced at her. "Listen to this CD. It's Robert Miles," he said, inserting the disc into the player. "There aren't many artists of his caliber, who can reach so deeply into human emotions and into the human spirit. I really like him, really love listening to his music."

Lisa agreed with Mark. The melodic sounds of the music gradually filled the car and set her in a romantic mood.

They were already on the highway, gliding with the flow of traffic. Mark stayed in the middle lane, holding the wheel with his right hand. His elbow rested on his lap. His left hand was occupied with a cigarette, which he flicked from time to time through the open window.

"You're an excellent driver," Lisa said out loud. "You're not speeding, not changing lanes too much. Most of all, you aren't yelling at crazy drivers even though they cut you off sometimes, like that old lady in her pompous Cadillac did. Look at that, she changed lanes again, right in front of you, like she's the only one on the road!" Lisa exclaimed with indignation. Then she looked at Mark. "You're an exceptional driver, one who sets examples to others." Her lips curved with a playful smile as she complimented him. Mark drew on his cigarette.

"You may tease me but I actually am a good driver. I haven't gotten a ticket in years, knock on wood." He looked around for some wood, and not finding any, knocked on his forehead. "Close enough, don't you think?" He smiled with satisfaction.

Lisa laughed. She felt so comfortable, so free with him. It was as though they had known each other for a long time.

They exited the highway and turned onto a small side road, lined with tall, colorful trees. Mark drove a few miles, then turned into a cul-de-sac and stopped in front of a six-story building with a wide, shiny glass facade. Neatly trimmed bushes and tall trees, ablaze in red and yellow, framed the building. It was an amazingly beautiful and peaceful place.

Mark turned off the engine and lit another cigarette. He stared into the distance in front of him. Lisa looked around, wondering where they were. Puzzled, she asked Mark. To her surprise, he said simply that he lives up there, in the building across from where they were parked. He turned to look at her, shifting in his seat.

"I didn't want to tell you in advance...I was kind of afraid that you might turn down my invitation."

Lisa gave him a long, thoughtful stare. Mark drew on his cigarette. His eyes looked apologetic and soliciting at the same time.

"I thought you might want to see how I live, to see me in my natural environment, so to speak."

He smiled and looked straight into her eyes. "No obligations, of course. If you want, we can go to some other place, like a restaurant or something. His left hand with the cigarette made a wide circle in the air. Keeping his direct stare on her, he took another drag. "So, what's it going to be, Lisa?" A trace of a smile and a bit of challenge reflected on his face.

Lisa looked at him, still silent, thinking of his proposition. She tried to stop the blush that crept treacherously up her cheeks. She hadn't been prepared for this situation, and struggled to make the right decision. On the one hand, she considered his "surprise" inappropriate. He should have asked her in advance before he brought her here. On the other hand, she didn't want to look like a prude, and make a big deal out of nothing.

Mark seemed to read her thoughts. "I know I should've asked you earlier. I realize you have every right to be mad. But please, don't be. Please forgive me. I was motivated only by good intentions, and I was afraid that you would simply reject my proposition before I'd be able to present my strongest argument." His look was kind and innocent.

"And what would that be?" Lisa asked.

"That I'm a terrific cook. I want to prepare a special dinner for you. You won't be able to tell my food from the food that's served at the best restaurants," he said proudly.

Lisa smiled and nodded, "Okay then, let's see."

They parked the car and Mark led her to the large, glass foyer, and then to the elevator, where he hit the button for the third floor. He opened the door to his apartment, helped Lisa with her coat, quickly removed his, and hung both coats into the closet. "Do you want me to show you around?" he asked.

"Sure," she said, feeling an authentic curiosity to see how Mark lived. She was glad after all that she hadn't turned his invitation down.

Mark took her into the living room. The custom-made rug covering most of the dark parquet floor in the room caught Lisa's attention. It was a deep brown color with a dark green border framing a scattering of green leaves. Although it was heavy-looking, it felt very soft and comfortable. On the left, in the center of the wall, was a big fireplace made of beige-brown marble tile. Adjacent to it was a wet bar that matched the tile on the fireplace.

Mark flipped a switch and the fireplace blazed to life with dancing flames. Lisa stepped over to the bar for a closer look at his fine selection of liquors and imported wines. The variety of bottles, with their different shapes, colors and labels, was impressive.

She looked at him with a playful grin. "Wow! You seem to be a great fan of good liquors."

Trying to analyze her intent, he concluded with a skeptical look, "I'm not an alcoholic. I just like to collect fine liquors. I buy them from around the world, and in fact, I only drink on rare occasions. Like when I have visitors or friends over," he said, a hint of defensiveness in his tone.

"Or women?" Lisa interjected.

Mark smiled. "Women," he said. "They are the most lovable and romantic creatures in the world."

He had moved closer to her and let his hand briefly caress her hair. "Tonight might be one of those special events," he said softly.

Lisa started to blush under his direct, intense stare, and berated herself for reacting so emotionally. She was, after all, a grown woman. Looking for a moment's respite to control herself, she said, "I really like that leather armchair of yours. It looks very classy with its tall back and soft, deep seat."

"It's very comfortable, too." Mark turned his head away from her and toward the chair. "It has a hidden danger in it, though. You won't want to leave it once you sit down in it. You'd risk becoming an armchair-potato."

They both laughed and Lisa's tension melted. She looked around. Although his living room didn't have a lot of furniture, everything was in harmony: the coffee table was centered on the sofa, which had a matching armchair. An elegant, stainless steel floor lamp gave a soft light from the corner of the room. The stereo system in the other corner completed the living room. In all, the room looked masculine, but also stylish.

Mark dimmed the light in the room and showed Lisa to a long balcony that ran across the living room and extended all the way to the kitchen.

Lisa admired the view of the park surrounding the apartment complex.

The full trees, bright with fall color, filled her sight. Lisa inhaled the fresh air and felt the liveliness flow throughout her body. *It must be such joy to sit here with a cup of tea or coffee after a long day at work, breathing in this invigorating scent of nature,* she thought as they returned to the wide hall.

Mark opened the door to his bedroom, and Lisa caught sight of a simply patterned modern rug, neutral-colored walls, and a dark four poster mahogany bed.

He then opened another door that led to the master bathroom. It was a spacious, white-tiled room with a tulip-shaped white sink and a Jacuzzi. The Jacuzzi brought yet another delighted smile to Lisa's face.

Continuing with the apartment tour, Mark led Lisa to a den located farther down the hallway. They stepped onto a bare hardwood floor. The first thing Lisa noticed were bookshelves that dominated the far wall, pushing up against both sides of a narrow window with wooden blinds that was located in the center of the wall. On the right-hand side of the room there was an elegant oak table that held a computer and a printer, alongside of which stood a black leather chair. There was another oak wood bookstand that stood to the right of the table. The left side of the room was occupied by a brown leather couch and a black steel floor lamp.

Lisa glanced around one more time before leaving the room. She felt that this room symbolized Mark's basic nature. It looked rather more Spartan than luxurious. Nothing extra, nothing opulent; yet, it was thoughtfully planned down to the smallest detail in a way that would make studying or working there very efficient and even comfortable. For a moment, Lisa imagined herself sitting on the couch with her legs covered by a warm woolen blanket, reading a book under the light of a floor lamp while Mark worked at his computer. The idea made her heart pound a bit with pleasure and longing at the same time.

Across the hall from the den was another bathroom that Mark briefly showed to her; next was the utility room with its laundry machines. She saw an empty laundry basket, detergents, bleach, and a lot of tools in boxes that were neatly arranged on tall wooden shelves. Everything looked clean and well-organized.

Intercepting her look, Mark mentioned casually, "I built these shelves myself. I sometimes like to fix or remodel things. I really like to do physical work to keep my muscles alive, you know, especially after those boring long days at work when I'm just sitting at my desk. If it weren't for my hobby, my muscles would probably have atrophied by this time." He flexed his big bicep, making it bulge under his tight shirt sleeve, as if to make sure it was still there, and looked at Lisa, smiling. "I'm a natural handyman. I don't have two left hands, you know. I can do anything with my hands." He stopped under her amused gaze. "Well, maybe almost anything with my hands," he conceded as he straightened his arm and let it rest by his side. Lisa smiled at him, impressed by his skills.

They returned to the living room and went into the adjoining kitchen. White oak cabinets, midnight blue counter tops, a tall, contemporary refrigerator and a wooden table with four chairs by the window created the picture of a well-maintained kitchen.

This apartment was the complete opposite of her own. Mark's didn't have many accessories or decorations, no flowers or anything impractical like the things Lisa scattered plentifully in her apartment. Instead, Mark's condo looked very functional and organized. It looked very masculine; yet it was cozy, too.

"What do you think about a glass of wine?" Mark asked her casually.

"I don't know," Lisa started.

Mark smiled at her. "I have a great red wine that's so smooth and flavorful, you'll ask for your glass to be refilled as soon as you try it."

They settled in the living room and Mark pulled two crystal glasses from beneath the bar and filled them half-full with dark red wine from a bottle bearing a French label. He handed a glass to Lisa.

"Just smell it. Do you feel its wonderful aroma?"

Lisa took the glass from his outstretched hand and inhaled the air from the glass. A warm, flowery aroma filled her nostrils. "Wow, it smells great," she said.

"To us," he toasted, and emptied his glass in two fast, deep swallows.

Lisa sipped her wine, feeling its warmth flowing gently into her veins.

"Do you like it?" Mark asked with satisfaction, already knowing her answer. Lisa nodded. The wine was incredible.

Mark put his glass on the bar and showed Lisa to the armchair. "Why don't you relax in here while I'm in the kitchen."

Lisa didn't object and appreciatively sank into the comfy piece of furniture. Mark pulled the cigarette pack from his pocket, lit one, and threw the pack on the coffee table.

"Do you want me to turn on some music?" he asked, moving to a stereo system.

Immediately, the room filled with the romantic lyrics of Joe Dassin. He turned back to her. "So, do you think you'll be fine here? I won't keep you waiting long," he promised.

Lisa nodded. "Don't worry, take your time. I feel very comfortable here." She stretched in the armchair to prove her words.

When Mark left, Lisa tucked her legs under her and closed her eyes. After her busy day at work, this place was so relaxing and comforting. The wood crackled quietly in the fireplace; the gentle music flowed from the CD player. Warmth and tranquility filled Lisa's body and spirit. She sat for a while, enjoying the feeling, and then forced herself to open her eyes, fearing she'd fall asleep. She lowered her feet back to the floor, lifted her glass, and sipped some wine. Then her eyes dropped to the cigarette pack. Lisa wasn't a regular smoker; she never craved cigarettes. In fact, she didn't even keep cigarettes at home or carry them with her. She smoked occasionally, though, usually at parties or with her girlfriend, Sonya. Yet now, she felt an urge to try one of the cigarettes that Mark had left on the table. She pulled one out and, not seeing any lighter around, approached the fireplace and lit her cigarette from there. She took a deep drag and blew out the stream of grayish smoke. The sudden light-headedness forced her to retreat to the armchair.

Reclining in the seat and stretching her legs, Lisa took the wine in her right hand while holding the cigarette in her left hand. Thoughtfully listening to the music, she sipped on her wine and dragged on the cigarette alternately. Suddenly the music stopped and Lisa heard the sounds of sizzling oil and running water from the kitchen. In reaction to the wonderful smells that emanated from the kitchen, Lisa's own stomach started grumbling and she decided to join Mark.

She put out her cigarette and, still holding her glass of wine, went into the kitchen. "The music stopped," she announced from the doorway.

Mark turned to her from his magic at the stove—a pan in one hand and a flat wooden spoon in the other. A smoldering cigarette rested between his lips. All four burners held saucepans and pots full of stewing or frying foods.

"Wow!" Lisa exclaimed. "You look like a real chef!"

Mark shook the pan he was holding and put it on the gas. "Everything's ready. This stew is especially delicious. Do you want to try some?" He pulled one piece of meat from the pot with his big spoon, and looked at Lisa, who still stood in the doorway. "Come on, Lisa. Come inside. I'm not going to bite."

Lisa stepped into the kitchen and Mark held the spoon out to her, blowing on it before offering some to her. Lisa opened her mouth and tasted the juicy and tender morsel of meat, which melted in her mouth.

"So, how is it?" Mark inquired.

"It's amazing," Lisa said, as she involuntarily licked her lips. When Mark promised to prepare a meal of restaurant quality for her, she'd been skeptical, but had been prepared to compliment him anyway for his dedicated effort. Now, her compliment was genuine.

"Where did you learn to cook like that?" she asked. "I'd love to get some of your recipes."

"I've never formally learned to cook." Mark took the pan from the stove and emptied the contents into a ceramic bowl. "Do you smell that?" He wafted the steam to his nostrils. "I added red wine and a special sauce that I just made. I never follow a recipe. I prefer to experiment with different ingredients, led by my own taste and intuition. What I consider the most important part of creating a really good dish, though, is that it's always tasted while it is being made. That way it never gets over-salted or over-spiced."

"Well, my cooking's quite the opposite." Lisa laughed. "I have all the ingredients and spices in certain proportions per recipe, all sitting ready on the table. Then I wash, cut, shred or slice, depending on what I'm cooking, and then simply place everything in the pot or pan or oven and set the timer. When the time's up, so are my dishes."

"I know. Women usually cook that way," Mark said. He glanced at her empty glass. "Lisa, I'm sorry for keeping you waiting so long." He pulled out the chair and helped her in. "Let me fill your glass first and then please give me another few minutes and the dinner will be ready."

He quickly stepped into the living room and came back with the bottle of wine. He poured the red, aromatic liquid into her glass and lifted his glass from the counter next to the stove. They both sipped on their wine.

"Do you need some help serving or anything?" Lisa offered.

Mark assured her that it was not necessary. "What kind of man would invite you for dinner and then make you work?" he protested.

"Never mind; I was just asking," Lisa replied. Trying to occupy herself, she couldn't find anything better to do than light a cigarette from the pack on the table and draw in the smoke. Slowly blowing the fluffy threads into the air, she watched them stream towards the ceiling and then gradually disperse.

She hadn't finished her cigarette by the time dinner was on the table, but she quickly stubbed it out in the ashtray and focused her attention on the food being presented in front of her. Steam from a rich soup in a wide glass bowl tickled her nostrils with its appetizing aroma. The stew was in a ceramic bowl; raw vegetables were arranged on a plate; baked potatoes were drizzled with butter. Everything looked and smelled irresistible.

They ate, drank and talked. Lisa told him about Irving, how smart and clever and funny he was. Mark mentioned his children—his young son whom he loved playing Nintendo with and his lovely daughter, who he enjoyed taking to the expensive kids' stores and buying cute clothes and toys for. Lisa refrained from asking him the details of his divorce. She didn't want to talk about her deceased husband, either.

Their conversation flowed easily and time passed quickly. Mark seemed very interested in her work as a massage therapist, wondering how hard the job must be for a petite, slim lady like Lisa, with her small, tender hands. Lisa reassured him with a laugh that, although her hands were small, they were strong enough to make the toughest man cry on the table under her manipulations. Besides, she pointed out, it wasn't physical strength that was important in her job, but the technique.

At the end of the dinner, Mark made some coffee, opened a box of chocolates and suggested taking everything back into the living room. He turned on the music, dimmed the lights, and lit two candles on the bar. Lisa was sitting on the sofa when he approached and held his hand out to her.

"How about a dance?" he asked, and before she knew it she was standing and pressed against his wide chest with his arms around her.

He leaned down and kissed her. She grabbed his neck and pulled him into her, her lips melting on his hot mouth. They were barely moving to the sounds of the blues, kissing, and hugging. Lisa's clothes were slowly unwound and dropped onto the floor. Nearly naked, she was draped in Mark's hot body and arms. He lifted her and carried her into the bedroom. She felt weightless in his strong arms. He lowered her onto the bed, leaned over her, and covered her with his hot kisses...and the rest of the night was lost to them.

CHAPTER FIVE

Lisa opened her eyes when daylight streamed into the room through the partially-opened blinds. She rolled over to the right, expecting to find Mark there. The last thought she remembered having before she fell asleep last night in his arms was the delightful awareness of security and comfort. It felt so unbelievably right when he cuddled with her in her sleep, so natural, like they'd been sleeping together for years. She still felt the strength of his large body and tenderness of his strong arms around her, and it seemed that she was accustomed to it by now. To her disappointment, the other side of the bed was empty, although the warmth of his body was still in the bedding. Oh God, she missed him already.

Lisa sat up in bed, grasping her arms around her legs. She called quietly, then a little louder, "Mark, are you there?" There was no response. Hesitating to yell, Lisa decided to go and look for him. She looked around for her clothes but, except for her boots, all of her clothes were in the living room. Lisa pulled the sheet off the bed and wrapped it around her body. She slipped her bare legs into the boots and started down the hall.

Mark was in the den. He was sitting at the computer working. Lisa snuck up behind him and quietly put her arms around his neck.

"Got you," she whispered in his ear.

Mark turned around quickly and pulled Lisa onto his lap. "You're a sleeping princess," he teased.

"I'm not," Lisa retorted. "Usually I get up early in the morning. But last night you—"

"Oh, now it's my fault that you've overslept until almost to noon." He kissed her and then noticed her bed sheet wrap, which had almost fallen off her naked body after her sharp landing onto his lap. He carefully unfolded what was left of the sheet and carried her back into the bedroom. They made love, and talked, and then made love again. The alarm clock on the night stand showed around 2 p.m. when Lisa stretched her body in joyful exhaustion.

"Mark, I can't feel my legs!" she sighed.

"Are you implying that I have to carry you in my arms for the rest of our lives?" he joked, obviously pleased with her compliment of his performance.

He lit his cigarette and they stayed in bed for a while longer with Lisa's head resting on his chest and his left arm around her. The wonderful feeling of belonging to each other was one Lisa carried with her for a long time after that day.

"Are you hungry?" Mark asked, finishing his cigarette. "How about we drink some coffee in the kitchen and then go to a Chinese restaurant or something?"

It seemed like a wonderful idea to Lisa, except she wanted to take a shower first. She looked around for something appropriate she could throw on. Mark's robe, which was hanging on the chair, wouldn't work because it was too huge. Mark appeared to read her thoughts. He opened his closet and pulled out one of his shirts. "This will serve as the perfect gown," he said as he causally threw it on the bed. I'll be waiting for you in the kitchen." He leaned over her and kissed her before leaving the room.

Lisa took the shirt and slowly put it on. It was scented with the whisper of his manly smell. She stayed still in it for a moment and was suddenly overwhelmed with emotions. Wearing his belongings, folding its long sleeves to make it fit, created the invigorating sense of attachment and closeness to this man. She had forgotten these feelings long ago with the death of her beloved husband. It was as though a light had suddenly illuminated the tunnel she'd been living in. She realized how insufficient her life was with nothing but her motherly duties, her job and house chores. She was so used to it that she had convinced herself that her life was full enough for her to be happy. Everything had changed today, making her realize what she was missing, what she had been unconsciously craving for all of these past, long years. Her heart was filled with sweet waves of anticipation as she considered the wonderful beginning of her new life. Filled with new feelings and thoughts, she went into the bathroom, took a quick shower and headed to the kitchen.

Mark was sitting at the table sipping his coffee and smoking a cigarette.

"How many cigarettes do you smoke a day?" Lisa asked, as she barely remembered seeing him without a cigarette.

"You'd be better to ask how many packs I smoke a day," he answered. "About two."

He got another cup, poured some coffee into it and handed it to Lisa. Then he showed her to the chair across the table. He seemed to be a little concerned.

"Is everything all right?" Lisa asked, surprised by his mood change.

"Yes, everything's fine." Mark drew on his cigarette and scowled.

Lisa became a bit worried. "Mark, you're answering like my son, Irving. 'Fine!' It's not an answer. Can you be more specific?"

"Oh, it doesn't matter. I just had a bad day at work yesterday," Mark started halfheartedly. "I finished this project I've been working on for weeks, and when it was finally ready for production my *wonderful* boss gave it back to me and requested more outrageous changes."

"You really hate your boss, don't you?" Lisa said, smiling, and noticing how sarcastic the word "wonderful" sounded in Mark's mouth.

"He acts like he's all that, but he doesn't know anything about engineering. He built his career just sucking up to his boss's ass." Mark swiftly stroked his hand. "I hate people like him! I'll never be one of them."

"So, what happened then?" Lisa asked, reaching for a cigarette.

"Well, we had a big argument. He invited the people from the quality assurance department to voice their thoughts about the project." Mark grinned sardonically.

"And?" she asked. Mark glanced at her with amusement.

"What do you think happened, Lisa? I'm a professional. I'm very good in my field. In fact, I'm the best consultant they've ever had," he said evenly. Lisa continued staring at him without comprehension.

"Of course I won! The project was accepted into production as I had created it. And believe me, Lisa, with my design the client's going to benefit the most. I've built a variety of machine lines for many different companies that I've worked for, and I know what I'm talking about. I'm still receiving compliments from my past clients."

Mark smiled. There was both a calm sense of confidence as well as a trace of arrogance in his demeanor. And there was something else, almost undetectable. It was a trace, a whisper of sorrow, and it was pain, and innocence in the face of the life's unfairness. Lisa was imbued with both deep admiration and tenderness for this man. She swiftly rose from her chair and hugged him as she lowered onto his lap.

"Why are you so upset? You should be happy," she said, breaking into a smile.

"Well, that's how my reaction is to those people." Mark looked at Lisa forlornly. "I get really depressed when I encounter this stupid aggressiveness." He drew hard on his cigarette and continued slowly putting the words together so she might better comprehend what he was going to say.

"I'm suffering from depression, Lisa. I've tried many things to get rid of it, but all I get is an inconsistent success. I've talked to a variety of psychologists, tried different drugs. Nothing seems to help. I'm especially depressed when I'm alone with my thoughts." His wide, winding brows creased as he frowned.

"Well, you're not alone anymore," Lisa exclaimed fiercely, and kissed him with reassurance. Mark gave her a tender smile.

"You don't know what you're talking about, Lisa. To become close to a man who suffers from depression isn't easy. Look at yourself. You're so petite and fragile. You'd end up draining yourself."

Lisa pushed away from him slightly. "You don't know me, Mark. I may look small and delicate on the outside but I'm entirely the opposite inside. I lost my husband after only one year of marriage. I had to drop out of college and forget about my career goal. I've been raising my son alone, and as you can see, I've been doing just fine." She paused, looking squarely at him, and then continued. "Believe me, I know what depression is. My knowledge of it comes from experience, not from books."

"What was your career goal?" Mark said as he looked at her pensively.

"I studied pre-physical therapy. Completed one year. All "A's", by the way," Lisa bragged. "Physical therapy is a very competitive program. One has to have a great GPA, excellent references, and volunteer work. There are a lot of requirements to get into it."

"What made you quit then?"

"Well." Lisa looked aside. "After my husband died, I had to get a full-time job. My son was only one year old when... when it happened... and everything..." She stopped, not knowing how to explain any further.

"Now that you have me you can return to school," Mark said passionately. He caressed her hair, and smiled at her blushing cheeks. "I'll be working, supporting you and Irving, so you can quit your job and concentrate on your physical therapy program." He paused, looking thoughtfully at her. "Anyway, this masseuse job doesn't seem suitable for you. Look at your small hands." He laughed, squeezing both of her hands in his one big palm.

"I'm perfectly suited to my job," Lisa objected, but she was deeply touched by his words. "Do you know what time it is?" She glanced at her watch. It was almost five in the evening and she had to pick up Irving by seven.

They quickly dressed and went to the nearest Chinese restaurant. Then Mark drove her home. He parked his car close to hers and they kissed. She had to rush to be on time to pick up Irving. When she stepped out of the car Mark lightly pulled her hand, making her sit back in the car.

"I'm so glad I found you, Lisa," he said bluntly.

"Me too." Lisa stroked her hair backwards, stunned by his words. What he just said was exactly what she was thinking. She was so glad she found him. Those words had been in her mind since they first met. She was comforted to know that he felt the same way.

When Lisa got to Irving's friend's house the boys were playing basketball on the backyard court. Irving was excited. On their way home he talked nonstop about his day, especially about fishing.

"Mom, Derek's dad caught this big fish!" he exclaimed as he spread his arms widely to demonstrate the size of the fish. "Would you believe it?"

"No, I wouldn't," Lisa said laughing.

"It's true, Mom. I saw it myself," Irving exclaimed again, nodding hotly, not noticing a bit of teasing in her words. "I caught a few fish too. Not as big as his dad though, but still very big. And Derek caught some too! Derek's mom cleaned my fish and wrapped it in a plastic bag so I could bring it with me. Are you going to fry it tomorrow?" he asked.

Of course, Lisa would be more than happy to cook the fish that her little provider brought home. She was very proud of her son.

They had some tea after they got home. Actually, Lisa had tea and Irving had milk. And they both had cookies. Then Lisa let Irving go to bed and he fell asleep very fast. He was exhausted after the day's activities with Derek. Lisa also went to bed. She fell asleep dreaming about Mark. She missed his arms around her and she longed for the comfort of his big, warm body.

Chapter Six

The next week went pretty much the same. Lisa rushed to work in the morning, then drove home in the evening, and again rushed to work the next morning, and hurried back home in the evening. The only difference between this week and all the others for the past four or five years was that Lisa was suddenly observing her life as an onlooker. Surprisingly enough, there wasn't much in her life to be excited about. She was stunned by the sudden realization of how monotonous and insufficient her life actually was. Her life was like a circle. One big, endless circle where look-alike evenings were replaced by look-alike mornings, which were then imperceptibly but consistently repeated again the following day. *Where will I be in a year or five years or ten years from now?* She found herself wondering. *Nowhere,* seemed to be the only conceivable answer. Her eyebrows were constantly furrowed, forming a tense vertical wrinkle as her mind continued wondering. *Is my masseuse job something that can provide a decent and secure life for me and Irving? What will happen to my job once I'm too old for it? Will it be possible for me to find a different job to provide for Irving and I?*

Lisa couldn't comprehend why these simple and obvious questions kept appearing in her head only now. How would she and Irving survive if she didn't have her masseuse job anymore? What else was she qualified to do? Lisa found herself tightly squeezing her hands together. Breaking the clench, she shook her hands, restoring the circulation. Was it indeed true that her hands would become weaker as she aged? If so, she wouldn't be able to work as much as she was working right now. Her rates would decrease as well as her income. Lisa automatically brought her hands close to her eyes and carefully examined them. Although satisfied with what she saw, she wasn't able to stop worrying.

Gosh, how inexcusably irresponsible she had been, living today like there was no tomorrow.

As she sat contemplating her future, suddenly something sharp, quick and invisible, like lightning, pierced through Lisa's body, and made her heart skip a beat. Distracted from her negative thoughts, she listened to the silence, and a moment later the ring of the telephone broke it. Lisa promptly grabbed the phone, already knowing who was on the other end of the line.

"Hello," she said into the mouthpiece.

"Lisa, hi." It was Mark's deep voice, which she would have been able to tell from a million others. In fact, and to her surprise, Lisa noticed that somehow she'd learned to predict his calls. It had happened several times. Like the previous day, she had been in the kitchen washing the dishes. Out of the blue, she stopped what she was doing, left the dishes in the sink with the water running and went into the living room. It was like she was hypnotized. She didn't think about what she was doing, and afterwards she wasn't able to figure out what had motivated her. She just moved without comprehension, like a zombie, until she stopped right in the middle of the room, wondering why in the world she had walked there. Then the phone rang and uncovered the mystery.

It was like she had a sixth sense or something. She smiled to herself as she greeted Mark.

"Mark, I miss you so much," she said, and her eyebrows raised in surprise from her own words. To tell the truth, she usually wouldn't have verbalized anything like that to a man that she'd just recently met. It would've sounded like she was desperate and she would've never been able to admit it even if she was. But it was different with Mark. She'd become strangely, unbelievably attached to him right from their first glance. It felt so natural to have him in her life, like they were meant to be together and it was only a matter of time before they would unite "for better or for worse."

"I miss you too, Lisa." She heard him dragging on his cigarette. "I am looking forward to seeing you for our Friday night date. I can't wait to hold you in my arms."

"Mark," Lisa said, hesitating. "As much as I want to, I can't see you tomorrow. Basketball season started at the school and Irving's on the team. They have games on Friday nights. Tomorrow's supposed to be a big game, and I wouldn't dare miss it."

Mark paused. "Lisa, you're killing me." He was slowly stretching the words in disbelief. "The only thing that kept me energized during the week was the thought of seeing you. Are you positive that there's nothing that could be done or arranged differently so we can meet at last?" He hesitated for a moment, then asked. "How about after the game?"

"It'd be too late. I have to take Irving home, feed him, get him ready for bed and then—" Lisa bit her lip, berating herself for ruining her date with Mark.

"That's fine. I understand," Mark said. "It's just that I've missed you so much and really wanted to see you tomorrow night." He dragged on his cigarette. "My friends have a birthday brunch on Saturday. They invited us both. So, I'll pick you up on Saturday at 11:30 a.m. Will you be ready?"

Of course she would be. She couldn't wait to see Mark and, expecting that they would be seeing each other on Saturday, had already arranged for Mary to come and watch Irving.

They talked for a while longer, discussing their days and how anxious they were to see each other.

"Who was that?" Irving asked when she finally hung up the phone.

Lisa paused, taken unaware by this seemingly simple question. "Was that a guy?" Irving pulled a portable computer game from his pocket and turned it on.

"It was just one of my friends." Lisa sensed a blush in her cheeks. She realized that she didn't have an answer to this question. How was she going to explain this to Irving if she had trouble understanding it herself? How could it be that she could be so deeply in love with a guy she barely knew?

"Is he going to live with us?"

"I don't know, son. We aren't at that point in our relationship yet." Lisa paused, amazed by his grown-up, direct question. "Why do you think he's going to?"

"Well." Irving made a face. "You're just always on the phone with him. And you talk about him a lot!" he said, gazing at her with reproach.

"Irving, are you getting jealous?" Lisa exclaimed with laughter. "Come on, you know that your mom loves you more than anything in the world. Nobody would ever replace you in my heart. You know that!" She held her arms out to him. "Come here, son."

Irving grudgingly took a few steps toward her. His face reflected the struggle he was going through. He tried to keep a frown on his face, but her words had already filled him with pride and relief. Lisa approached him swiftly and grabbed him into her arms.

"How great, and cute, you are," she said laughing, kissing and caressing his hair.

"I'm not." Irving started to blush. "I'm almost eight, Mom!"

"Of course you are, sonny," she started with a smile, but Irving interrupted her, throwing his portable game on the couch.

"Can Billy come over so we can watch this video? He already called me three times. Can he? Please!"

"Of course he can come over, but both of you would have to eat dinner first."

The agreement was made, and Irving jumped to the phone to call Billy, leaving Lisa amused at how easily youth can throw off their emotional burdens and move on.

CHAPTER SEVEN

Thursday came around. From the morning it started out haphazardly. First, Lisa forgot her car key inside the house and didn't realize it until she got to the car. The night before it had fallen from her key chain and she put it on the dresser, intending to fit it on the chain later. But she never did. Blaming herself for being so absentminded, she turned back to the apartment and picked up the key. *This should be a great example for Irving of what usually happens to a person when they put off things that need to be done right away,* she thought wryly. Although, it would be better to set positive examples for him instead. Lisa grinned as she took a quick glance in the mirror. She didn't consider herself too superstitious, but nevertheless, she found that some signs are meaningful. The superstition that returning home for something forgotten in the house would begin a bad day usually turned out to be true for her. A glance in a mirror was supposed to counteract the bad luck.

Today, however, the bad luck didn't seem to be frightened away so easily. Lisa rushed to the salon praying she would be there on time for her first session. Opening the door to the salon, she discovered a pitch-black room, scaring herself to death that she might have mistaken the salon's entrance with another storefront. Running outside, she looked around to make sure that the door was the correct one. Finding that it was, she was only partially relieved. Why were all the lights out?

She went back inside and felt her way to the back kitchen, where she found the girls drinking coffee under the dim light of candles and the shadow of their boss. The news was that construction workers accidentally knocked out the electrical wires, so the electricity in some of the nearby buildings, including their salon, had shut down for an indefinite amount of time. Their boss was furious and was taking her anger out on the staff. She'd had to turn down clients, and losing their business infuriated her. She reminded the girls over and over how hard she'd worked to build up the clientele list and obsessed over the fact that it was now in jeopardy. The girls remained silent and exchanged glances. Margaret gestured with her index finger at her temple, indicating that her boss was crazy. Of course what had happened was outrageous, but it wasn't their fault that the electricity was shut off and that they couldn't provide service to the scheduled clients. As far as their commissions were concerned, they wouldn't benefit from standing there in the dark kitchen and not working either.

When the electricity was finally fixed everyone was relieved and there was peace at the salon again. Everything gradually returned to normal and the incoming clients didn't have a clue about the recent electrical power outage and the chaos it had caused in the salon. They received their treatments as scheduled, on time and at their best. Nevertheless, the employees still seemed stressed, especially Lisa. At the end of the day she felt unbelievably drained and couldn't concentrate well. Almost mindlessly, she plodded to the parking lot, sat in her car, turned on the engine and put it into reverse. Suddenly a jolt hit the rear of the car and the vehicle wheezed, then abruptly died. Lisa's upper body was thrown forward by the inertia, then back into her seat. *Wow! That was something I was really looking forward to today. A car accident!* Lisa rolled her eyes in disbelief then let out a deep forlorn sigh and got out of the car.

A yellow pillar was jutting out of her car, right between the edge of the back door and the trunk. The original color of her car was scratched out with wide and bright yellow stripes. She bit her lips, ready to break down into tears. The bad luck today seemed to be picking up steam. She headed back into the car and turned the key. The engine creaked and halted. Lisa tried it again, and then once more, with a similar result. The ignition screeched and wheezed, not seeming to get anywhere. Lisa angrily hit the steering wheel. Now she would need to take the car to the body shop. Or worse, have to have it towed there, for God's sake. Her Saturday date with Mark was looking jeopardized by this twist of fate. How was she going to break the news to him? She already turned down their Friday date because of Irving's basketball game, and now she didn't see any possibility of going to his friends' Saturday brunch! And how in the world was she even going to make it to Irving's game if her car was still stalled? She wouldn't be able to take care of the car until Saturday since the mechanic was already closed and tomorrow morning she needed to go to work. Lisa hit her vehicle in despair. Just going to work tomorrow was going to be a challenge now. It looked like the dark forces were definitely getting in her way today.

Lisa took a deep breath and tried to compose herself, since getting angry wasn't helping her situation. She decided instead to turn her bad luck around and to concentrate on what she needed to do. She remembered her husband teaching her some techniques on how to start a malfunctioning car. Trying one more time to start the vehicle, she pushed the gas pedal slowly to the halfway point, and then, while still holding the pedal, she turned the key in the ignition. Now, to Lisa's great satisfaction, the engine turned over, bringing the car back to life. Lisa carefully pulled out of the parking lot and slowly guided the car onto the road, managing to make it home. As she rushed upstairs she formulated a plan on how to accomplish everything that needed to get done.

As she stepped into her apartment, she grabbed the phone and called Margaret, and asked her for a lift tomorrow. Lisa's home was on Margaret's way to work and she said she was happy to pick Lisa up and take her back home afterwards. Margaret was very sympathetic to Lisa's problem and gave her plenty of advice on where to find the best mechanic and the best deal to repair the car. Finally, she brought up the morning incident, complaining about the terrible headache that it had given her and mentioning the tons of extra-strength Advil she had to consume. They discussed their "mad" boss, and their stressful jobs. Lisa liked Margaret. She was a funny and easygoing person, and she had a wonderful ability to turn things around so that even the worst nightmare would sound like a joke in her interpretation. As Lisa spoke with Margaret, laughing at her stories and at themselves, she felt a comforting relief as the tension, which had solidly occupied her upper shoulders and neck from the beginning of the day and had not gone away, now began to slowly disperse. Lisa felt the blood flow coming to her stiff neck, warming it up and releasing the stress.

"Margaret, I adore your spirit!" she confessed when they were wrapping up.

"I know, everybody does," Margaret said, laughing. Lisa hung up the phone, smiling.

Next she dialed her neighbors, the parents of Irving's friend Billy. Since Billy was also playing on the team tomorrow, Lisa asked them if they would be nice enough to take her as well. They said they would be glad to, so another problem was solved relatively easily. And at last, she made her final call.

"Mark, my car's broken," she started.

"What happened?" He sounded worried. Are you all right?"

"Yes. I'm fine." She hesitated for a while, berating herself for what she was going to say.

"But it seems I won't be able to make it on Saturday," she almost whispered it in the mouthpiece.

"Why? I don't understand. You're hiding something from me, Lisa. Have you had a car accident? Are you injured?"

"No, it wasn't a car accident." She paused. "Although, come to think of it, it was. I hit my car on a pillar, it got damaged and I had a hard time getting it started. I can't risk leaving it unattended for another week, as I depend on this car every day. Saturday is the only day that I can make it to the body shop," she added hopelessly.

"That's all?" She heard him let out a sigh of relief.

"Isn't that enough?" Lisa's brows rose in amazement. She wasn't expecting this kind of reaction from him.

"Lisa, what I was trying to say is that you don't have to worry about the car. It's nothing." His deep voice sounded so reassuring. "I'll come over on Sunday and fix your car. It will run and look even better than before. Nobody will know the difference."

After their conversation, Lisa sat still for a moment with the phone clamped between her knees. *It was God's help that brought Mark to me,* she thought. The day that had started upside down in the morning, and had gotten worse and worse, had nonetheless resulted in a happy ending. Not believing in signs after all! She grinned. What might have happened if she hadn't glanced in the mirror to counteract the bad luck from returning home for her key? Lisa put her cordless phone on the stand and proceeded into the kitchen. She didn't want to guess what might've happened. That unfortunate chain of events today could well be considered a coincidence, but it could also be justified by the fact that she returned home for her key. Whether coincidence or not, Lisa wasn't going to discard the little things that she knew about signs, even though some people would call it superstition.

Chapter Eight

Saturday at 11:30 a.m. sharp, Mark's Acura honked in front of Lisa's living room window. They drove to a small, cozy Italian restaurant. When they stepped inside, a few people were sitting at the round table against the wall. A large pastel painting in a white frame above the table portrayed a beautiful young woman carrying a big straw basket full of grapes over her shoulder. A handkerchief covered her hair and revealed only one small piece, almost the same color as the straw basket. The picture was so alive and full of energy that Lisa involuntary stopped for a moment to admire it.

"I'm Jerome." A low voice behind her announced. Startled, Lisa looked over at a short man who had suddenly appeared. He smiled broadly at her and energetically stretched out his hand. "Mark's told me a lot about you," he confessed, focusing his direct, unblinking stare on her as he shook her hand. With his big, round stomach and short, curved legs he resembled a Gingerbread Man. Yet, his posture, his look, and his overall appearance projected self-satisfaction and vitality. "Street-smart" was what people would call him.

"Nice meeting you," Lisa shook his hand. "I've also heard many good things about you. I know you're Mark's best friend."

Obviously flattered by the compliment, Jerome grinned appreciatively. He opened his mouth to reply when Mark moved between them, shielding Lisa from him.

"Romy, leave Lisa alone for a moment. Let her sit down first and then you can throw all of your many stories on her."

"As you wish! Follow me. We're all already situated at the table." Jerome/Romy retreated without visible disappointment.

Lisa threw a quick look at Mark. He read the question in her eyes correctly.

"Romy's my best friend and it's our normal way of communicating with each other," he explained aloud, smiling openly at Jerome. "Right, Romy?"

"You should hear how I communicate with him!" Jerome, who now sat across the table, said as he burst into peals of laughter.

Mark pulled out a chair for Lisa and sat down next to her. "How long have you two known each other?" she asked.

"All of our lives!" Jerome exclaimed. "Ever since I can remember, Mark was always around." He laughed. He spoke very loud and clear, emphasizing words like "remember," "Mark," and "always" and articulating with his hand as if he was giving a speech in front of a large audience.

"Now, I've always got my wife around instead," he said with a nod to the woman next to him. "But as for the good old times." He winked to Mark.

The woman on his right gave him a long, heart-freezing stare. She was wearing an old-fashioned, double-breasted blue jacket and a lacy white blouse. She was a head taller than her husband but was still sitting tall with her back straight and her chin lifted up. Her short, dark brown hair, permanently waved and with a neat part, was smooth and shining.

"Let me introduce my wife to you, Lisa. This is Connie, the flower of my life," Jerome said, grinning.

Waving her hand toward her husband in a disrespectful gesture, Connie looked at Lisa. "Don't take him seriously, he's already drunk. It's very nice to finally meet you Lisa. Mark couldn't stop talking about you."

"Okay, time's up!" Jerome rose from his chair with a glass in his outstretched hand. "Cheers everybody," he said, as he downed his glass in one gulp.

"Jerome," his wife said as she punched him in the side. "That's enough already!"

"What have I done?" He turned his smile to her.

"You forgot to introduce us," the woman at his left interjected.

"He'd never forget to take his drink though," Connie said sarcastically as she attempted to take away the glass that her husband just refilled. She didn't succeed, since he turned faster than she grabbed. He swiftly stretched his hand with the glass far away from her reach and laughed with satisfaction at how furiously mad his wife had become.

"This is Nora and her husband Steve," he said, introducing the couple. "Very religious people, but still! In the process of searching for their true faith."

"Thank you. You finally noticed us," Nora said, ignoring his last remark. "Nice meeting you," she greeted Lisa.

"Nice meeting you, too." Lisa smiled at Nora. Mark sat in silence, watching the scene with a grin.

"They always fight. Jerome and Connie I mean," he whispered in Lisa's ear. "As long as I've known them they have behaved like this. It's unbelievably amazing how people who fight so often could still be together, yet they have been married for years. They have two children, a big house, and they honestly think of themselves as a good and happy family." Mark was going to say something else when a young waitress approached and asked him what he would like to drink. He lifted his face to her and paused, studying the girl with interest.

"I'll take whatever you recommend. I'm at the mercy of your taste," he finally answered with a broad smile.

"What if my taste is awful?" she laughed.

"Such a beautiful woman must have good taste." His smile now spread to his ears.

"Iced tea, then," she said confidently.

"Iced tea, it is," Mark concluded with satisfaction.

Lisa felt the blood rising up to her face and beads of sweat starting to form on her forehead. When the waitress came to take her order, she could hardly force herself to murmur something about plain water.

Mark turned his head to look at her. "Lisa, you should've ordered the iced—"

"No, I'm fine with water," she interrupted abruptly.

"What?" he asked easily, and lit a cigarette. "What's wrong, Lisa?" His eyes looked innocent.

"Nothing," Lisa said. Shaking her head and changing the subject, she turned to Nora. "I've heard your daughter's attending a Catholic school. Does she like it there?" Nora seemed very pleased with the question.

"Yes. In fact, she can't stop talking about her new school. She's very interested in religion and she asks a lot of questions about the world. You know. What came first and how it came, and–" Nora didn't get a chance to finish the sentence when Jerome giggled out loud.

"Of course she's asking questions. She's just ten years old and she's confused! I would be too if I were in her shoes!"

"You're a confused man when you're in your own shoes," Nora returned with indignation. Jerome broke into laughter once more.

"Correct me if I'm wrong, but from the first grade and every freaking year after that your daughter went to a new school, didn't she?" He counted on his fingers. "First grade, Montessori school. Then that academy. Now what grade is she in? Third! And what school is she in now?" He looked around victoriously. "Now, it's a Catholic school! Isn't that just great? Where will she go next? Hebrew school?"

Lisa gazed across the table. A polite smile floated across her lips but her mind was far away from the topic being discussed. What had just happened? Did Mark really flirt with that young waitress or had it simply been her imagination? She thought about it in despair. Most of all, her own reaction to that episode had truly frightened her. Maybe it was just a playful chat he was having with that attractive young waitress. Why should she take it so seriously? He was just being polite, that's all. Well, a little *over* polite. But then again, he only placed his order. He had simply ordered a drink! Iced tea. Period. Then, why was she having these uncomfortable feelings? Why was she becoming so obsessed with this that she wasn't able to relax, and was having trouble following the conversation at the table? Lisa rubbed her temples, struggling to organize her own thoughts, when Mark wrapped his hand on her shoulder and pulled her closer to him.

"Are you getting bored? Let's go dance," he whispered into her ear, his soft lips brushing her cheek. The touch of his strong, warm body made her forget about everything. All her doubts flew away with the easiness of the wind as her heart pounded with gentle waves of tenderness and happiness. She couldn't explain it with words, not even in her mind, but she knew that he was the one. She knew that it was inevitable that they would be together. And that was the only thing that mattered. Everything else was just fuss.

Mark rose from his chair, one hand still on her arm, and pulled her to her feet. They danced and they ate. And Lisa discovered that, on top of all his other talents, Mark had a great sense of humor. It was kind of a dry English humor, which made him even more appealing. If, of course, he could be any more appealing.

The conversation at the table flowed smoothly with jokes and funny stories. Even Jerome's wife, Connie, unbuttoned the collar of her lacy blouse and enjoyed the laughter with everybody. Her husband didn't waste the opportunity though. As Connie turned her attention away from him, he quickly poured some alcohol into his glass and drained it in one gulp. A cheerful smile spread across his face and he winked at Lisa in conspiracy as their glances met. Lisa giggled. It looked so funny to see a grown man behaving like a mischievous schoolboy. But then, it wasn't only humor in his act. Somehow he showed a great care and love for his wife. It was somewhere deep inside this seemingly tough man, and it was very touching.

Time went by pleasantly and quickly, and nobody could believe it when the brunch was over.

"How about we all go to our place?" Jerome proposed. "We have a nice house and a pool table."

"I've made great cookies," Connie interjected. Lisa loved the idea. She glanced at Mark.

"With pleasure." He smiled down at her.

45

"Nora, Steve, how about you guys. Are you coming?" Jerome asked the couple.

Unfortunately, they couldn't make it. Steve had work to finish and Nora had to take her daughter to a ballet lesson.

They accompanied Nora and Steve to the parking lot and when the couple left they sped off in their cars to Jerome and Connie's house.

In the car Lisa felt slightly light-headed. She reclined her seat back and looked out the window. The colorful trees were shining under the rays of the sun and shadows passed through them. The weather was beautiful and so was Lisa's mood. The glow of the sunlight was so bright that it beamed into her eyes, blinding her. She stretched and bent her legs to the right, setting them on the seat while she turned from the sun toward Mark. Burying her ear in the headrest, she looked at him thoughtfully, searching his profile. He noticed her stare and reached up with his right hand to touch her hair.

"Are you tired?" he asked softly.

No, Lisa wasn't tired. In fact, she was filled with energy, happiness, and passion. She moved in the seat to its left edge and cuddled her face on Mark's chest. His right hand slid down from her hair to her shoulders and firmly but very gently hung around her neck. Lisa's head was trapped between his strong bicep and his shoulder.

He looked down at her; his lips slightly touched her forehead. "Lisa, I can't drive like this," he said, laughing, as she twisted under him trying to free herself from his embrace.

He released her and pulled out his cigarette pack from the pocket of his jacket. He lit it quickly, blew the cigarette smoke into the window, and looked over at Lisa again.

"It was a wonderful brunch, wasn't it? I could tell you liked my friends." He took another drag on his cigarette.

"I could tell you liked that girl!" The words inadvertently flew out of Lisa's mouth. She realized what she just said only when Mark looked down at her with confusion.

"What? What girl? What are you talking about, Lisa?" He sounded amused, like he thought that Lisa was a bit tipsy.

Drawing herself from him, Lisa dove out from under his arm and back into her seat. "The waitress. Your 'iced-tea' girl," she reminded him courteously. "Remember now?"

To her surprise, Mark burst out laughing. She stared at him, confused. First, this episode with the waitress from the restaurant. Lisa thought that the memory of it had been gone from her mind for good but now, out of the blue, it suddenly came fresh and alive to the surface, which made her a little nervous. And then this wild laughter of Mark's!

"What's so funny?" she finally broke down and asked, a bit more sharply than she intended to. Mark stopped laughing but a small smile remained on his face.

"I'm sorry, Lisa. I didn't mean to laugh at you. But I thought that you might have been jealous, which was kind of funny." She continued staring at him, still confused. Mark turned his head to the front window, searching the road.

"Because I didn't care about that waitress at all," he explained evenly. "But I wanted you to be jealous. Not intentionally, but instinctively, I suppose," he added, smiling thoughtfully. "See, there's a whole psychology system which lies under that. Look at me. I'm almost forty; middle-aged, divorced, not much of a significant man. Whereas you're a very attractive, young, intelligent woman who might find out one day that she deserves better. That's why I have to be creative. I want you to think that I'm the man who's irresistible to young women." He ran the back of his fingertip up over her cheek and smiled widely. "Then, per the universal woman's logic, you'll be attracted to me even more. Am I right?" Mark's eyes shined with a sort of humor but they also expressed some certainty.

"What in the world is the universal woman's logic?" Lisa exclaimed, purposefully sounding indignant. "It's not true. You're stereotyping women!" The last line didn't sound as strong and confident, though. Against her own will she had to admit that there was some, although very peculiar, point in his statement. Nevertheless, Lisa was prepared to disagree with Mark and stand up with all her might on the behalf of all women when a sudden thought hit her and she lost all her steam. It seemed shockingly, unbelievably fallacious, but there was only one simple explanation to all of Mark's absurdity about women: he wasn't as arrogant and self-confident as he appeared to be. The discovery that such strong, masculine and smart man such as Mark would need to seek reassurance from outside sources to prove himself amazed her. Her heart filled with tenderness for him. Moved by these impulses, she leaned back into him and put her arms around his neck. Mark glanced down at her. His lips gently touched her hair; his gaze was warm. Neither of them said anything, but they understood one another beyond words.

CHAPTER NINE

In a short time Mark turned onto a small private street and parked by a large, two-story brick house. They walked together along a reddish-brown sidewalk. When they entered the house they saw their reflection in a mirror on the closet door at the end of a small hallway. Next to the mirror was a shoe rack with slippers, which they put on before entering the large living room. Lisa looked around, taking in the magnitude of the room. There was large, heavy furniture of an earlier era, a thick, dark burgundy rug, tasteful pictures in golden frames, and a large granite fireplace. The interior of this room had been well planned, and the decor was expensive and beautifully matched. Nevertheless, to Lisa it looked somewhat pompous and stuffy, like an exhibition in a museum. There was something in the room that didn't fit with the rest. It was a large, wide aquarium, which was built into a partial wall at the opening of the dining room. Three aquarium lamps illuminated it, causing the water to sparkle and shine. Colorful fish slipped smoothly through the water. This particular area brightened the house and filled it with positive energy. The aquarium drew Lisa's attention and she walked closer to it to gaze at the fish.

"Do you like it?" Jerome said as he approached her. He looked very pleased with her interest in his "beloved child," as he referred to it.

"Did you finally put in the automatic pump?" Mark asked before Lisa could respond. "Last time I was here the pump was manual."

"He sure did," Connie said. "I'd have thrown this tank and its fish away before now. I was sick and tired of cleaning it."

"I assembled the pump in the basement and drilled holes for the wires to go into the tank from there. Let's go down to the basement. I'll show you the equipment," Jerome said to Mark.

"And we're going to the kitchen," Connie said, smiling at Lisa when the men left. "The kitchen is the best room in every house, right?" she said as they walked there together.

To Lisa's surprise, the spacious, well-lit kitchen did, in fact, look very impressive. Shiny multi-paned windows stretched along one wall, and a wide glass door opened to the porch where colorful trees rustled in the breeze, making the kitchen feel warm and cheerful. The modern cabinets were paneled in dark cherry wood. In the middle of the room was an island with a granite counter top and a stove in the center. Across and to the left of the window was the eat-in area. A round table was fully covered by a yellow tablecloth with fringe on the end. There was another small, white lace cloth in the center of the table and an ornate crystal vase holding red and white roses. The seats of six tall, cherry chairs were fitted with red and white cushions.

"I crocheted it myself," Connie said, referring to the lace cloth. "I like to crochet sometimes. Of course, these days we can buy everything in the store so our kids know nothing about crafts, or cooking," she said as she pursed her lips in disapproval and continued, "but nevertheless the homemade things are different. Nothing can compare to them."

"I like it in here, it's a very warm and comfortable place," Lisa said, unable to refrain from the compliment.

"We spend the majority of our time in the kitchen, so it should be as comfortable as possible," Connie said proudly.

Lisa didn't object, not because it seemed a bit dangerous to argue with Connie, but because Lisa absolutely agreed with her in this case. Come to think of it, Lisa's kitchen was also an "all-purpose" room where she cooked, ate, played chess, and even watched TV with Irving. Lisa also loved to have coffee in the kitchen or simply enjoy it there with her girlfriends. And that's not because she didn't have any other place in her apartment for entertainment, because she did. Her living room was comfortable, with a television, DVD player and other leisure attributes. But somehow the kitchen felt more private, more comfy, or something like that.

Connie filled the teapot with water and placed it on the stove. She pulled a big glass plate from the cabinet, then filled it with fresh, homemade chocolate chip cookies and placed them on the table. "Maybe I should serve this on the porch?" she asked, looking at Lisa thoughtfully and then answered her own question. "No, I'd rather not. It's kind of cold and windy out there today."

Lisa was suddenly startled by a soft voice behind her asking, "Mom, where's Dad?" She turned around and was surprised to see a little girl standing there. She had entered the room so quietly that Lisa hadn't noticed her until she spoke.

"He's in the basement sweetie, with Uncle Mark," Connie answered, and introduced the girl to Lisa. "This is my daughter, Anna." She smiled.

"Nice to meet you," Lisa said, grinning down at the girl. "How old are you?"

The girl looked back at Lisa. She kept silent while focusing her dark brown eyes on Lisa's for a long time. Lisa remembered the same look from her old teacher in high school when she didn't know the correct answer to a question. Now, as the girl kept staring, Lisa caught herself wondering what she had done wrong. To her relief, the girl turned her face to her mom, who answered for her.

"Anna's seven," she responded and then added with edification in her voice. "You could've answered that yourself, Anna." Then she took a cookie from the plate and handed it to the girl. "Go see what your dad and Uncle Mark are doing in the basement."

When the girl disappeared as quickly and as tranquilly as she had recently materialized, Lisa asked Connie, "Is Mark actually Anna's uncle?"

Connie smiled. "No, he isn't. He's just been a friend with us for a long, long time and he's known Anna from the time she was in diapers. I don't recall how it first happened but I remember that she always used to call him "uncle," and I wouldn't correct her and neither would Mark or Jerome. Mark actually enjoys having her call him her uncle," she explained. "Mark likes Anna a lot. My daughter's not an easy child; she has a strong personality, you know."

"I bet she does," Lisa said as she remembered the girl's stare.

"And Mark was able to find a common language with her," Connie continued. "She adores him." She paused and then added, "Mark's very good with children. He's very much the opposite of Jerome, who doesn't know how to talk to his own kids. It's very sad that Mark can't have his own children live with him."

"You mean because of his divorce?" Lisa asked.

Connie gave her a long, searching look. "I don't think I should say much about this," she began, hesitantly. "It's Mark's personal life and I'm not the kind of person who talks about other people's personal lives. All I will say is that Mark's not like most men. When it comes to children, he's the best. It was he, not his wife, who spent nights with the babies when they were crying or sick or getting their first teeth. He was the one who went to parent's meetings at school and checked the children's homework. He always had time for them, even though he works very hard."

"He must be missing them then," Lisa said, tempted to know more details, but she cut herself off. She didn't find it appropriate to talk about Mark's life behind his back. She changed the subject. "My son's pretty much the same age as your daughter. He's going to turn eight this December."

"Is he a Capricorn?" Connie inquired with interest. "It's a good sign. Usually Capricorns are hard-working, charming and successful," she said when Lisa confirmed Irving's Zodiac sign. "My daughter's a Pisces, and she inherited all the features of her sign. She's quiet, smart, and extremely receptive. And she's a compassionate girl, although she holds all her emotions and feelings deep inside. Try not to believe in Astrology too much," Connie said with a laugh.

Lisa was surprised that Connie knew about Astrology. Somehow she thought that women like Connie only believed in practical things that they could either see or do. *Once again, don't stereotype people*, she told herself. *They will amaze you with their uniqueness and unpredictability.*

"Where're my cookies?" Always cheerful and loud, Jerome's voice broke in as he, Mark and Anna showed up in the kitchen.

"Please find your seats. Everything's ready," Connie invited. Surprisingly, she didn't berate her husband for his bad manners.

The cookies were fresh and soft and they tasted great. Connie was a very hospitable hostess and a terrific cook, Lisa had to admit. They all had a lovely time. After tea they went to the porch where they sat for a long time on a bench under a big, leafy elm tree, just relaxing, taking in the fresh air, and enjoying nature.

Then Jerome went inside and brought out a couple of bottles of beer from the refrigerator, this time intercepting his wife's disapproving look. She didn't say anything, but invited Lisa to see the garden, leaving Mark and Jerome to their beer. Connie and Lisa took their shoes off and headed for the yard. The garden was big enough for several trees, including a few peach trees, multiple rose bushes and numerous other beautiful flowers. In the right-hand corner of the yard, Connie even had an area where she grew her own tomatoes, sweet peppers, cucumbers and green onions. These veggies, depending on the season, actually went to her kitchen from this garden. It was wonderful! Lisa imagined that one day she would have a garden like this herself, and she and Irving would eat their own home-grown vegetables. "Irving, would you like some green onions? Go to the yard and pick a few please," she'd say, and Irving would run outside to pick them and they would very much enjoy eating them. Lisa smiled, envisioning this picture.

They walked with bare feet on the neatly trimmed grass. It was soft and tickled their feet.

"It's very healthy to be in contact with the soil," Connie commented.

Lisa agreed. "Our feet have millions of receptors corresponding to the internal organs of our bodies. We actually activate them by walking on the ground," she kept up.

"I was thinking of buying a house somewhere in Wisconsin, close to a lake so we could go there in the summer and enjoy nature," Connie mentioned thoughtfully.

"That's a wonderful idea," Lisa exclaimed. "Anna would definitely like it there. Children like being around the water."

"Yes, it's true. I'd love to have it for her." Connie paused. "But I'm afraid that my sweetheart will spend all the time there with his fellow drinkers."

"Who's your sweetheart?" Jerome's voice rose from his place on the bench. But before Connie could reply he proposed— "It's almost dinner time and I'm starving. How about we order food from the Chinese restaurant across the street and have a nice dinner together?"

"It's a lovely restaurant," Connie said as they approached the bench. "The food's always good and fresh there, and it's not expensive. We often order from there and the owners know us and always give us a good deal."

Mark rose from the bench swiftly and put his arm around Lisa's shoulders. "As much as we'd love to, we have to be leaving soon," he said, politely declining the invitation. "It's already late and Lisa has to get home to take care of her son, Irving," he explained.

"Who's with your son now?" Connie inquired.

"He's with his babysitter, Mary," Lisa replied. "She's a very good lady and she's taking excellent care of Irving."

"So why hurry?" Jerome interjected. "The dinner will take just a couple of hours and you'll still be home on time." Lisa glanced at Mark.

"No, we should be going." He pressed Lisa closer to him. "I have to take Lisa home and you guys also need your rest from this long day."

"As you wish," Jerome said as he made a dismissive gesture with his hand and looked away from them.

"Come on, let them go. You always try to force people to do what you want," Connie said with indignation. "It's impolite and it's also annoying, you know!"

"I'm the one who does that?" Jerome asked but then smiled openly at Mark and Lisa. "Okay, guys, if you've got to go then you've got to go." He held his hand out to Mark. "I had a great day today. Happiest birthday in many years." He shook Mark's hand and then held his hand out to Lisa. "It was very nice to have you here, Lisa," he said, smiling at her. "I enjoyed your company and hope that we can all get together again."

"Me too," Connie added. "I'm very pleased to have met you, Lisa."

"Thank you. It was nice getting to know you too. I had a wonderful time," Lisa said.

The couple accompanied them to the car and Connie waved goodbye to them as they pulled away. Lisa also waved to her from the car, looking back over her shoulder until Connie became very, very small and then completely disappeared from view. Lisa turned over and lounged comfortably in her seat.

"It was a wonderful day, wasn't it?" she recalled.

Mark's hand reached out to caress her hair and then slid to her shoulder, squeezing it lightly. Lowering his head to her, he whispered into her ear. "I've missed you all day long. I couldn't wait to hold you in my arms, to touch you, to kiss you." His hot breath burned her skin; his eyes conveyed a clearly promising message. There was both the compliment and the desire, and an openly revealed intention in his statement and in his gaze that made Lisa flush under his direct stare. She turned away to look out the window.

"Where are we going? You said to Jerome that you're taking me home," she reminded him, just for the sake of buying some time to gather herself together.

Although Mark didn't say anything, he certainly noticed her confusion. His eyes lit with humor and his lips opened in a smile. "I couldn't wait to find any excuse to leave, and taking you home was the first one that popped into my head," he confessed, looking passionately down at her. "But you didn't think I'd let you go so easily tonight, did you?" He pulled out a cigarette from his packet and glanced toward Lisa, his eyes filled with passion. "Cigarette?" he offered.

Lisa accepted. Mark pulled out another cigarette, lit them both and held one out to Lisa. She drew the hot smoke in, noticing that this time the smoke wasn't as bitter as it was before. To her surprise, the smoke felt like a soft, fluffy cotton wool that filled her up with relaxation and comfort. Amazingly enough, the cigarette felt absolutely differently for her today than it had before.

"What kind of cigarettes are these?" She asked.

"Marlboro lights; it's one of the better brands," Mark replied absentmindedly. "Jerome likes you, you know," he said. He sounded like he was continuing on the subject that was on his mind. Lisa glanced at him.

"I'm flattered," she said. "But I wouldn't expect otherwise." Her eyes filled with a playful smile.

"Jerome's compliments are actually very hard to come by," Mark said, shaking his head. "Jerome's a womanizer but he has never respected women that much. Therefore, getting a compliment from Jerome is worth a lot." He grinned at Lisa.

"I don't understand. How could he be such a womanizer? I thought that they got married right after high school!" Lisa exclaimed, ignoring what she thought was a compliment.

Mark looked down at her with an odd expression. "I didn't say that he was dating women only before his marriage."

"Does Connie know about this?"

"Know about what?"

"That Jerome's—" she paused, looking for the appropriate word. "Seeing other women," she finally completed the sentence.

"Of course she does." Mark drew on his cigarette and smiled at her confused glare. "You have to understand, Connie sees it in a different way. Jerome makes much more money than she does – she couldn't have her lifestyle without him. He gives her a sense of security. If you think about it, Connie has everything a woman needs. She's a wise woman and understands that men have their needs. As long as her family doesn't suffer from it, then she can look past it."

"I don't know," Lisa said, shrugging. "It seemed like they were a happy family to me. They have two kids. I've met their youngest daughter and she's a very cute and well-behaved child."

"Oh, please," Mark interrupted. "Their oldest daughter, Sara, got married at eighteen, right after she graduated from high school, and immediately moved with her husband to New York, far away from her parents. And Anna? What a poor child! She sees her parents fighting every day and just bottles up her feelings, keeping her mouth shut." Suddenly, he became very agitated and distressed, as though the topic Lisa opened had touched fresh wounds in his heart. He lit another cigarette and hastily drew on it.

"What can you possibly know?" he said with condescension. "You came from a happy and loving family—but this girl, this girl—" He circled his hand in the air. "Being a child, she never even got a chance to feel like one, to think, to behave like one!" he said, finishing the sentence temperamentally. "The only time that she can allow herself to be a kid is when I'm with her. When I talk to her, read books to her, or when I teach her to rollerblade. Then she blossoms. That's why she likes me so much."

He blew the stream of smoke out through the crack in the car window and then directed a thoughtful gaze to the road in front of him.

"You must be missing your daughter a lot," Lisa whispered quietly. Mark didn't say anything. He only dragged on his cigarette and continued looking into the distance.

The miles had flown by and they were now turning onto a familiar street, surrounded by trees full of yellow and green leaves. Mark parked the car, walked over to Lisa's door and held out his hand.

"Your hand, madam!" He snapped his heels like a bellboy. He looked funny and sexy at the same time.

"With pleasure." Lisa smiled and stretched her hand out to him. Mark gently took her hand and turned it palm-side up. His eyes concentrated on hers as his lips descended to her palm, heating the skin with his hot touch, and then moved on to her wrist.

"So romantic," she managed to say as her skin erupted into goosebumps.

"The romance has just begun." Mark swiftly pulled her out of the car and into his embrace; his muscles tightened under his shirt and his heart started to beat faster. Lisa suddenly felt her legs get weak under the weight of her body. She wrapped her arms around his neck for support when suddenly her legs left the ground. She flew up into the air and swiftly landed in Mark's arms. Everything happened so fast that Lisa didn't even get a chance to get frightened.

"Does this madam like the service?" Holding her like a feather in his big, strong arms, he smiled.

"She likes it; she really does." Lisa leaned her head onto his shoulder.

"I thought so," Mark said and proceeded to the entrance of the building. With her in his arms, he opened the lobby door and stepped into the elevator. The elevator brought them to the third floor. Mark opened the door to his condo and nudged it shut with his foot. Walking with her to his bedroom, both of them full of laughter, they fell onto his bed and then time was lost as Lisa found herself escaping in his bed sheets to freely soar in the fluffy clouds, weightless and without a care...

***

It was around eight in the evening when she came back to reality. They quickly got dressed and rushed to Mark's car. Glancing around at the dark, Lisa sighed.

"How could it be so late already? I hope Mary put Irving to bed on time."

"You have nothing to worry about. From what you've told me, Mary has proven to you many times that she's a very responsible and reliable babysitter, and that she's very good with Irving. Hasn't she?" Mark assured her. His confident voice soothed her, and she voiced her agreement.

On the way to her house, they were passing a Wendy's when Mark suddenly realized how hungry he was. "You must be starving," he said. Lisa's stomach answered for her with loud rumbling and growling. Unfortunately, there was no time for anything other than fast food. They turned off the road and headed towards Wendy's. There weren't many people there at this time. Lisa ordered a salad and Mark ordered a burger and a cup of coffee for each of them. They quickly ate and Mark hurried to drop Lisa off.

When they got to the house it was completely dark. Only the full moon lit their way. Mark parked the car and walked Lisa to the entrance of her building. She pulled out the key from her purse and unlocked the door. Mark opened the door for her and leaned against it to let Lisa in.

When she stepped over the threshold and smiled at him, he held his arm around her shoulders and carefully dragged her to him and kissed her.

"I had a wonderful day," he said. He kissed her again and then once more before he left.

Lisa went upstairs to her apartment. It was dark, peaceful and quiet, and only the hallway was lit. That was a good sign. It told Lisa that Mary had everything under control, that she'd put Irving to bed on time before going to bed herself, and that she'd turned the doorway light on for Lisa so she wouldn't come home to a dark house. Trying to be very quiet, Lisa tiptoed into the apartment and saw Mary was sleeping on the couch in the living room, making slight snoring noises.

She went to Irving's room and found him sound asleep on his right side, his blanket crumpled down in his bed, his pillow on the floor. Lisa smiled. Irving had a habit of turning and shifting and kicking while he slept, sometimes ending up with his head in the opposite corner of the bed and his legs on the pillow, or something of that sort. "You're probably playing war games in your dreams," Lisa always teased him. She approached his bed on her tiptoes, smoothed out the blanket and carefully covered her son. Then she lifted the pillow and cautiously placed it under his head. He smiled in his sleep, stretching comfortably on the pillow. Lisa gently kissed him and left the room.

After finally getting into her own bed and crawling under the bed sheets, she realized how exhausted she was.

The moonlight shone through the window, leaving a wide patch of light on the ceiling. Lisa glanced out the window. The full, unusually clear and bright moon shone powerfully in the dark sky. The picture of the night horizon was the last thing Lisa remembered before closing her eyes and drifting into a deep sleep.

CHAPTER TEN

The headache was unbearable. It pressed her head from all sides simultaneously, causing a sharp, twisting pain that radiated to both of her temples, the back of her head, her eyes and her neck. Terrible nausea arose from deep in her gut and accumulated in a heavy knot in her throat, giving her the urge to vomit. Lisa opened her eyes. The room was dark and stale and the air was dense and foggy. Something in the corner, close to the door, caught her attention. It was a cloudy, unstable silhouette that resembled an old woman in heavy, gray, baggy clothes. Struggling with her headache, Lisa tried to make out the image of the woman. She had shoulder-length, thin, grayish hair and her right hand was leaning on a black cane with a twisted top. Lisa couldn't see the woman's eyes in the dark, but she sensed her heavy, motionless stare. A shiver of fear went through her body. She couldn't move, couldn't think. Her gaze was riveted on the woman. Suddenly the air in the room started to move. It began with a few random waves that gradually turned into a whirlwind. Inevitably increasing in speed and power, the waves filled the room.

Lisa soon noticed that the waves were caused by the woman's left hand as she waved it in the air. Suddenly, Lisa was lifted from her bed, her arms spread wide at her side, her body parallel to the floor. Under the woman's control, the waves created a large, powerful funnel. Lisa felt her body pulled into the center of the funnel and was hopelessly sucked into and dragged along with it. Lying flat, she spun at its base, rising higher and higher with each rotation. Finally, Lisa almost reached the ceiling of her room. She looked around desperately, trying to grab onto anything in sight that could help her escape this whirlwind. But to her horror, everything she tried was hopeless. The tornado now accumulated in one strong, dense thrust and headed towards the window, carrying her with it. Lisa couldn't look down, but she knew that the woman was there, guiding her movements with her left index finger. Glancing in the direction of the moving air cluster, Lisa saw huge black clouds hanging above the ground and a wind gone berserk outside.

The picture was awful and astonishing at the same time. New horizons were created there; they lured Lisa with their mystery. They attracted her to them. An intangible yet powerful force dragged her to nowhere, paralyzing her with its power. Lisa felt an enormous desire to give up and accept the inevitable. At some point she felt a strange desire to explore what was unknown, but some instinct forbade her to go there. It told her to resist, resist with all her might. Losing all hope of rescue, she gathered herself and all of her will together, hoping to find the strength to defy what was overwhelmingly powerful. "No!" she screamed in horror. "NO!"

Suddenly, everything was gone. Lisa opened her eyes. Her heart beat so quickly that it almost pulsated out of her chest. Beads of sweat covered her forehead. She looked around and found herself lying in her own bed. It was quiet and peaceful. The window was closed and the moonlight softly filled the room. Lisa glanced at the bedside clock. It showed 3:15 a.m. She sat up in her bed, grasping her arms around her legs. It was a nightmare, an awful and horrible one, but still just a nightmare. Even realizing that it was just an awful dream, Lisa's whole body still trembled from the horror. Everything that she just experienced looked and felt so real that it continued to frighten her almost unbearably. She turned on her lamp, got up from the bed and opened the window. The cold night air entered the room, refreshing her. Momentarily, her fears were gone. "Stupid me. Forgot to open the window before going to bed," she muttered. Knowing that sleeping in discomfort causes bad dreams, she found it inexcusable that she had failed to ventilate the room.

She headed to the kitchen to grab a glass of water and then returned to her bedroom and stretched out on the bed. She turned the light off and closed her eyes, trying to fall asleep. But her mind was still focused on the terrifying pictures from her dream. She wondered what would have happened if she had allowed that wind to drag her out. Lisa turned from side to side trying to think of something else. Then she started to count imaginary pink elephants. She stopped counting when the 50th elephant slowly stepped out after the 49th elephant. Nothing seemed to help. She was sleepless. She turned on the light and pulled out a book from the drawer. It was a book that she had started to read weeks ago but never found a chance to finish. Now was the perfect time to know how the events in the novel would unravel.

Lisa closed her book when morning sunlight entered her bedroom. She stretched and yawned. Suddenly she felt an intense urge to sleep and wanted to take a nap for an hour or two. *Like a baby, confusing day with night*, she thought. However, Mark was going to arrive a little later to help her with her car and Lisa didn't dare greet him in her pajamas. She got out of bed and went to the bathroom.

The contrast of hot and cold water from the shower refreshed her and renewed her energy. Finishing her morning routine, she came back to the bedroom and opened the closet, searching for something appropriate to wear. She didn't want to look dressy but at the same time she wanted to look gorgeous. It must be something that looked casual and spur-of-the-moment, but was still elegant and stylish. She finally settled on a pair of tight blue jeans she'd recently purchased from Loehmann's, and a white DKNY shirt with a wide, midnight-blue stripe down the center and a cute, small zipper at the neck. Looking in the mirror she smiled at her image with satisfaction and turned on the radio.

"Good morning to all of you," the cheerful announcer's voice said as it filled the room. Trying not to awaken Irving with the loud noise, she turned the radio down and went closer to hear the weather forecast.

"Looks like today we're going to have clear skies with a bit of wind, but still in the upper 60s," the pleasant voice announced. Lisa turned the radio off and headed to Irving's room. To her surprise, he was not sleeping. Already dressed, showered, and with combed hair, he was sitting on the rug with his back turned to the door, occupied with his toys. He had metal soldiers equipped with different weapons that he always loved to play with.

"Irving," Lisa exclaimed in astonishment. "How long have you been up, sonny?"

Irving turned towards her.

"Mom, good morning! Look what I've got here!"

Lisa came closer and kneeled down beside him. There were two armies of the green and silver steel soldiers that were attacking each other over different terrains. Irving was imitating and reproducing battle cries and weapon sounds. The soldiers were falling from wounds and dying with honor.

"Irving, where's Mary?" she asked when the battle finally finished and the green army raised their flag.

"She went home, Mom," Irving said. "We didn't want to wake you up because you probably came home very late." He glanced at her. "I brushed my teeth and took a shower and ate breakfast with Mary. Then she rushed home since she had some stuff to do, and I was trying to be very quiet," he added proudly.

Lisa patted his head and thoughtfully lifted a few pieces of fuzz from his shirt.

"Irving, we're expecting a guest today," she started. "He's going to fix our car—" She paused, searching for a stronger reason to justify Mark's visit. Irving's reaction truly surprised her.

"Awesome, we won't be spending much money to repair it then, right?" he asked as he turned back to his soldiers.

His practicality amazed Lisa. *What a wonderful generation*, she thought.

The doorbell interrupted her thoughts. Lisa rushed to the hall and opened the door. There stood Mark, smiling widely at her from over the threshold. He wore blue jeans and a tight, thick-thread, knitted white sweater, which emphasized his broad, masculine chest. He looked very casual, but appealing and sexy at the same time. With her hand on the doorknob, Lisa stared at him until his gentle cough unfroze her.

"May I come in now?" He grinned.

"Of course!" Lisa stepped back and opened the door wide, inviting him in.

"Coffee?" she offered. They proceeded to the kitchen and Lisa began making coffee and setting up the table with the cake and cookies that she bought for the occasion. She was taking out the coffee set from the upper cabinets when Irving entered the kitchen.

"Mom, I beat the game," he announced, referring to the Game Boy that he carried in his hands.

Startled, Lisa almost dropped the porcelain cups that she was holding. She was going to call to Irving after the table was set, but now she blamed herself for how things turned out, causing Irving to feel second-best. Wrong-footed, she put the cups on the counter.

"Irving, this is Mark. Mark, this is my son, Irving," she said, introducing them.

"So, what's the game that you just beat?" Mark inquired cheerfully.

"It's Bomberman. See?" Irving came closer to Mark to show him his game. Mark took the Game Boy and started passionately pressing the buttons, asking Irving about the rules. They became occupied and excited over the game with the same degree of interest.

"Do you know that there's a new version to this game that's coming out on CD?" Mark asked.

"Yeah, my friend Billy told me," Irving replied. "He's going to buy the game soon and we're going to play it from his computer."

"Wonderful, then," Mark concluded and glanced at his watch. "Time's up." He rose from his chair. "Do you want to help me work on the car?" He grinned down at Irving. Irving's excitement reflected in his eyes and his wide-open mouth.

"Can I, Mom?" He looked at Lisa, pleading.

"Sure, you can," Lisa answered. "But what about the coffee and the cookies?" she inquired, looking disappointedly at the set table. "Everything's ready."

"Can we have it to go?" Mark asked, smiling.

"Yeah, can we have it to go, Mom?" Irving repeated.

"Well guys, I adore your work enthusiasm," was all she could say, considering the situation. She poured the coffee into a coffee jug and handed it to Mark. She then put cookies and a few slices of cake in a paper bag and gave it to Irving.

"I'm not invited?" she asked when Mark and Irving headed to the door. She knew that the question was a rhetorical one, but thought she would ask anyway. Mark turned around and looked at her tenderly.

"It's a man's job, Lisa," he said with a smile. "We want you to relax and enjoy your time. Let us take care of the rest. Right, Irving?"

"Yes, Mom. A man's gotta do what a man's gotta do," Irving said, mimicking some movie hero. Then he eagerly pulled on Mark's sleeve. "Can we go already?"

"Okay, then," Lisa concluded aloud when the door closed behind them. "I guess that now I've gotta do what a woman's gotta do." She opened the refrigerator, thinking about preparing dinner and smiled, recalling Irving's serious "manly" attitude.

Lisa decided to make some chicken noodle soup and chicken breasts for the main dish. For the side dishes she settled on mashed potatoes with gravy and sautéed green peas with fried onions. She turned on some music, threw an apron on, and began washing, cutting and shredding the meat and vegetables. She was busy with her routine when the front door loudly flew open and Irving dashed into the apartment, running to his room. Lisa quickly wiped her hands with a kitchen cloth and headed after him.

"Mom, we need to go to the store to buy some car paint," Irving announced as he rushed through the clothes in his closet.

"What are you doing then?" she started to say, and then froze in astonishment. Irving's shirt, once striped blue and white, had now turned into one pale, grayish color and was hanging out from his very dirty pants. Irving turned his head from the closet to her. Stunned, Lisa clapped her hands over her mouth. Irving's face reminded her of a monster in a fairy-tale movie they'd seen. He looked as excited as he did dirty.

"Mom, Mom! Mark said that I have to change to go to the store!" He rambled as he hopped on the floor with impatience. "What should I wear?" he asked.

Lisa pulled a fresh pair of jeans and a t-shirt from the closet, and a pair of the socks from his drawer, then headed to the bathroom. She didn't want to let him go without taking a shower but under his pleading stare she settled for him washing his hands and face. While Irving was washing and changing, she went to her bedroom to find her old black t-shirt. This t-shirt was a part of the negotiation, as Irving agreed to wear it over his clothes next time he worked with a car. Lisa handed the t-shirt to him when he was already on his way out. Promising to wear it, he pushed it under his armpit and ran, jumping over the stairs.

An hour passed. Dinner was ready and waiting on the stove, though it was too early to eat. The dishes and kitchen were clean, and even the laundry was done. Lisa looked around with satisfaction and decided to go outside to check on her hard-working men. She found both of them in the parking lot. They were occupied talking over the open hood of her car. Mark was standing with his back to her. He was wearing a baggy blue shirt. One of his hands was occupied holding a cigarette while the other was holding a big, grayish-white cloth. Articulating with that cloth, he explained something to Irving who listened to him with an open mouth. Lisa was only a few steps behind them when Irving noticed her.

"Mom!" he exclaimed in disappointment. "You shouldn't have come. It's supposed to be a surprise!"

Mark turned around. "It's okay, Irving," he assured him. "We're done here." He closed the hood and proudly showed Lisa the car. "What do you think? Do you like it?"

The car looked beautiful and clean. It shone under the sun and looked like a brand new car. Walking around it, Lisa came closer for a thorough inspection. To her amazement, the scratches left by the nasty yellow pillar were gone for good. Not a tangible trace was left.

"Mom, you should hear how the engine was roaring when we were fixing it," Irving gushed. As he promised, he was wearing her old t-shirt over his clothes and he looked like a real handyman in it.

"I poured oil into the tank," he bragged. "I checked the oil level with Mark and it was too low!" His eyes were lit with happiness and pride.

Lisa grabbed his shoulders and hugged and kissed him. "You're my lovely, lovely little mechanic!" she exclaimed. "I'm so proud of you!"

"Wait until you drive the car!" Mark interjected. "We want you to check it out; start it and get it running first. Then you might want to compliment us even more. Right Irving?" He winked at Irving.

"Mom, Mark said that we're going to a movie tonight. Isn't it great! Are you going to drive us there?"

"Have you already decided on the movie?" Lisa asked.

Of course they had. They both wanted to see *The Terminator* with Arnold Schwarzenegger and now they were hoping to get her approval. Lisa didn't have anything against this movie. Besides, she was thrilled with the possibility of all of them spending time together.

"I'm in," she declared.

"Yes!" Mark and Irving exchanged pleased glances.

"But you have to take a shower first and then eat before anything else," she said, cooling down their excitement.

"Yes, ma'am!" Mark ran his hand across her hair and called Irving. "Let's go, partner. I'm starving. Those who work hard always eat well. Right?"

"Right, I'm hungry like a horse," Irving said and all three of them headed to the apartment.

"So, were there a lot of damages?" Lisa asked on their way.

"Not much." Mark smiled. "We found some disconnected wires that we fixed, and some bad spark plugs that we replaced, and then this and that... Overall, your car's in a good condition. It will serve you for awhile," he said, gazing at her.

Lisa was overwhelmed with emotion. She felt an enormous desire to lean on him, to feel his warm arms around her. She felt marvelous. Everything was marvelous. It was the first time that Mark and Irving had met and they had obviously hit it off. Mark fit in. He blended into their family so naturally that it seemed like it was meant to be. He was like the missing part of a puzzle that, when added, made everything complete. They went back into the apartment and Mark and Irving took turns showering, then rushed into the kitchen. The dinner was already on the table, and they attacked the food as if they'd been starving for days.

"Oh Mom, this soup's yummy," Irving said while stuffing himself.

Lisa smiled as she watched Irving eat, talk casually with Mark, and compliment her food. Both of them were having a great time. They were sharing their funny stories about fixing the car, interrupting each other and laughing. And her heart was once again filled with warmth. That was all that Lisa wanted, wasn't it? To have a family again. To have a father for her son and a husband for herself. To gather together at a table. To love and to be there for each other. Was it too much to want? Or was it not her fate at all?

After their early dinner they went to the movies. Mark bought the tickets and escorted Lisa and Irving to their seats. Then he went to the concession stand and bought popcorn and a large Pepsi for each of them. They sat directly in front of the screen with Irving in the middle. The lights dimmed, the movie started rolling, and the room was filled with intense, fascinating action. In the breathtaking moments Irving would lean over to Mark and ask him who he thought would win, and Mark would whisper back into his ear. At times, Mark would glance over at Lisa with a look of understanding and playfulness, stretch his arm behind the seat and slightly touch her shoulder. She would exchange glances with him, and her eyes lit up with an emotion and a desire to stop time and to have the moment last forever.

Back at Lisa's apartment after the movie, Lisa left Mark to take care of the coffee in the kitchen while she guided Irving to the bathroom. While he was brushing his teeth she made his bed. Walking into his room, Irving jumped right under his covers and stretched out in comfort. Lisa sat next to him on his bed, covering him with a blanket.

"Did you have a good time today honey?" She smiled.

"I had a great time, Mom," Irving replied. "Can we go out again like this next weekend?" He looked directly into her eyes.

"Of course we can." She softly stroked his hair. "I'm looking forward to it." She kissed him good-night and headed toward the door. She was almost out of the room when Irving asked. "Mom?"

"Yes, honey."

"Why does Mark smoke so much?"

"I don't know." She paused shortly. "Bad habit, I think."

"That's fine, Mom. He's still cool," Irving said quietly.

"Good-night sonny, I love you."

"I love you too, Mom."

She closed the door and headed to the kitchen.

CHAPTER ELEVEN

Mark was sitting at the table facing the window, smoking a cigarette and sipping on his coffee. Lisa closed the kitchen door and quietly snuck in, hugging him from behind. Without giving him a chance to turn around, she slid under his arm and swiftly landed in his lap, leaning against him as she cuddled and kissed him.

"Lisa," Mark laughed, trying to safely put down the cup on the table. "You're making me spill the cof—" The last word was swallowed as Lisa's lips melted onto his, drowning him in her hot, thirsty mouth. Mark hastily smashed his cigarette into an ashtray. He grabbed her hair and slightly tilted her head away from him. Looking into her eyes with unbridled passion, he gathered her into his arms and carried her to the bedroom, locking the door after him. He lowered her to her feet but continued holding her tightly, nibbling on her neck, her cheeks, her eyes and sinking into her lips with a fanatical, unrestrained desire. They were hugging, kissing, touching. Something impossibly passionate, something wild and unfettered came into them. Breathless, madly tearing off their shirts and tight jeans, they knocked over the bedside lamp as they made love. Everything was so much more romantic, sensual and electrifying than it ever was before.

"I've melted from head to toe," she finally murmured in exhaustion.

Mark pulled out a cigarette. "Should we go back to the kitchen?" he asked, gesturing toward the cigarette. Lisa nodded, got up and threw on her clothes.

Lisa opened the window and the vent in the kitchen as Mark lit up a cigarette. She sat down and pulled out a cigarette. Mark was looking pensively at her, a soft, tender smile on his face.

"Imagine how we could have this all the time if we lived together," he said, blowing thin grayish smoke up to the ceiling.

A mixture of excitement, confusion, and anxiety electrified her. Could it be that the moment she had been waiting and longing for ever since she met him was about to happen? Was he going to propose today? Lisa glanced at him, trying to read his face, his eyes, his posture, to see if she had correctly interpreted his words. But Mark was sitting there, looking comfortable and relaxed. A thoughtful, tender smile was frozen on his lips. His eyes suggested something but his face was unreadable.

"Mark," she said and then hesitated, fiddling with her cigarette between her fingers.

He sparked the lighter and held it for her. She lit her cigarette, holding his eyes in hers as she sorted out her thoughts.

"Mark," she said again, fighting for time. "Why did you divorce your wife?"

Mark's face darkened. His wide left eyebrow curved up and he looked at her as if she were an inattentive schoolgirl.

"I thought I explained it to you already. My ex-wife and I were entirely different people. We talked past one another and couldn't live together under one roof. What's more important is that she poisoned our children. My son is a wonderful, handsome, and clever boy, but he has this attention deficit disorder. What he needed was maybe more attention, more love and more patience, and he'd quickly have reached the level of the kids his age. But it was hopeless to talk to her. She just threw him into the special ed school with mentally disabled children. What could he have achieved there? His mind would have just deteriorated!" Mark angrily slapped the table. "And my daughter. We had a special connection with each other, which made my wife jealous. She couldn't stand that my daughter loved me more than her. I could bear almost everything that my ex did, except how she ruined my kids. I tried everything that I could, but it was out of my control to change anything in that house. Living there as a passive observer was something I couldn't bear. I basically packed my bags and moved to another state in despair." He rested his chin on his hand and his eyes settled on hers. A still silence filled the room.

That was what Lisa couldn't understand. She couldn't imagine any woman in the world who wouldn't work hard to keep a man like Mark, even if it would mean compromising her own ego. This was especially true for his ex-wife, who had Mark as a father of her two wonderful children.

"Mark," she said, "how did it turn out that you didn't get custody of your children?"

He scowled. His right arm, which rested on the table, involuntarily tightened. "It's my pain, my sentence," he said as a sudden twitch jerked his face. "Judges automatically favor giving children to the mother unless she's a complete nut case or an alcoholic," he said, his big hand clenched into a fist. "Unfair American laws that discriminate against the fathers' rights." He waved his hand. "The only thing I got was the weekly visits, which wouldn't be enough for me to raise them the way I'd want to.

Those visits only allowed me to provide them entertainment and spoil them. But I needed to be a real father to my children. I wanted to build their character, teach them about life and show them the world. I tried to communicate that to my ex-wife, tried to explain to her that I want only the best for my children, that they would grow and blossom with me. Everything was pointless. She was stupid and stubborn and argued only for the sake of winning. The children's interests weren't even her concern." He shook his head and took out another cigarette.

Lisa's hand unconsciously stroked Mark's arm, calming him down. Empathy, compassion and tenderness filled her heart. *It's unfair the way life turned out for this wonderful man,* she thought and then halted in astonishment as a simple, breathtaking idea occurred to her. Maybe it was meant to be? Maybe it was all part of God's greater plan, that Mark's divorce would be followed by Lisa and him ending up together? She looked at him, stunned.

"What are you thinking about?" Mark asked softly.

"I love you Mark, I've always loved you," she wanted to say, to scream. But she was speechless. She could only lift his hand from the table, and, full of love for him, bury her face into his palm.

Mark gently tore his hand away from her face.

"Lisa," he started to say with a cough. "I was going to tell you; to ask you," he paused, and then looked straight at her. "I'm much older than you."

"Not much, it's a pretty normal difference in our age," she interrupted.

"Wait, don't interrupt me please. I'll get off track," he begged. "I'm older than you, and I'm a divorced man who's supporting two children—" He rubbed his forehead and continued after a thoughtful pause. "I love you, Lisa. I've loved you since I first saw you."

Lisa's heart skipped a beat. She sat, frozen to her chair, waiting for what he was about to say.

"And your son's a great boy. He's smart, and funny and we have a great deal in common with each other," he said, paused again and then finished, "I'd like for all of us to live together. What do you say, Lisa?"

Lisa's heartbeat increased as she felt her cheeks blushing. She pulled out a cigarette from the pack, lit it and took a deep drag from it. "Ahhh. I—" She stretched the words.

"Lisa." Mark said as he looked pensively at her. "I can't be married right now. What if it won't work? Even though there's an obvious attraction, and the chemistry is right between us. What if we're both mistaken? I can't stand another failure. I'm dedicated to giving my whole heart, my soul, and everything to my family. I'm afraid of failure. Think about this. You wouldn't want yourself or Irving to be hurt if this doesn't work out."

There was a lot of sense in what he just said. Obviously he was right. It would be greatly selfish of her to ignore everything but marriage.

"Let's live together for a while, see how things go, and then we'll get married," Mark said earnestly.

Lisa tenderly ran the back of her hand over his sharp bristled cheek. "Where would we live?" she asked.

Mark let out a deep sigh of relief. "We can either live in my place or in yours." He lit a cigarette.

"Well, your place has only one bedroom." Lisa circled her hand in the air. "Let's live here. Both Irving and I love this place. Irving has good friends in this neighborhood; he's accustomed to the local school and everything."

Mark lit up the room with his smile. "Okay then," he concluded, and then offered, "Another cup of coffee?"

They sat there for a while longer, drinking, talking and smoking, and then Mark left. This time he left so he could come back for good. When the door closed after Mark and his steps gradually receded into the silent night, Lisa walked into her bedroom and spread the sheets out on her bed. A bright, happy smile lit up her face as she thought about making the bed the next time, laying down the pillow for Mark, falling asleep in the comfort of his big, strong arms, and waking up from the kiss of his so hot, so manly and yet so gentle lips. Those lips, which she had definitely, totally, madly fallen in love with. The lips which had seemed familiar from their first kiss.

Which side of the bed does he prefer? She wondered, and grinned at the thought. It was so enjoyable, thrilling really, to think about questions like that. Those questions gave her the realization that she wouldn't be alone anymore. She had a lover, and a friend by her side, and even though he had said it was only a "trial" relationship she knew in her heart she was going to share the rest of her life with him—for now and forever. For better or for worse.

Lisa dove under her bed sheets thinking of Mark, almost feeling his strong, warm body against hers. She stretched comfortably on the pillow and fell into a deep, easy sleep, a wishful smile shining on her face

Part Two

CHAPTER TWELVE

Loud voices interrupted Lisa's dreams. She opened her eyes and looked around. The flight attendants were pushing lunch carts from the ends of each aisle. The smell of food filled her nostrils. Lisa wiggled in her seat, stretching her arms and legs to energize her body, which had gone numb from sitting in the same position for so long. She bent forward and crossed her arms in front of her, then side-to-side, and she stretched her legs. She noticed that Irving was suspiciously quiet and a sideways glance showed he was sleeping quite sweetly, his headphones still on. *No wonder*, Lisa thought. Rocking back and forth for several hours in a plane could make anyone fall asleep. Not to mention that they'd woken up before sunrise to get to the airport in time for their flight.

Irving was in such a deep sleep that she hated to wake him. She hesitated for a moment, then finally stroked his hair softly and kissed him.

"Mom, I'm still sleepy," he murmured, and moved to the corner of his seat, further away from her. He pulled his legs up onto the seat, wrapped his arms around his knees, laid his cheek on them, and tried to go back to sleep.

Lisa grinned. "Irving, you're going to miss lunch," she insisted, touching his shoulder patiently. "It'll be a while before we arrive and have dinner. You'll be starving by then."

Irving tossed in his seat, rubbed his eyes and yawned widely. "You fell asleep too, Mom," he said. "I was bored and I didn't want to wake you up."

"Oh, that's so sweet of you, Irving. Let's go freshen up in the bathroom. It will help you wake up," she suggested.

They waited for the flight attendant to serve their food. Lisa laid it out on the table and they walked to the bathroom. She watched Irving study the cold water running through his fingers before splashing it on his face.

"Irving, the sooner you do it, the sooner it will be over with," she said, laughing.

He washed his face carefully with soap and then rinsed it with cold water. After he finished, she dried him with a paper towel and quickly washed her own face. The cold water and the walk down the aisle got their blood flowing and energized them. They returned to their seats and enjoyed their meal.

After lunch they played a game of slapjack until an action movie started. Irving watched the movie with interest. Lisa watched for a while and tried to follow the plot, but she soon became lost in the rapidly changing fight scenes and characters, and her eyelids grew heavy. The world around her faded away, and her mind drifted back into memories.

***

Isn't it ironic how life can be unpredictable, or, even worse, unfair? Sometimes, it presents appealing and promising opportunities in your path, and you're thrilled. You're happy to realize that you're not forgotten, not lost in this endless universe. And then there it is, finally. The thing you were waiting for so desperately is laid out in front of you. It's close, it's right there, just on the horizon. All you have to do is reach out and take it. But you never once try to question it; you go for it blindly, arrogantly, ignorantly, assuming that it is what you thought it was. That's how life teases you, laughs at you and lures you into its trap.

Lisa ran her fingers through her hair and then crossed her arms over her chest.

Although...maybe it's not life that should be blamed for the wrong turns and unfulfilled promises. Maybe it's people who bring it on themselves. Maybe it's fate, that unavoidable destiny that rules the world and gives each and every one of us what we deserve. Lisa let out a deep, thoughtful sigh. She tried to be objective. Nothing is inevitable or unpredictable. Aren't people given signs, insights and warnings throughout their lives? Just be sensitive enough to listen, and wise enough to hear. *Foolish people have eyes but do not see and ears but do not hear,* isn't that what the Bible says? That could definitely be said about her, since she hadn't heard and she hadn't seen. No matter what she called it, life or fate, she had received many signs that she neglected to pay attention to. Not only that—she was proud and arrogant enough to interpret those signs to be good omens. Like the time she ran her car into the pillar. Her car halted then, leaving her date with Mark in jeopardy. She believed that all the dark forces must have come together to stand in her way. She was upset, angry and frustrated. Things seemed to fall apart at that moment. But in truth it was a sign to prevent her from falling into the trap. She just wasn't attentive enough or selfless enough to understand that at the time.

Lisa's lips formed an ironic smile. At times she had felt that something wasn't right about Mark, that something wasn't in place, or was missing, but those feelings never fully surfaced. They were always foggy, building up in the back of her mind, but, like flimsy dreams, they disappeared faster than they came. Lisa recalled the episode at Mark's friends' brunch party at the Italian restaurant. She remembered how Mark flirted with the attractive, young waitress and how she'd been embarrassed and devastated. But at the same time she couldn't explain her feelings...or she hadn't wanted to? It still amazed her how she didn't see the true picture back then. Mark humiliated her in front of his friends by talking the way he did with that waitress. But, with his reasoning, Lisa justified his behavior and instead blamed herself for being paranoid. She rationalized. She was given a glimpse of his inner self but she ignored it, seeing only what she wanted to see. She already had a vision of who Mark was in her heart and fell in love with it, and she was more than willing to accept anything that would keep this image of him intact.

She was enchanted by Mark, covered by a sweet fog that only a man could create. She was like a different person around him; she easily and willingly justified everything about him. Lisa remembered thinking very poorly of his first wife, who failed to hold onto him. She looked down upon that woman, not considering the fact that Mark's explanations for his divorce were vague and seemed to bring up even more questions, especially the part where he moved to a different state, far from his children, whom he said he loved very much. Those questions stayed in the back of her mind no matter how many times he justified them to her. If only she hadn't ignored those glitches in her heart, if only she had acknowledged them, then they would have shown her the truth of Mark's personality. But she hadn't. Her mind had been set and she ignored any holes she saw in his explanations. Lisa thought that Mark was sent to her by Heaven. Yes, he definitely was sent to her. But it wasn't by Heaven.

Lisa drifted back in her memories to one of her most mysterious and frightening dreams; the dream that sent her a definite sign, a message she wouldn't care to recognize until much later.

It was the dream that had started with an old woman who seemed to be from a different world, and she was trying to pull Lisa into it. The woman created a powerful sucking force that she used to try to drag Lisa into the unknown. The pictures of the mysterious horizons in her dream still flashed in her mind. Lisa remembered how much she had been afraid of it, yet was lured into it. She was almost ready to let herself go and give into the old woman's power when something inside of her, some instinct, told her not to give up, to resist with all her might. In the dream, she listened to her insight and was able to overcome the dark force. In reality, however, the dark force came the next day, when Mark proposed. Lisa had expected a *marriage* proposal, but it had turned out to be something else; it was a well-justified proposition to live together. And although she was sort of disappointed, Lisa was convinced by Mark's reasoning to go for it, and ignoring her inner alarm, she was happy and excited and impatient to explore the new lurching horizons. She dismissed her dream then. But so many times in her memories she went back to that dream, wondering what would've happened if she had given up and let the forces drag her in. Ironically enough, it seemed that her real life answered that question for her.

Lisa believed that everything in life happens for a reason, even though that reason is sometimes far from the realm of our comprehension. Therefore, everything that happened to her was *meant* to happen. Maybe the whole point of human existence on this earth is for human beings to understand those reasons and live their lives accordingly. Maybe all that she went through was meant to strengthen her or refine her soul, and perhaps... perhaps to show others that there is always a way out of the darkness and into the light.

CHAPTER THIRTEEN

In the beginning, everything had seemed to be great. The next Friday after work Mark had come over with his belongings in a couple of black leather suitcases and carrying his suits in a garment bag. Lisa and Irving helped him unpack and the three of them had a special candlelit dinner that evening. The next morning Mark took Irving and Lisa to Best Buy. They wandered around the aisles looking at the variety of entertainment sets that the store had to offer. Lisa stopped by the televisions. Action, drama and sports all surrounded her. The televisions were much sharper and crisper than the old 27-inch television she owned.

Glancing back, she noticed that Mark and Irving were gone. She walked around and found them two aisles away. They were both playing some computer game. When Mark saw Lisa he left the game and they went to choose the items that Mark wanted to purchase for their living room. Irving joined them a while later. Mark bought a great entertainment center and 34-inch television. It came complete with a compact media center with 6 Dolby digital surround sound speakers.

On Sunday morning huge boxes of parts and pieces for their new entertainment furniture were delivered to their house. Mark and Irving started the massive assembly job while Lisa did the housework. For the entire next week, their evenings were occupied with assembling their system and stretching the wires to connect them to speakers that they nailed to the walls.

By the following Saturday everything was finished. Mark and Irving called Lisa over, dimmed the lights and turned on the music. Lisa sat down on the couch, surrounded by sweet, soft opera music. Later, coffee and cookies were brought from the kitchen, Mark turned on the TV, and the three of them watched a movie on HBO together.

Lisa's living room turned into cozy home theatre. Every day Lisa hurried home from work to enjoy another wonderful evening with her family. They ate dinner in the kitchen with the door open, listening to soft music. After dinner they drank coffee, sat on the sofa in the living room and watched movies. Irving would sit with them, sometimes doing his homework at the coffee table, sometimes playing chess with Mark. He was excited about having Mark live at their house. He'd liked him ever since their first meeting. Irving shared his school stories with Mark, and asked him many of the questions that he always wondered about. Lisa was thrilled at the way Mark found answers to all of Irving's challenging questions.

Irving proudly referred to Mark as his father when he was with his friends, although he still called him "Mark" to his face. Mark was very well aware of the fact that Irving called him **"dad"** in front of other kids but to Lisa's slight disappointment he thought that Irving didn't mean it, and only said it to sound like he was from a "complete" family like the rest of his friends. Nevertheless, it seemed that Mark definitely cared about Irving. He gave him the computer that he brought from his house, which was much newer than the one he'd had. He also bought him various computer-tutoring programs and a couple of strategy war games.

After setting up his old computer in Irving's room, Mark went shopping for a new one. Actually, they shopped a lot during those first days. Lisa found herself checking out expensive things, which she had never allowed herself to look at before. It was fun to shop for clothes with Mark. She began to think it was really a misconception that men don't like to shop. She decided that they probably do, but are afraid to confess it, considering that shopping isn't a "manly job." Or maybe it was only Mark who liked to shop. He could walk through aisles and not get tired or bored looking at all the items. Lisa would go to a store and scan the selection. If nothing caught her attention, she would continue to the next store until she found what she wanted.

With Mark however, it was a different story. On one of their many outings to the mall, they walked into a boutique with women's clothes first. Lisa quickly checked out a couple of the sections and was ready to go to the next store. Mark looked at her in astonishment. "Lisa, you didn't look at anything!" he exclaimed.

"I did," she retorted. "There's nothing that I like."

"Oh, come on, I'm sure there is," he challenged with a smile. He started scrupulously searching through items on the rack. To her surprise, he found two beautiful, appealing items on his first try. One of them was an evening blouse that had white and black diagonal stripes and a well-known designer label. Lisa was surprised not only at Mark's good taste but also that she hadn't spotted the items herself. Within a few more minutes, Mark found black silk pants to match her new blouse. The black pants and striped blouse soon became one of Lisa's go-to outfits for special occasions.

They also visited other stores in the mall that day. Lisa was proud to learn to look patiently through everything in the store before leaving. They visited only two more stores and bought Lisa all the clothes that she needed, spending a whole lot less time than she usually did when she shopped using her method.

In one store, Lisa and Mark were browsing together through a rack when a young, leggy sales girl walked by in tightly fitting black pants. Mark's eyes followed her with a sideways glance as she passed. The girl seemed to feel his eyes on her and she turned around and approached him. "May I help you?" she asked as a wide, professional smile lit her face.

Mark's smile was even wider. "Do you carry such wonderful pants as the ones you're wearing?" he inquired.

"Yes, definitely. We carry them in all sizes and a variety of colors in the second section, right after this one," she answered gladly.

Mark kept pinning her with his eyes. "I want those pants," he said as he pointed at her legs, smiling broadly. "But I'll only take them if they come with your beautiful legs," he said with a laugh.

The girl looked at Lisa in confusion, smiled politely as if it were a great joke, and then retreated quickly.

Lisa felt the warmth of her face as it burned with embarrassment, especially after the girl's glance. She looked at Mark and found him continuing his search. "Lisa?" He turned around to face her. "It seems that there's nothing else that good on this rack. Let's go to the next one."

He was smiling openly at her like nothing had happened, and seemed completely unaware of her humiliation. Lisa recalled his explanation of why he flirted with the young waitress at the Italian restaurant during his friend Jerome's birthday party. He was afraid that one day Lisa would find him old so he wanted to show her that he was still attractive to younger girls.

Lisa shrugged. If Mark had to confirm his own ego that way, she'd be more than happy to play his game with him. He had suffered enough throughout his life and Lisa didn't want to add more by making a big deal out of his small whim. She didn't voice her feelings and they ended their shopping that day by buying a few more things for each of them. Right after they left the last store, they went into the mall restaurant, where they had a fancy dinner with red wine. Lisa thought that Mark spoiled them by taking her and Irving out to restaurants almost every weekend. They all enjoyed it though.

However, what Mark had said about it being hard to be around a person who was suffering from depression turned out to be very true for Lisa. A few weeks after the incident with the saleswoman at the mall, she left work a little earlier than usual. She popped into the grocery store to pick up some bread and olive oil that she needed, and then promptly drove home, thinking she had plenty of time to make dinner before Mark arrived from work.

When she stepped inside her apartment, something felt very different. Worried, Lisa threw her grocery bags on the kitchen table and rushed to Irving's room. To her relief, Irving was sitting at his desk and was occupied with playing a new computer game.

"Irving, honey, why are you sitting in the dark?" she asked, turning the light on. "And you didn't even come out to greet your mom like you used to," she added with a slight reproach. "I hope this computer won't take the place of your mom in your heart." She stroked his hair softly and kissed him.

"Sorry, Mom. I didn't hear you coming," Irving said distractedly, looking a little confused. "This is an awesome game," he continued, turning back to his computer. "Look, they're hiding behind those walls." He referred to the fighters while hitting hastily on the keyboard. "This is me, see?" He pointed to a man with a huge weapon.

"Have you finished your homework?" Lisa asked, staring at the blur of fighters and weapons. She couldn't figure out how Irving knew who was on his side, because they all looked the same to her and were moving so fast.

"Yeah, I didn't actually get that much homework today. We had a substitute English teacher and a substitute for History. So I only had to do my Math today."

"Okay then, I think," Lisa said thoughtfully, looking at his monitor, which was flashing with fires and blasting war sounds from its speakers. "Why don't you look at some of the tutoring programs that Mark gave you?" she asked. "I think they're very interesting and can prepare you for your tests in school, don't you think?"

"Yeah, sure they can Mom," Irving said, still occupied with the game.

"I'm going to start dinner and then we'll eat together when Mark comes home," she said. "Hopefully, you'll be done with your game by then." She grinned at Irving.

"Mark's already home," Irving mentioned, his gaze still fixed on the monitor.

"Mark's home?" Lisa asked, thinking that she had heard Irving incorrectly.

"He's sleeping in the bedroom, Mom."

This was a surprise. Mark had never come home this early before. There was definitely something wrong with him today. Lisa hurried to the bedroom.

CHAPTER FOURTEEN

The door was half-open and the light that she turned on in the living room shone into the darkness of the bedroom. Mark was lying down on the bed on his stomach, his face buried in the pillow. The blanket covered his long body so that only a part of his dark hair could be seen on the white pillowcase. Lisa's worries rose. She kneeled in front of him and gently touched his forehead with her palm. The gesture was automatic, like she had done so many times with Irving, to check if he was ill.

"Are you okay, honey?" she asked softly.

"I'm fine," he said hoarsely, his voice muffled from the thickness of the pillow.

Lisa's heart jumped in her chest, and then hung in there and halted. She had never seen Mark this way before. Something terrible must have happened, something unbelievably terrible. Mark wasn't moving; he was just lying there with his head in the pillow and his arms around his head.

Was he sick, was he hurt, was something wrong with his children? Lisa thought these in fear. She was imagining all the worst possible things that could have happened.

"Mark," she murmured, stroking his hair gently. "Tell me, please. You can tell me anything. I'm here for you," she said, her voice encouraging.

Mark turned around slowly as though it was suddenly hard for him to move his large body. He looked at her, his gaze searching her face. It seemed like he was weighing all the pros and cons of sharing the news with her.

"I got fired from work today," he finally blurted out. His eyes held onto hers and they were full of irony.

Lisa was stunned into silence. She was ready to giggle, but considering the situation, she composed herself. Being fired from work was surely not a funny thing but it was certainly a relief since Lisa had assumed something much worse.

Mark got up. He stood beside the bed, clad only in his sweat pants. His expression was contrite and earnest at the same time. Lisa blamed herself for undermining his grief. She smiled at him. "Let's go to the kitchen. I'll make you some coffee."

Mark followed her in silence into the kitchen. He looked very uncomfortable.

"I didn't mean to disappoint you, Lisa," he said, lowering into his chair and lighting a cigarette.

"I'm not disappointed at all!" Lisa objected wholeheartedly. "These things happen. They can happen to anybody!"

Mark shook his head and sighed. "It's not the fact that I lost my job but the way that I reacted to it that makes me so upset." He jerked his hand with his cigarette.

Lisa put a scoop of ground coffee into the coffee machine, added some water and turned it on. While the coffee was brewing, she sat down at the table across from him and pulled out a cigarette from the pack on the table. It crossed her mind for a split second that she was having a sudden craving for a cigarette, but she shook her head and dismissed the thought.

"It's understandable that you're upset," she said as she blew out a grayish stream of smoke and reached for his hand across the table. "Anybody would be—"

His head jerked up, his eyes lit with a sudden rage. "Who cares about anybody?" he sneered.

Lisa's hand drew back quickly and her heart jumped to her throat, making it hard to breath. Her hands felt suddenly cold and cramped, making her almost drop the cigarette. Mark looked at her and color washed up on his face.

"Lisa," he said, reaching out to touch her hand, which was clenched on the table. His expression conveyed guilt and shame. But there was also pain—deep, hard, unbearable pain that he was obviously trying to push away with incredible effort. Lisa swallowed hard. She bit her lip in disappointment with herself. Wasn't it she who had so deeply and heatedly convinced Mark to confide in her? Now, when the time came to lend Mark a hand, all she could do was to get upset about him yelling at her. She gazed at him. He looked so vulnerable and yet courageous, so appealingly masculine. She loved him more than she ever had before. Apparently, something more than losing his job was making him upset enough to lose his temper. Lisa licked her lips.

"Mark—" her voice was soft and gentle. "Why did they fire you?"

He drew heavily on his cigarette and turned to face the window. "I came to the plant for my normal check-up duties. I was talking to the workers and explaining the drawings to them. While we were going over the details I realized that the job could be done more efficiently if there were some changes made to the original design. It was easier and faster to show them right there how it would look, so I rolled up my sleeves and started to work." He took another drag on his cigarette and for a moment studied his big, strong, hairy hands thoughtfully. Then a dry smile formed on his lips. "My boss came to the field when the job was done. I was surrounded by workers who had come to see my work. They praised me and shook hands with me. I was about to give them instructions on how to make other machines when my boss entered the circle. He looked furious. He wanted to know what was going on.

The foreman started to explain that I had just shown them an incredibly genius, simple way of working the machine that they'd been struggling with for a while. The boss screamed at everyone to get back to their workstations. His face was dark red by that time. I glanced around and everybody looked as confused by his behavior as I was. That silent disapproval by everybody made him even more furious." Mark crushed his cigarette in an ashtray and started up another one. "He was shouting something about the design, quality assurance control and a plan. I tried to explain to him that the changes I suggested and wanted to implement proved to be more efficient than the original layout in the design. That previous machine couldn't even make it through the tests. We risked not going into production by the deadline. I'd proved that my enhancement to the machine solved the problem. But everything I tried to tell him was in vain. He wouldn't listen. The only thing he cared about was his ego, as the chief designer of that machine. Since he couldn't find anything with my design to object to, he cried in anger, 'You're fired!' I said, 'Fine;' then I took my bag and headed for the door."

Mark heavily drew on his cigarette and continued. "When I was walking down an aisle between machines to the exit, the foreman stopped me and whispered, 'I'm honored to have had a chance to work with you, Mark.'" Mark smiled grimly. "I'm not blaming him for not standing up for me before the boss. He has a family to feed."

"What's that smoke?"

Startled, Lisa turned to see Irving at the doorway. His face was contorted with a scowl. He squeezed his nose with his fingers and wheezed. "I'm suffocating; I can't breathe!"

Lisa jumped from her seat and opened the window, waving her hands in the air and trying to drive away the dense grayish clouds of smoke that had filled up the kitchen. She looked at Mark. He was pouring some coffee from the coffee machine into the cups. His expression was unreadable, but he seemed eager to continue with his story.

"Have you done your homework?" Lisa asked Irving.

"Yes, I have, Mom. And you already asked me that question!" He looked at her with disappointment. "And I'm hungry, Mom. How much longer is it before dinner's ready?" he cried.

Lisa smoothed her hair from her forehead. Guilt filled her heart. She had totally forgotten about dinner and her son. She stole a sidelong glance at Mark. He was standing silently by the coffee machine, deep in thought.

"How about I make you some sandwiches and juice and bring them into the living room so you can eat there and watch a movie?" she asked with an exaggerated, winning smile. Irving looked at her and Lisa felt her cheeks blushing.

"Whatever," Irving said as he shrugged and turned around. "I can't stand the smoke in here anyway," he tossed back at her as he walked away.

Mark grabbed the cups of coffee and put them on the table. "Do you want a sandwich?" Lisa asked, pulling out bread, mayonnaise, ham, and some vegetables from the refrigerator.

"No, I'm fine," Mark said as he gestured at the ventilator. "Let's turn it on," he suggested, and flipped the switch. "It will suck the smoke out."

It was a great idea. Lisa wondered why she hadn't thought of it before. She made a sandwich for Irving, poured some grape juice into a glass cup, then put everything onto a tray and carried it into the living room. Irving was sitting on the sofa, browsing through the TV channels. Lisa softly stroked his hair. "I love you, sonny."

"Yeah, yeah," Irving muttered, looking at the TV screen with exaggerated interest.

"Sonny, you know that I do," Lisa said putting the tray on the coffee table. "I made a special sandwich today." She smiled as she reached out to hug and kiss him, and then returned into the kitchen. She closed the door behind her so the smoke wouldn't penetrate into the other rooms. Mark was sitting at the table, thoughtfully stirring the sugar in his coffee. Lisa grabbed her cup.

"Mom, I need a napkin!" Irving's loud and demanding voice came through the door and into the kitchen. She understood that he was upset and angry for being left out. Nevertheless, his behavior was inappropriate, she thought as she headed into the living room with a napkin. She quickly returned to the kitchen.

"What's happening to the world?" Mark said, looking at her in despair. "Aren't people appreciated for their sharp minds or original ideas anymore?" His face jerked convulsively. "Ordinary, boring people who never would have been able to reach the top: are they ruling now?" He groaned, rubbing his forehead. "How could this be? I don't understand it. These people aren't able to progress; they aren't capable of doing anything productive except whatever political crap they have to, so they can end up above everyone else. Their plants and fields would be demolished if it wouldn't be for people like me. They should praise me;

instead they do whatever it takes to get me out of their way." Mark hit the table with his clenched fist.

Lisa's heart was filled with love as she looked at him. She understood his pain. It must not have been easy for a bright, gifted and ambitious person like Mark to work under a less skilled, unappreciative boss.

"Mark," she murmured, putting her comforting hand over his. "I'm going to say the banal thing, but the world isn't perfect. There's a lot of bureaucracy and unfairness in it but there's also—"

He didn't let her finish. "No buts, Lisa," he cried. "Can't you understand that if things are the way that they are, then this world isn't for me?" He moaned and hungrily drew on his cigarette, finishing it in almost one last hit and immediately lighting up another. "I simply can't stand stupidity," he continued bluntly. "I was trying to adjust, to cope with it somehow. I even developed some techniques to stay silent when I heard my colleagues speak pure gibberish at meetings or workshops." He laughed, his eyes filled with a mixture of sadness and irony. "And you know what? It helped a little, but I'm a hard worker who's not about the politics, and although I managed to control my tongue, my eyes would give me away. Sometimes they would see in my eyes what I was really thinking about them, and it infuriated them. They hated me and tried to block my path." He gulped hard, thoughtfully looking at Lisa.

"Mark," she said as she took a drag on her cigarette, trying to compose her thoughts. "Maybe you take it all too seriously. Maybe it's not worth the headache. We have a life besides our jobs, and that's what really matters. Whatever we do during the day, whatever idiots we stumble upon, whatever stress we're going through, it's all temporary, it's all just fuss. At the end of the day we come home to the embraces of our loved ones, and that's what's permanent!" Lisa paused and then smiled, her eyes lighting with humor. "Night after night, weekend after weekend, year after year and to the end of your life you'll be stuck with your dearest, your beloved ones. Isn't it great? How does it sound? Isn't it exciting?" She slowly blew the narrow grayish stream of the smoke to the ceiling. "Maybe these kinds of thoughts should concern you more and you should cast out your other dilemmas?" she joked, trying to ease his tension.

"You're my lovely little shrink!" Mark laughed.

"Well, I studied psychology," Lisa remarked with a bit of pride in her voice. "I got all A's, by the way."

"Oh, those psychologists," Mark said with scorn. "I tried different counselors. They dig deep into your childhood, blaming your parents, especially your mother. However, there are many other factors that may affect a person. Like a chemical imbalance, your brain constitution, or just nervous energy. But actually, nobody seems to know the real cause of depression. They try to treat it but none of them go out of their way to help you. They don't look at the problem involving the entire system. Instead they pick out the separate, individual symptoms, trying to isolate them. Once, after all my interior resources were exhausted trying to overcome depression, I agreed to use antidepressant drugs. Although I knew in the beginning that it wouldn't help, I still took them. I did it to satisfy the doctor and out of my helplessness. The doctor was a woman who seemed like a bright and clever thinker. Yet the drug didn't work. It only made me feel sleepy, dizzy, and weak. Most of all, it slowed down my concentration and even affected my sexual performance." He let out a deep sigh and looked at her sadly.

"I think that in this case drugs should be the last resort," Lisa said, while lighting another cigarette.

"Then what, Lisa?" he cried. "What should I do? Look deeper down into my childhood? Well. My parents got divorced when I was eleven years old. My mom worked hard with two jobs, that's why she didn't have time for me. Growing up, I was a very curious boy with many questions. My mother bought me books so that I'd read them instead of bothering her. I spent all of my free time lying on the living room couch, reading books. Without being noticed, I started to live a life of the heroes from these books, and my imagination took me away from the reality of my life. Everything that happened in reality wasn't as interesting and fascinating as it was in books.

I found myself having difficulty talking with my peers. And as a result, they'd avoid and tease me. It hurt me a lot, Lisa; it really did. I decided to make them interested in me and want my friendship. In order to get that, I decided that I'd need to be well-built, so I started weight training. During all of my free time the only thing that I'd do was work out, lifting massive weights and working my abs, so I could have this six-pack. I noticed that my peers started to respect me for my new appearance. They wouldn't risk teasing me anymore. But still, we didn't have anything in common; we didn't click." Mark took a deep drag on his cigarette. "I remember the days when my father lived with us," he continued. "My father would never have allowed me to be a couch potato. We used to bike, play sports, fish. I kept wondering if I would've become a different person if my father would've stayed with us. One day when I was a freshman in college I felt very down. I told my mom how bad I felt and asked her if she knew or did anything that made me feel that way. She just cried in response, telling me that she didn't do anything wrong, and that my best interests were always her first concern. I then called my dad and asked him if he knew the roots of my suffering, thinking maybe if I knew the cause I'd be able to fight it. Do you know what my dad said?" Mark grimaced. "He said that it wasn't his problem, that he never heard about it and whatever I was talking about had nothing to do with him. His words made me feel even more alone and secluded." Mark looked searchingly at Lisa. "Maybe that's my problem. Maybe that's why it's hard for me to build relationships, to make people love me?" he muttered as a trace of pain flashed across his controlled face.

"That's not true," Lisa objected heartily. "You don't know what you're worth. You are loved. You have so many great friends. Look at yourself; you're smart, charming and handsome. Any woman would kill to be with you. Any company would be honored to have you!"

He let out a wistful sigh. "Maybe you're right. After my divorce I felt miserable. I missed my children and felt alone for a long time. And I hate to be alone." He smiled tenderly at her.

"You aren't alone anymore, Mark!" Lisa reached out for his hand. "You have Irving and me by your side."

"I'm so happy that I found you." He smiled, leaning back in his chair, looking over at his watch. "Lisa, do you know the time?" he exclaimed. "It's really late; Irving should have been in bed by now."

Lisa got up quickly, lost her balance momentarily, and grabbed onto the counter to prevent her fall. For some reason she felt dizzy and tired. She headed over to the living room and found the empty plates and napkins that Irving had left behind him on the coffee table. Lisa then went to Irving's room to check on him and found him asleep on his bed. *Time goes by so fast*, she thought. Children grow up fast. She didn't even notice when Irving had gotten responsible enough to go to bed by himself. And on time!

She adjusted Irving's blanket and went back to the kitchen. Mark was standing there, brewing the coffee. He looked fresh and relieved. He looked himself again.

"I suddenly feel very hungry," he said, smiling at her. "Do we have anything to eat?"

Lisa was exhausted. Her head was splitting and yet she felt very glad that she had helped set Mark's mind at ease. This realization mobilized her inner resources, giving her strength.

"Would you care for some dinner?" she asked.

"A sandwich is fine."

She started to prepare the sandwiches for them both while Mark finished making coffee. They sat down at the table and Mark bit into his sandwich. Lisa sat there, staring at her sandwich. She didn't feel like eating it at all now. Her headache was growing worse and worse. The cigarette smoke filled her up, making her nauseous. After Mark finished eating, Lisa cleaned up the table and put her untouched sandwich into the refrigerator. Mark approached her from behind and gently pressed his lips against her neck. Then he turned her around and kissed her. The kiss was deep, long and soft.

"Let's go to bed," he whispered into her ear. "I can't wait to hold you in my arms."

I have a terrible headache, she was going to say, but she changed her mind and swallowed her complaints after he added passionately, "Making love with you lights up my life."

Mark turned the kitchen light off and they went into the bedroom, wrapping their arms around each other.

CHAPTER FIFTEEN

Mark's routine didn't change for the next week. He didn't have to go to his office anymore but searching for a job ended up being even more demanding. He still continued to wake up at 6 a.m. on the dot, take a quick shower, shave, have a cup of coffee with a cigarette and, right after that, he'd go to the coffee table and engage in the hard work of looking for a job. He laid out the classified section and thoroughly reviewed the job ads. When he found one that was of interest to him, he'd carefully cut it out and glue it to his note pad. Finishing with the newspaper he switched over to the computer and continued his search by browsing through various job sites. He e-mailed his resume to the addresses that he picked out and also called recruiters whose numbers were listed. He ended up taking a lot of phone interviews and driving all over to different cities for personal interviews. At the end of the week, he looked exhausted but satisfied. Two companies had made him offers. He accepted an offer from a well-known and prestigious company located in downtown Chicago. The position he was hired for looked very appealing in terms of his job responsibilities and the conditions were much better than those of his previous job. He was asked to start immediately, on the following Monday morning.

Mark was very excited about it. Lisa made a special pasta dish, accompanied by meatballs, and set the dinner table with a bottle of red wine and candles. She lit the candles, put a CD into the stereo, and they all sat together in celebration of Mark's new job. Mark poured some red wine into the tall crystal wine glasses. He dropped a little into Irving's glass as well and clinked glasses with him.

"Mark!" she exclaimed with confusion. "Irving's not supposed to have wine. He's too young for that!"

Mark grinned at her. "I just gave him enough to smell it; there's not much to drink. Besides, do you know that red wine's said to be good for your blood?" He looked at her with his chin extended. "French people, you know, won't sit down at the dinner table if there's not a bottle of good red wine there."

"Mark, we're not French," Lisa retorted with laughter.

"Well," Mark said, "statistics say that the French happened to have 15% fewer people with cancer than Americans; the women there are all slender and beautiful and the men all look like Apollo," he stated his point.

"Well, I give up," Lisa chortled. "You're like an encyclopedia! But still, let's give Irving a glass of water instead."

"All right." Mark said, filling a glass of water for Irving and handing it to him. "Now, a toast: to your mom!" he declared.

"To you, Mom!" Irving repeated enthusiastically, and both of them hit their glasses against Lisa's.

"How come you know so much about wine and French people?" Lisa asked.

"I told you that I read a lot," Mark said, smiling.

"I don't like reading that much," Irving interjected. "Why read if you can watch a movie!" he exclaimed as he threw his hand in the air. "Unless a book's a school assignment, then only silly people will read it," he added with conviction.

"Irving!" Lisa scolded, looking at her son in astonishment. "What might Mark think about you? You didn't mean what you just said, did you?"

Irving began to blush. "I read *Goosebumps*," he said to his defense. "It wasn't an assignment either!"

Lisa tried to hide her amusement from the child's inventiveness. She exchanged glances with Mark.

"I accept that," Mark said, looking seriously at Irving. "It's a good book and very popular with kids your age. However, I can bring you a book called *Treasure Island,* which is written by Robert Louis Stevenson, a very famous author. It's full of the kind of adventure that you can't find in *Goosebumps*. It's an adventure of pirates, treasure hunting, betrayal, and revenge. As soon as you start reading it you'll get so carried away by its thrills and adventures that you won't be able to put it down until you finish it," he promised.

"Sounds enticing, doesn't it?" Lisa said, ruffling Irving's hair.

"Sure," Irving replied without much enthusiasm. "Did they make a movie?"

"Irving, a book and a movie are two different things," Mark said. "When you read a book, you interpret it in your own way; you make your own conclusions. In a movie, everything's already laid out for you as the movie producer sees it."

While Mark and Irving were talking, Lisa cleaned up the table and washed the dishes.

"Some coffee or tea?" she offered.

"I'll have some coffee," Mark said, raising his hand.

"Irving, how about you?" she asked. "Some cookies with tea or juice?"

"Juice please," Irving said. "Can I have it in my room, Mom?" he asked. "I started on this new level before dinner that I want to finish. Can I?"

"Okay," Lisa agreed. "But that's only because today's Sunday. I don't want you to make a habit out of it," she added.

Irving jumped up from his chair, heading straight to his room. "You're going to be smoking anyway," he murmured from afar.

Lisa didn't say anything. To her shame, she couldn't really object to her son's words. Surprisingly for her, she seemed to be getting used to the routine of smoking cigarettes and having a cup of coffee. It'd be nice to have a balcony or a porch where they could go for a smoke, but there wasn't one. Besides, it felt more comfortable to sit there at the table, drinking coffee, smoking, and talking in the coziness of their own kitchen instead of being outside in the cold.

She opened a window, turned on the vent and closed the kitchen door to keep the smoke inside the room and prevent it from going into Irving's. She lowered herself onto a chair by the window and stretched, leaning back against the chair. It had been a long day and she was feeling a bit tired. She was grateful to have a chance to relax. She took a slow, deep drag on her cigarette and watched Mark pour the coffee for them both. Then he pulled out a cigarette and grinned at her. "You seem to be enjoying the moment." His look was warm and gentle.

"I sure am," she said frankly.

The kitchen was clean; the aroma of the steaming coffee delightfully filled her nostrils. Mark was sitting at the table across from her, simply adoring her. At that moment she had all she needed to feel happy, accomplished, and complete. She needed as little as that and as much as that, all at once.

"You look a little tired," Mark said attentively. "Is everything all right?"

"Yes, I'm fine." Lisa sipped her coffee. "I just feel a little overwhelmed from working on my day off, that's all." She smiled at him.

"I told you." Mark looked at her with slight reproach and added softly, "Don't go to work, Lisa."

"Well, I had to." Lisa let out a deep sigh. "The other massage therapist who normally works on Sundays went on vacation and I had to substitute for her." She made an indefinite gesture with her hand and smiled. "I had to do it." Mark looked straight into her eyes, his expression serious.

"Lisa, I'm not talking about a particular day, I was talking about you quitting your job permanently." He reached out to touch her hand that was lying on the table.

"This massage job isn't meant for you Lisa. It requires a lot of physical strength and long hours to make a relatively good living. Look at you. You're slim and tender. Your hands are small, soft, and delicate. Both of them easily fit inside one of my fists," he said laughingly as he took her other hand and covered both of them into his big hand. "Those hands are made to be caressed, to be kissed, not to be engaged in hard, sweaty work," he said passionately.

"All of it isn't based on physical strength, Mark," Lisa said, taking her hands back. She looked at them. "They might look small and weak but there's a lot of strength in them, and also a lot of a proper technique that can make any male client squeal," she said as she tried to open Mark's fist with both of her hands to prove her point.

"Lisa, stop breaking my finger," he whined, laughing, twisting his fist from her as she decided to open his fist by pulling his finger first. "You know what I'm trying to say, don't you?" He took his hand from the table to light a cigarette. "Lisa, I'm serious. Please don't behave like a little girl. What I'm saying's very important. I know that masseuse job isn't for you. I know that you can do better." He took a drag on his cigarette and slowly blew out the gray stream of smoke. "It wasn't your fault that you didn't make it through college. It was a tragedy; you were left alone with your son and had to go earn money to make a living." He leveled a soft gaze at her. "But now you have me, Lisa. I'm here to support you in your endeavors. I know you were taking prerequisite classes to become a physical therapist. You have this drive and passion and ability to be an exceptional physical therapist. You'll have a lot more opportunities and resources to help patients than you do now." Mark held her in his gaze.

Lisa lit her cigarette. She felt the warmth of a blush on her face. Mark noticed her confusion. "Lisa, I'm not a stranger to you," he said wholeheartedly. Your best interests and the best interests of Irving are my top priority." He gestured with his hand, emphasizing his words. "Do I even have to tell you that?"

Lisa took another drag on her cigarette, trying to sort out her thoughts. She was looking for a persuasive argument to deny his offer and not hurt his feelings at the same time. She didn't consider herself ungrateful. Life had already taught her to appreciate even small things, the things that some people may take for granted. She appreciated Mark's offer very much. The possibility of going back to college was very desirable to her. It stirred up all the dreams and ambitions she had repressed after the death of her husband. It filled her heart with hope and excitement for the future. Still. How could she just go ahead and quit her job? She didn't have any savings to live on, except Mark's willingness to support her. She knew in her heart that Mark was the one; she had felt that right from their first meeting. And, with time, she had grown to know it for sure.

They'd been living together like a real family. They actually were a real family. Lisa thought of Mark as nothing less than her husband, and she knew that he felt the same. Still, they hadn't been legally married. What Mark was asking was for her and Irving to live entirely on his income. But only God knew how long it'd be until she'd finish school and find a job in her new field. All that time she and Irving would be a burden for Mark! He might not realize it now; he might deny this fact with all his heart, but Lisa couldn't exploit his kindness. It was unacceptable to her. She never wanted to be a burden to a man, even though this man was Mark. Lisa blew the cigarette smoke out the window, trying to sort out her thoughts, but her face gave her away. Mark seemed to read her mind.

"Lisa," he said, leaning back in his chair. A look of doubt and disappointment was reflected on his face.

"If we don't have faith in each other, if we don't trust each other, then what's all of this about? What are we doing here? If that's what it is, then everything that we're trying to build here doesn't seem to make any sense." He spread his hands in a helpless gesture; his eyes focused directly on hers, his gaze steady and firm.

"That's not what I meant," Lisa exclaimed vigorously. She felt a sudden pressure in her temples, like blood had just flooded her head. A flash of fear overwhelmed her. Mark took a deep drag on his cigarette.

"Lisa, you know that I'm not a boy anymore. I have life experiences and heavy baggage behind me. I put so much blood and soul into my family, especially into the children. I thought that I had something but it was like a bad investment, and I ended up with nothing." He crossed his hands on the table, and looked at them longingly for a split second. "My heart was turned upside down. My life stopped making sense." He looked at her with pain in his eyes. "I can't waste my time knowing that our relationship won't go anywhere. I'm committed to put everything into this family and I'm expecting to have the same dedication in return." He tapped his fingers on the table and then continued. "But if we can't reach a mutual understanding at the beginning, then maybe we have to sit down and talk seriously about whether or not we made the right decision starting this family."

Lisa suddenly found it hard to breathe. How did this start? What had she said or done to suddenly break everything that she cared so much about? Somehow everything was going in an unexpected direction. Her thoughts were getting mixed up. Her brain was drawing a blank. She lifted her head to look at Mark, her eyes wide open with astonishment, tears ready to come out. She made an impossible effort to hold them in.

"Mark," she said, her voice trembling. "It's not that I don't trust you."

"Lisa," he said, forcefully shaking his head. "Let's not quibble over semantics. I stopped trusting words a long time ago unless they were backed up by actions. Words mean nothing unless they're followed by actions." His eyes bored into hers with a meaningful look before he twisted away to stare out the window.

Silence filled the room. Lisa licked her lips, parted them, but not a single word could come out. She knew that she had to say something to explain herself. But only tears came, pouring down her cheeks. She wiped them with her sleeve, then lit a cigarette and inhaled the smoke deeply. "Mark," she said, weighing her words. "Please understand my point of view. I don't have any money to pay the rent and the bills without a job. This is an uncomfortable issue to discuss, but we need to address it before we make such an important decision."

"I didn't take you for your money," he interrupted quickly. "If I were seeking money I'd probably have looked somewhere else." He grinned at her. "I love you Lisa. And I love Irving like my own son. I want the best for you both. My only requirement is for all of us to row the boat in the same direction, otherwise it just sinks." He took a drag on his cigarette and looked straight into her eyes.

"So, what will it be? Are we going the same way?"

She smiled back at him. "Of course we are, Mark."

He leaned back in his chair, letting out a deep sigh of relief, then looked thoughtfully at her.

"You know, Lisa, I think we all need to take a vacation. We're all tired." He tapped his cigarette in an ashtray. "What do you say about going to Mexico? Cancun or something?" He looked expectantly at her and continued. "How long has it been since your last suntan? Look at you, you remind me of Snow White." He smiled and reached out to run his hand along her cheek.

Lisa couldn't believe that she heard him correctly. She couldn't remember the last time she had had a vacation. It was probably over three years ago.

"That'd be great." She hesitated for a moment. "Can we afford it?"

"Look, Lisa. I'm getting a fairly decent salary, and this company even gave me a signing bonus. I think that the best investment for my bonus is to go on vacation. Don't you?" His expression was a little querulous, but proud and happy nonetheless. "What do you think?"

"I love it! I really do," she said.

CHAPTER SIXTEEN

Margaret didn't take the news well. "You can't just quit your job!" she said, her eyes wide with shock at Lisa's betrayal. "You can't leave me all alone here!"

"I'm not leaving you alone," Lisa said, reaching out to hug Margaret.

"Don't even touch me. Traitor." Margaret twisted away from Lisa's grasp, her eyes shining with tears.

"I'm not a traitor," Lisa said, eyes wide with sincerity. She was deeply touched by her friend's reaction to her announcement. She paused, and then gave her a small smile. "I'm just trying to explore new opportunities. Discover unknown horizons." She waved her hand as if to show where she could find the hidden horizons. Margaret buried her head in her hands.

"Margaret," Laura interjected. "You're out of your mind! Lisa's future is laid out in front of her. Why would her best friend hold her back, unless you're jealous?"

"I'm not jealous of Lisa!" Margaret said, her face fierce, and then she stopped.

"Don't listen to me. I'm just upset that you're leaving, that's all." She looked at Lisa; her gaze softened with sadness. "It won't be the same here without you."

Lisa felt her eyes filling with tears. She was going to miss Margaret and the other girls. She was going to miss the back room with its coffee breaks and girl talk. She was going to miss the special, homelike atmosphere of their salon, the familiar smells, and her room with the massage table, equipment and products. She was going to miss her clients and even her boss, who, all-in-all, wasn't as bad as the girls' gossip made her sound. She might've been strict and arrogant but that was how a boss needed to be to run a successful business, wasn't it? Indeed, she was good at her job, and, as their place was prestigious in its field, the girls always had plenty of clients. Lisa's heart lurched as she looked around. What she saw wasn't only her work place. It was a part of her life. It was a part of who she was. Was she making the right decision by burning all her bridges? What if everything went wrong? What if her rejuvenated dreams were crushed by the harsh world? Lisa inhaled deeply, then exhaled. She held onto one thought. *Whatever will happen will happen.* But at least she'd be able to say she gave it a try instead of wondering how her life would've turned out.

Her boss asked that Lisa be loyal to the company and take care of her clients who were already booked. They both went through the schedule and agreed that Lisa would work part-time up to Christmas, so they wouldn't have to cancel the existing clientele. Lisa didn't mind at all. In fact, she was glad to continue working. It made the transition to her new adventure less abrupt and less frustrating. It gave her time to gradually get used to the thought that this wasn't a dream. She needed time to come to grips with the realization that her intentions to change her life upside down were not just in her imagination, and they weren't going to disappear if she opened her eyes.

***

The first morning without going to work seemed somewhat unreal to Lisa. She woke up as usual. Mark was already in the kitchen making coffee. He greeted her with a smile. Lisa joined him for morning coffee and a few cigarettes. They talked briefly of her plans to research the college's prerequisites and schedules, and possibly talk to the college counselor or at least to make an appointment with her. Mark advised Lisa to have her transcript ready before going to the meeting and to write down all the questions that she needed to ask so she'd be ready for the next step when the meeting was over.

When he left, Lisa woke up Irving and put his usual breakfast set on the table: Honeycomb cereal, a sliced banana and milk. Irving came into the kitchen with a big poster, which he carefully squeezed through the door. It was the science project that he and his group had worked on over the weekend. Mark helped them find information in the encyclopedia—a CD that he had recently bought for Irving. The boys printed out the colorful images and glued them to the poster. They also typed captions, glued them under the respective pictures, and supplied a descriptive arrow for easy navigation. The poster looked great and it promised to beat out all the other competitors. Irving was trying to prop up the poster against a chair to keep it safe, but it kept sliding down.

"Sonny," Lisa said, taking the poster from him. "Sit down and eat your breakfast. Let me take care of your poster." She found two pieces of cardboard and sandwiched his poster between them so it wouldn't get bent. When Irving was ready to go, she walked with him to the school bus, helping carry the poster. After she saw him off to school she came back to the house and, for a split second, froze in confusion, standing in the middle of her living room. Her apartment looked and felt somewhat different, although Lisa wasn't able to identify what actually had changed.

The sun shone into the room, making it warm and bright. Her plants turned their leaves to the rays and they looked fresh and nourished, as always. Despite the cold weather outside, it was warm and cozy inside her apartment. Yet, there was something different, something strange about it now. Lisa felt an inexplicable cold rising from deep inside her, making her heart squeeze.

Tiny, horrid goose bumps spread all over her body. She found herself shivering as though she were standing outside in the cold. She lowered herself onto the sofa, crossed her arms on her chest, and tried to think clearly. She had to get rid of these ghastly feelings quickly, before the fear possessed her completely. At any rate, she had to compose herself. She was at home at a time when she'd normally be at work. That explained why she was feeling strange. She had to get used to it, that was all.

Lisa looked around and scowled. Her thoughts seemed to be very rational and convincing. They were supposed to bring relief and put everything in place. Unfortunately, they weren't. She still felt alone and frightened and uncertain. Nobody seemed to be waiting for her anywhere. Nobody seemed to need her. Mark was at work. Irving was at school. Lisa visualized the salon where she'd worked for years. Margaret, Laura and the others were probably busy with their clients by that time, and the coffee in the back kitchen had already been made, and it'd be tickling her nose with its heady aroma. Are the girls going to talk about her when they gather in the back room? Did they miss her? Lisa imagined the answer was no. They'd probably already forgotten about her, which wasn't really their fault. Lisa had willingly left them and not looked back. So there was nobody to blame for sitting here in the middle of the day in tears. Nobody, of course, except herself. She had to accept the bare-naked truth—she wasn't part of a team anymore. They'd lose any interest in her as their friend now that they had nothing in common with her anymore. She was an outsider, a stranger to the girls whose presence in her life had only yesterday seemed so natural, routine and permanent. Lisa's anxiety rose. The fear was taking control of her. Now she wasn't sure that she had made the right decision in quitting her job. Worse yet, she was sure she had made the biggest mistake of her life.

Lisa smoothed her hair off her forehead. The desire to run to work and beg her boss to take her back overwhelmed her. She imagined herself coming to her room, setting up her massage table, lighting the candles. She visualized her clients, and almost felt her hands performing the familiar routine to the sounds of the soft, gentle music and sea gulls' squeals. To her surprise, those pictures brought some relief to her. She began to think through her decision. Obviously, leaving her job wasn't the end of the world. She was just getting a little emotional. Anybody in her shoes would freak out too. It was a normal reaction to such hasty and dramatic changes as the ones occurring in her life. Wasn't it?

Okay then, Lisa thought with some satisfaction. She paid tribute to her nostalgia, but afterward it was time to get over it and start to make a plan. Besides, tomorrow morning she was scheduled to go to the salon to see the two clients. So, in less than twenty-four hours, she'd be able to meet the girls and the clients again, and reminisce. And if the worst happened, and her college adventure didn't work out, she'd always be able to come back to her old job and do what she was doing, wouldn't she? These thoughts energized her.

Lisa got up from the sofa and inserted a CD into the stereo. The room filled with sounds of quiet, soft music. She smiled. Actually, now that she thought about it, she could admit there were some advantages to being free and home alone. She just needed to concentrate and keep herself on track. She needed to be determined and stick to the plan so she wouldn't waste valuable time.

Lisa wandered to the kitchen and pulled the phone book out of the cabinet. She skipped through the pages to find the phone number of the local community college's admissions office. Then she dialed the number and set up a meeting with a counselor. The counselor was booked for the whole week, but, fortunately for her, a cancellation had just been made and Lisa was offered that appointment. She gathered her papers quickly and put them into the folder, then headed off to the college.

The sharp corners and strong lines of the college's architecture absorbed Lisa as soon as she stepped through the entrance. Long narrow corridors, majestic, granite columns that reached the heights of the ceilings, and hushed classrooms all demanded respect. Somber professors marched along the corridors. In contrast to them, the students looked preoccupied, rushing in all directions with heavy bags and large textbooks in hand.

For a moment Lisa stood there in confusion, anxious about proceeding. She took a deep breath and closed her eyes for a moment before she moved ahead like diving into deep, cold seawater. She walked along the corridor to the center where it expanded with a wide, beautiful arch large enough to fit a cafeteria; then passed through the adjacent area with registrations and admissions offices where students were waiting in line. When the corridor narrowed again, Lisa found the room she was looking for located at the end of the hall. She hesitated for a moment, then quietly knocked and opened the door to the inviting voice from inside. A middle-aged woman in a black knee-length woolen skirt, white blouse and gold-framed glasses greeted her with a smile.

"Mrs. Malden," she introduced herself. "And you must be Lisa?" She smiled encouragingly at Lisa and indicated the chair next to the desk. "How can I be of service?" she asked.

Lisa dug into her Claiborne bag and pulled out a transcript with the credit hours she'd completed almost seven years ago. However, she had little hope that those hours would be accepted, considering the length of time that had passed since they were taken. Yet, to her delight, the counselor assured her that her credentials were valid, and could be applied toward her major. Lisa would need to request an official transcript from her previous college and have it sent directly to the Registration and Admissions office. The advisor appeared to be a professional and knowledgeable woman. At the same time, she had an open, friendly attitude, which comforted Lisa. Mrs. Malden provided Lisa with detailed information regarding prerequisites for admission into the physical therapy program and came up with a list of classes that Lisa needed to complete in her pre-physical therapy curriculum.

Leaving the counselor's office, Lisa was excited. She was all set for the next step, which was registering for the classes. Per Mrs. Malden's advice, she'd have to take four credit hours in Biology, which were Human Anatomy and Physiology, and then English and Sociology. That was ten credit hours altogether. Her schedule looked somewhat tough, as she'd have classes four days a week. However, because she'd registered late, all the other classes were already full. So she was happy that she was able to register at all. The next semester, however, she intended to book the classes as early as possible to make her schedule more compact and to free up more weekdays.

Mark was surprised when Lisa told him that she not only met with a counselor but had actually registered for the semester as well.

"You're not losing a moment, are you?" He looked thoughtfully at her. "Your schedule looks pretty intense. Do you think you took more classes than you can handle?" He sounded concerned.

"I'm *positive* I can handle it," Lisa said. "I want to complete the prerequisites and get into the physical therapy program as soon as possible. Why stretch out such a doubtful pleasure as doing my homework?" She laughed.

"I love your spirit." Mark smiled at her warmly. "You're as courageous and optimistic a woman as you are beautiful!"

They went to the kitchen for some coffee. There was one uncomfortable issue left that needed to be discussed. Lisa lit a cigarette and studied the narrow, bluish rings of smoke. She hesitated. She stalled for time, hoping that Mark would ask her first. Mark seemed to read her mind.

"So, what's the damage?" he asked, smiling.

Lisa handed him the bill that she had received together with her registration materials.

Mark looked at it briefly, went to their bedroom and returned with his checkbook. He quickly wrote a check, signed it and gave it to Lisa.

"I hope they won't call me to the principal's office for any misbehavior," he said as he grinned at her.

"I promise I'll be an exemplary student," Lisa said flashing a half-serious, half-mocking smile.

There was only one way for her now, she thought—the rough, thorny road that led forward to her ambitious mountain peaks. Lisa smiled. She was no longer afraid, nor was she doubtful. She had made a decision and her mind was set. She was determined.

CHAPTER SEVENTEEN

Irving's eighth birthday was on December 23. Mark suggested that they have a party at Chuck E. Cheese's. Irving invited all of his friends and Lisa made the reservation two weeks in advance. To her surprise, she was told that she was lucky as there were only two spots available for that date.

"Usually, people try to make party reservations at least a month in advance," the receptionist advised Lisa. Lisa thought she'd keep this information in mind for the next occasion. In the past, they celebrated Irving's birthdays at home with a few adult guests and their kids, and she hadn't known that this place was in such demand.

Irving was excited. Saturday morning Mark borrowed Jerome's van and they went together with Irving to pick up his friends. Then they came back to pick up Lisa and they all headed to Chuck E. Cheese's. Their table was ready. It was long, assembled from a combination of several small tables, covered with a tablecloth, and already set up with paper plates, cups and plastic silverware. The table was located perpendicular to the window in the middle of an extremely crowded room. Popular children's songs were playing as kids ran around everywhere. Sonya, her husband, and three-year-old son were already waiting inside. Lisa was very happy to see them. She also invited Margaret, who came alone, as her husband had gone on a business trip to California. She invited Laura and two other girls from work as well, and Mark invited Connie, Jerome and Anna. He also invited Nora, Steve and their daughter, who unfortunately couldn't make it, but who had sent Irving a nice birthday card that sang a song when it was open.

Lisa seated Irving and his friends on both sides of the table, starting from the window. In this way, the part of the table that was closer to the aisle was reserved for the adults. While waiting for the pizza to be served, Mark poured everybody their choice of a soft drink. By this time, the other guests had arrived and joined them at the table.

Jerome rose from his seat. "It's not a party if there isn't anything spicy on the table!" he announced as he pulled out a bottle of wine. He was so well prepared that he'd even brought paper cups with him.

"To the next generation," he declared and emptied his cup in one gulp. He snorted some air, coughed, and immediately filled his cup again.

"Don't worry," he assured everybody. "I have another one in reserve." He showed his left-side pocket.

Connie gave her husband a heart-freezing look. "You should be ashamed of yourself; there are children here," she exclaimed furiously.

"C'mon, Connie," Mark stood up for his friend. "The children are busy with their own business. They're preoccupied with pizza and in a few minutes they'll go to the arcade." He paused thoughtfully, as a wide smile came across his face. "Besides, our friends would probably be bored." He glanced to the section where Lisa's young co-workers sat. "If it wouldn't be for the wine, I probably wouldn't have enough courage to entertain them." He smiled and reached out to make a toast. "To beautiful women," he declared and touched his glass against the girls' cups.

Margaret pushed Lisa's leg under the table and gave her a "whoa" look. Lisa just smiled and shook her head. She knew that Mark was just trying to be a gentleman and nothing more. Still, she wished Margaret and the girls Mark had toasted to knew that as well.

In a few minutes, the children started disappearing in groups, running off in different directions and getting lost in the midst of happy, hyper faces.

"Let's go see how the children are doing," Margaret said as she grabbed Lisa by her arm, dragging her away from the table. Sonya followed behind them, holding her son in her arms.

"Mark's flirting with everyone," Margaret whispered forcefully to Lisa when they were far enough away.

"No, he isn't," Lisa objected as she rolled her eyes.

"He told me that I have gorgeous hair when he helped me out of my coat." Margaret looked unblinkingly into Lisa's eyes. Lisa felt color wash up on her face.

"C'mon, Margaret," she said. "You do have long, beautiful hair. It probably caught on to your coat when Mark helped you to take it off. He was just trying to be nice." She managed to make a smile.

It was a mystery to Lisa how some women took causal, meaningless compliments so seriously. If a man paid any attention to them, they'd started expecting a marriage proposal. It was even more upsetting that her closest and smartest friend Margaret acted this way.

"I just wanted to mention it, so you'd know." Margaret glanced at Lisa. "Mark's a handsome, attractive man. Women are attracted to him, and he's well aware of the fact. He's not losing a single moment to show it to everybody." She gave Lisa a warning look. "You have to be alert, girlfriend. That kind of man needs a collar in the form of a ring." They both laughed and headed off to join Sonya and the other kids at the games.

The party went well. It finished up with a mountain of icing that was actually birthday cake and had eight candles for Irving to blow out and make a wish upon. On the way home, they dropped off the children at their houses and headed home themselves. Irving sat in the back, occupied with unwrapping his birthday presents. Lisa took a sidelong look at Mark. He was steadily driving the car down the highway, staring at the road in front of him.

"Mark," Lisa started, and then hesitated. She opened the passenger window, pulled out a cigarette and lit it. Mark looked at her expectantly. "Did you say something, Lisa?" he asked.

She took a drag on her cigarette and let the smoke out the window.

"You were giving compliments to all the women around you." She looked at him. "Some of them seemed to think you were really interested in them," she added with an easy laugh.

Mark laughed in response. "Some women are so conceited," he said harshly, but when he looked at Lisa his eyes softened. "You remind me of my ex-wife," he said. "She used to say that I embarrassed her by paying attention to other women." He laughed. "I'm a man, Lisa. It's in a man's blood. It's sort of an instinct for any man to be a gentleman with the ladies." He looked pensively at her and then turned to stroke her hair. "Understand though, that nothing and nobody's above you in my heart."

Lisa smiled at him. She didn't consider herself conceited, and most of all she didn't want to resemble his ex-wife. As far as she was concerned, she didn't have anything in common with that cruel woman. Lisa threw her cigarette out the window, moved to the side of her seat and leaned to Mark's arm. She must've indeed been paranoid and ungrateful. Mark had arranged such a great birthday party for Irving. He had entertained the guests; he had picked up and took care of all the kids. He had taken care of everything just to make her and Irving happy. Lisa pressed tighter and closer to Mark. A wry thought entered her mind. Human nature is indeed inexplicable. Why is it that no matter how much one has, they always want more?

Mark looked down at Lisa passionately.

"You're sitting so quietly, like a kitten against my arm." Lisa just smiled. She felt so happy and secure, better than ever.

CHAPTER EIGHTEEN

Lisa's classes started on the second Monday of January. Surrounded by a diverse crowd of students, she made her way over to the Hall of Science for her biology class. Her first lecture was held in a large auditorium. Lisa sat down in the middle of the second aisle, pulled out her notebook and pen, and set them on the desk. A tall, slim woman entered the classroom with her head held high. Her gait was energetic and confident. She put her belongings on the desk, hung the visual aids on the board, and introduced herself. Without any further preamble, she headed to the blackboard and started the lecture.

"Principles of Anatomy and Physiology. The human body consists of several layers of structural organization, and those layers are closely associated with one another in various complex ways." Direct and to the point, the teacher began to cover the first topic. She briefly touched on each structural layer, then proceeded straight to the next topic. Lisa tried not to miss a single word and, at the same time, tried to write down as many details as she could. Although intrigued by the system of the human body, she soon realized that with all of the topics and information that would be covered in this one lecture, she'd need to study all the details in each chapter carefully at home to fully understand the material. After the lecture she was exhausted.

Following her schedule, she rushed to the second floor through the long labyrinth of corridors, making a few turns before finding her sociology classroom. Out of breath, she entered the classroom and grabbed the first vacant seat she could find.

The professor entered the room just as Lisa sat down. He was a middle-aged man wearing bright-colored pants and a black shirt. He started the lecture by introducing the topic of sociology to the class. He stood as he discussed social science and its history. His explanations were insightful. All the facts that he presented were supported by real-life examples. Throughout the lecture the professor gesticulated, emphasizing the main points. His expression was alive and energetic and his gestures were full of emotion and heart. Suddenly he paused, took off his glasses and placed them on the desk. Then he looked around the classroom, with his eyes full of mystery.

"Do you know what the crucial question of sociology is?" He raised his hand, index finger extended, and loudly exclaimed, "Why!" He looked around the classroom victoriously, observing the students' reactions. "Yes, 'Why' is the crucial question of sociology. Why do some people commit crimes, or suicide, become unemployed, take drugs? Is it due to individual, biological, or personal problems, or is the social environment a factor?"

Lisa listened to his every word with great fascination. He touched on popular topics like drinking, stealing, and drug abuse, and he analyzed the causes and judged them from an entirely new perspective, one that Lisa never considered before. The lecture was so fascinating that Lisa didn't move once throughout the entire thing, and she was startled when he dismissed them so soon. The teacher asked them to conduct research about people's interactions in their own community. The task was to observe and interview their neighbors at home and in public. The last part of the research required the students to arrive at a conclusion about the individual's ties within a group. Lisa was excited about this class as well as the assignment, which was due in two weeks.

After sociology, she had a two-hour break before her next class. She went to the cafeteria to have lunch and a cup of coffee. The cafeteria was fairly crowded. Students were talking, eating and even doing their homework. Lisa recognized a couple of familiar faces at a table in the middle aisle and headed toward it. The two girls at the table were from her biology class. They also recognized Lisa and waved to her, inviting her to join them.

Her new friends were Sandy and Kristina. They were high school graduates attending their first year of college. They were both nursing majors and therefore had to take a several science classes. Kristina began sharing what the junior students were saying about their biology teacher. She'd heard that the teacher was a single woman without any family or relatives and that biology meant the world to her. They said she also took her teaching very seriously.

"She's strict, determined and expects every student to be completely devoted to the class if they want to have a chance of receiving a fair grade. She never curves or accepts any excuses," she explained.

"She sounds like a machine that has a program in place of a heart!" Lisa exclaimed.

"She also teaches the lab class and will probably expect the students to know every single muscle, artery, vein, and even capillary of the cat that we're going to dissect," Sandy added.

Lisa's eyes flew wide open. "We're going to have to dissect a cat?"

Kristina looked at her with amusement. "Of course. A fuzzy, black cat that's going to scream under the scalpel," she whispered in a terrified voice.

"That's so nasty, Kristina," Sandy interjected. "It's probably a fifty-year-old cadaver." The girls all burst into laughter. They continued laughing, interrupting each other's sentences, and pantomiming the teacher's sober expression that they guessed she would use during the lab. Although the girls were a bit younger than Lisa, and they had different life experiences, Lisa felt very comfortable with them. Even though they had a humorous and careless attitude, the girls were very determined with their studies and goals in life. After lunch, Lisa and the girls exchanged their phone numbers and decided to get together sometime to study. They went to their next class, and Lisa decided to finish the last hour of her break at the library searching for scientifically-accepted methods to conduct a proper interview.

After the library she headed to her last class, which was an English class, in an upbeat mood. Lisa felt great. She wasn't alone anymore in this college; she wasn't lost among the large auditoriums and the many classrooms. She hadn't melted into obscurity in the crowd of people. She had made friends here, already loved her classes and was excited to study. She belonged to this college and had become a true, single part of it.

She sat at the desk in the first row and looked around while waiting for the teacher. Smiling, friendly faces surrounded her. Mostly there were people in their teens and early twenties. However, Lisa noticed two middle-aged women. They were both sitting together at desks in the second row across from Lisa. They were occupied in a quiet conversation, sometimes letting out a loud giggle before stifling it. The two women at the desk across from her didn't seem like they had ever doubted their decision to return to college. Lisa shook her head. She had thought that she was too old to go back to college, while these two women, who looked at least ten years older than she was, seemed like they naturally blended in. She realized that one's perception of the situation doesn't necessarily reflect the real situation itself. Her worries that she might look strange to others by quitting her job and going to college at her age were based more on her own fears and doubts than the reality of the situation. In fact, the choice that she had made in her life was indeed the right one. Lisa's lips curved into a smile. She needed to stop worrying and waiting for others' approval. This new step was a great opportunity for her and she should be grateful for this chance, considering the fact that she hadn't been able to fulfill her dreams before this point in her life.

The English professor interrupted Lisa's thoughts. He introduced himself, briefly touched on his background as a former editor-in-chief of a local magazine, and switched to the topic of the lecture. He introduced the class to the strategies of persuasive writing and asked everybody to come up with a good example of a persuasive situation. Almost all of the students raised their hands and the blackboard was filled with many written examples. Lisa volunteered the topic of an election board. The teacher assigned everyone to write the rough draft of their own topic by the next class.

Driving home in the car, Lisa could only think about all the homework that was assigned. She mentally planned all the things she needed to do for her classes. On top of that, she had to keep in mind her responsibilities to Irving and Mark; she had to arrange her time in such a way that she could stay on top of everything. With all of these thoughts running through her mind, Lisa didn't notice that she had already arrived at her apartment.

"Mom, can you please take me to Derek's house?" Irving asked as soon as she showed up at the door.

"What's the rush, sonny?" Lisa said, closing the door and heading into the living room to drop her heavy bag on the table. *It'd be nice to have my own study*, she thought.

Irving followed her. "Derek got a new game. There are other guys that are coming over too. Please, mom," he begged.

Lisa looked at him. "Irving, you know that you can visit your friends on weekends only," she said. "We've had this discussion in the past."

Irving flinched. "Yes, mom. But now that you're home early I thought..." He trailed off.

Lisa looked at him, exasperated. "Irving, I'm still very busy, if not even more than before. I have my studies, my homework—" she caught Irving's puzzled stare and smiled. "Yes, sonny. Your mom's also going to have homework, and projects, and tests, just like you do." She ran her fingers through his hair. "And I'm still your mother who has to do the shopping, and cooking and cleaning, to make sure that you and Mark are eating properly and wearing clean clothes."

"Can Mark take me to Derek's then?" Irving asked hopefully.

"Irving!" Lisa paused for a moment, bewildered by his persistence. "Mark's working really hard and...why are we having this conversation anyway?" She couldn't conceal the irritation in her voice. "Have you done all your homework?"

"Almost," Irving murmured in disappointment, and headed to his room.

"Make sure that you finish your homework, sonny, and I'll bring you something to drink," she said to him. She opened the refrigerator and took out some meat and vegetables for dinner. Something bothered her, some ugly irritation that rose from somewhere in her stomach up to her hands, and made them tremble.

She threw a carrot on the table. It landed with a loud sound, twisted and then fell onto the floor. Lisa opened the drawer and pulled out a cigarette. She closed the kitchen door, turned on the vent, opened the window, lowered herself onto the chair, and lit the cigarette. This was a surprise. She'd made the rule of visiting other kids only on weekends a long time ago because she was working during the week and couldn't take Irving to his friends. Irving had understood and hadn't ever complained before. Why was he so insistent today? What had changed that would make him behave so atypically?

Was it the fact that his mother wasn't working now and therefore he thought she had time or was even obligated to drive him around? Or maybe deep inside Irving had always felt less fortunate than other kids, and now all of those thoughts and feelings were finally showing themselves. If so, then she probably wasn't as good a mother as she thought she was. Lisa shook her head. *One guess is as good as the other,* she thought wryly. Then she realized she must have been really stressed out and frightened with all of the changes in her life that she'd almost made a big deal out of nothing. Indeed, since she was home much earlier than usual, Irving hoped that she might be able to drive him to Derek's. So he'd asked her. Any normal kid would have done the same in his situation! She'd overreacted and had arrived at some outrageous conclusion about something that had never been.

Lisa smashed her cigarette in the ashtray and inhaled the fresh outside air from the window. She made a few energetic turns, then a couple of sidelong stretches, and finally shook out both of her hands. According to her new friend Kristina, these exercises were supposed to make Lisa feel refreshed and rejuvenated. Smiling, she opened the refrigerator and pulled out the rest of the ingredients. This time the food was safely placed onto the table, proving Kristina's relaxation technique to be true.

Mark came home at about the same time that dinner was finished. They all ate in silence for a while. Irving was unusually quiet. He was carefully lowering his spoon inside the bowl and scooping up the soup, bringing it up into his mouth and lowering it again, up and down, up and down. He looked very intent on this routine.

"What's up, Irving?" Mark asked, and the soup that was on its way to his mouth sloshed back down into the bowl.

Irving glanced sorrowfully at Lisa before he confided to Mark. "Derek's dad bought him a new game. And everybody's going over to his house today."

"If you're done with your homework, I can take you there after dinner," Mark said casually.

"Yes, I finished my homework," Irving stared at Mark in disbelief. He looked like he wasn't sure if he heard Mark correctly.

Mark smiled and glanced at Lisa. "And what are your mom's plans for tonight?"

"I have to study." She grinned. "Just some boring stuff..." She glanced at Irving. "You guys are your own bosses for the evening!"

Irving's face lit with happiness. He wanted to jump up from his seat right away.

"Don't push your luck, though," Lisa cooled down Irving's fire. "Finish your food first, please."

The rest of the dinner was much more alive and interactive. They finished dessert and Mark and Irving went for their coats to go outside.

After they left, Lisa cleaned up the kitchen and took her textbooks to the bedroom. She seated herself at Mark's computer desk, opened her notes along with her biology book and began to study. It was clear right from the first page that all the layers of the structural organization that her teacher briefly touched on were in turn complex structural units that needed a lot of studying. These units combined together to carry out certain important functions. Atoms form molecules and molecules form cells, which then form tissue. Tissue joins together to make organs that build the system, and all the parts of the body interact and function with one another, composing the wonderful, amazing structure called the human body. It resembled a watch that had a variety of small circular wheels, cogs, and rods that each perform their own function and all together create a wonderful mechanism that tells time. And just as with a watch, we don't think about how it works, we just take for granted that it will, and we learn to depend on it.

It was almost 10 p.m. when she heard Mark and Irving coming. "Where have you been?" Lisa couldn't believe that it was so late already.

"I went to drop off Irving. Since there were four of them playing a new video game, I thought they'd be busy for a while. Plus, I didn't want to disturb your studying." Mark smiled. "So, I called Jerome and we got a couple of beers at the bar while Irving was playing with his friends." He paused. For a split second, he looked at Lisa through his designer glasses with a bit of confusion and guilt. Then a soft smile came across his face. Lisa stared back at him and whatever remarks she was going to make to them for coming back late momentarily flew away. She turned to look at Irving. He was standing at the door with his coat in one hand and a box in the other. He looked happy and eager to share his story.

"I got a new game," he bragged, waving his hand with the box.

Mark swiftly turned to Irving. "Are you still here?" he asked. His voice intentionally became strict; his expression was very serious. "What did you promise me?"

"I'm already in bed," Irving said, quickly disappearing into his room. "Good night," he yelled through the door.

"Good night, Irving," Mark replied.

"Good night, sonny." Lisa headed toward the door, thinking of checking on him before he fell asleep.

Mark leaned comfortably against the wall and held out his right arm to hug her. He pulled her to himself and whispered into her ear, burning her skin with his hot breath. "Irving's a big boy, he can manage to go to bed alone." Mark's lips slowly slipped to Lisa's neck, then to her cheek. He pressed her tightly against him and covered her face with soft, hot kisses. Lisa held her arms on his chest and gently pushed herself from him. She was thrilled to feel his big strong arms around her. She loved when he kissed her that way. The sensation of his masculine, warm body made her dizzy as always. She wanted to be kissed and cuddled and...and to fall into a deep sleep. She was extremely tired and she didn't want sex tonight. Mark's face suddenly darkened. He looked directly into Lisa's eyes.

"Am I being punished for having a couple of drinks with Jerome?" His eyebrows furrowed as he scowled. He let her out of his embrace and turned his back to her while heading to the kitchen.

Lisa rushed after him. "Mark, you misunderstood me!" He was already sitting at the kitchen table, lighting his cigarette. "Mark, I'm not trying to punish you or anything like that. In fact, I was glad that you were able to take care of Irving while I was studying. He looked so happy!"

Mark just blew out the gray stream of smoke into the space between them. "Children always like me; it's the women I have trouble with." He looked at her, his eyes lit with irony.

"Mark, I'm just incredibly tired and I want to get to sleep," Lisa held out her arm and reached for his shoulder.

He took another drag on his cigarette and turned his face away from her to blow out the thick and heavy smoke. He looked hurt and upset. Lisa's heart lurched with pity for him and guilt at the same time. She couldn't leave him alone in a mood like that. She slid herself onto his lap and brushed her lips against his bristled cheek.

He hesitated. "If you want to go to sleep, then go to sleep," he said, trying to resist, but his last words melted in her mouth.

She slid her hands under his shirt to reach around his back, clung to his chest and covered him with soft and gentle kisses.

Mark smashed his cigarette into the ashtray, lifted Lisa into his arms, and carried her into the bedroom.

Chapter Nineteen

The month that followed was intense. Lisa attended the lectures and labs. She studied Physiology and Anatomy, learning about cell division and gene action, the skeletal-muscular systems, and joints. She ascertained research methods and ethical issues in social research, the evolution of culture, and traditional American values. She was getting proficient in persuasive techniques and presentations. She spent hours in the library doing research for her projects. She was studying at home and in the college cafeteria during her breaks between classes. She was going to the Biology lab during weekends with Sandy and Kristina to learn every single muscle of their cadaver cat. She was writing essays and research papers and she was making speeches and taking pop quizzes and tests. She studied hard to achieve the highest grades, since the physical therapy program was very competitive and hard to get into. Plus, she was doing volunteer work in the hospital for the program requirements. On top of that, she was squeezing in the cooking and the cleaning, and only the dream of her upcoming spring break vacation helped her make it through.

She thought a lot about the vacation. She visualized every single detail, saw the ocean waves rolling in, and felt the hot sand on her skin. She pictured romantic nights with Mark, walking together alongside the shore, and talking and kissing under the shining and mysterious moonlight. She visualized exotic dinners at the restaurant—the table would have a basket full of freshly baked bread accompanied with golden butter and sparkling white wine that would be served in tall, crystal-clear glasses. She imagined musicians with big sombreros and heavy guitars playing beautiful melodies. She almost lived the vacation through the succession of wonderful images in her head, and that may have been what scared her luck away.

When a little more than two weeks were left for this so-awaited escape, Mark was fired from his new job. He was in the kitchen smoking his cigarette when Lisa came home with bags of food. His presence at home was unusual for this time. His posture and facial expression told her what had happened but she didn't want to believe it. She placed the bags on the table and started unpacking them, praying in her mind that her assumptions were wrong and that there was a good reason for this unexpected occurrence. She dragged on, opening the refrigerator and cabinets and filling them with the food, not saying a word. She would wait until he was ready to talk. By a sidelong glance, she saw Mark still smoking and staring straight ahead. Her hopes that he'd start talking first grew smaller with every passing second. When all the bags were unpacked, Lisa paused for a moment, standing there in the middle of the kitchen. She was waiting, hoping for some magic to happen, for anything that would prove her assumptions wrong. Nothing happened, though, and Lisa slowly lowered into the chair across from Mark. She pulled a cigarette from the pack on the table and lit it.

"Where's Irving?" she asked.

"I took him to Derek's; they wanted to do homework together," Mark blew out the smoke and looked at Lisa. His expression was ambivalent. "They fired me." He made a flippant gesture with his hand and dragged heavily on his cigarette. His statement was an unnecessary one. In her heart, Lisa already knew what had happened, but had refused to believe her instincts. Mark's words destroyed her last glimmer of hope for something magical to happen and save them. Unfortunately, magic happens only in fairy tales, and she had to accept the bitter reality. Silence filled the room. Lisa's heart skipped a beat and then stopped altogether. The blood left her face. She felt a deep tenderness and empathy for this man, but at the same time she was filled with a great sorrow and misery for herself. Everything was falling apart; everything. Thoughts raced through her mind. What if Mark didn't find another job soon, how would they survive then? What would happen to her education; would it even be possible to complete the semester? Should she just go back to work and forget about her Biology class, along with its cadaver cat and crazy teacher and, more importantly, her new friends? Should she just forget about everything and pretend like it never happened? Act like it wasn't her, who after so many worries and doubts, had finally believed Mark about her bright future and a wonderful career? Who completely gave all that she had into making everything work out? Lisa tried to swallow, but found her mouth was too dry. A dreadful feeling was overwhelming her. She struggled to stay calm, but her face gave her away.

"Don't worry, you'll be fine," she heard him say, a hint of anger in his voice. "I have savings in my bank account, and I have some other sources of income." He tried to smile, but failed. "We'll just have to cut down on some expenses, like restaurants, shopping." he paused. "Unfortunately, we'll have to return our tickets as well, but that's all of the damage that I can see."

Oddly, Lisa felt a great deal of relief and confusion at the same time. She regretted her terrified thoughts about the impact of Mark's job loss on her life. She felt absolutely selfish and totally egotistical.

"Who cares about those restaurants or vacations!" She sounded very sincere and she really was. An appreciative smile lit Mark's face.

"So what happened?" Lisa lit a cigarette and inhaled the warm, bitter smoke.

"Women bosses. I make them furious or something." He shrugged. Lisa looked at him blankly.

"I had a one-on-one meeting with her, you know, like one of those regular meetings where employees have to discuss their goals and dreams and other politically correct crap with their managers. Just a waste of time and energy." He let out some rings of smoke and grinned. "I made an attempt just for once to turn the conversation into a productive one. I tried to discuss with her the necessity of buying new equipment to build our new machines. I explained to her the advantages of this acquisition, stating that our machines will be more competitive and modern. Budget-wise, they would soon pay for themselves and start bringing in a profit. Whereas now, the equipment is constantly breaking, which requires additional money for repairs and a bigger work force. Overall, the machines are too old for the market. I deeply regret, however, that she couldn't comprehend anything I said to her. She's one of those uptight, dressy, bossy women with long, glued-on nails and thin straws for a brain. She accused me of being too smart and stubborn and suggested that if I didn't like it there then I better pack up my things and leave. Then I lost it and told her what I really think about her and her abilities as a manager." Mark smiled wryly. "You had to see her. She flung the door wide open and left her office screaming and yelling in this high-pitched voice. Her face was red; her eyes were bulging out. She looked old and ugly. She looked insane. Our director was passing by at that moment. He froze in the middle of the aisle, staring at her in shock and confusion all at once and then he gave me this kind of sympathetic look for having to work for that woman." Mark paused. For a moment he looked directly into Lisa's eyes, and then he continued. "I picked up my things and went home." He spread his hands in a helpless gesture. "So, here I am, miserable and unemployed."

"You aren't miserable." Lisa let out her hand to stroke through his hair. "You're still my lovely Mark, smart, intelligent and handsome. A man who makes women crazy."

Mark laughed. "You always make me feel better. How do you do it? What's your secret?" He looked passionately at Lisa; a mocking smile came across his face. "Maybe if I knew the trick, it'd be easier to stay firm. Maybe, I'd be able to not lose it each time I face such stupidity and incompetence." He let out a deep sigh of regret. "Why did God grant me such a brain but at the same time fail to give me the wherewithal to change anything?" Mark reached out with his hand to grab a cigarette from the pack and mindlessly crumpled it under his fingers while looking into Lisa's eyes, searching for an answer to what seemed to be a most painful and crucial question in his life.

Lisa stared back at him in a silence, trying to sort out her thoughts. She didn't know what to say. She didn't have any special secret, nor did she know any tricks. She just loved him. That was all; and that was everything.

"Did you try to talk to the director and explain the situation?" she asked softly. Maybe he can set her straight." Mark smashed his cigarette into an ashtray in a sudden gust of rage and then turned to the window and immediately lit another one.

"My director's a nice, sweet person. He's this kind of old-fashioned person who wouldn't sneeze without apologizing beforehand. He's smart, but he's too soft and weak. He's unarmed and helpless against aggressive people. Besides, he's going to retire soon, so he would settle for anything just to have his own peace of mind. No matter how much he valued me and how low he thought of her, he'd never fight with her. So what I did seems to be the only appropriate solution..."

"Mark!" Lisa gave his hand a light squeeze and then released it. "I understand you, I truly do. But sometimes the situation goes beyond our control and we have to accept the inevitable. It wasn't your fault; it wasn't anybody's fault."

Mark looked at her with amusement in his eyes.

"Yes, I know what you think," Lisa exclaimed firmly, as if he was arguing with her. She spoke vigorously, trying to arrange the whirlwind stream of her thoughts into a smooth and logical flow, trying to explain, to justify her every word. "Yes, your boss is an unfair and cruel woman who left you without a job. But at the same time she's a poor woman who deserves pity. She doesn't know what she did. She's blind to her faults and can't see wrong from right. It's like a severe disability and you should be sorry for her."

The amusement in Mark's eyes faded. He gave Lisa an odd look and his eyes resembled those of a concerned and worried parent of a sick child. "I have to be sorry for her?" Mark said the words slowly and carefully, as if Lisa were the disabled one. "Are you out of your mind, Lisa? What are you talking about? Is this some kind of crap that was invented thousands of years ago specifically for the slaves' ears, to keep them blind? Somebody slaps you on one cheek, and you just give them the other, is that what you're saying?" His face was contorted, his voice cracked from irritation. "I'm not anybody's slave, Lisa," he spat. "I never was and never will be, and nobody in the world, nothing will make me one. You understand that, Lisa? No *one* and no *thing* will ever be in charge of my life. That's my, and only my, privilege—to be my own master, to control my own life. No one can take it from me, no one, including you, Lisa. It's my territory; it's a stop sign, a red line that not even you'll ever be allowed to cross. If I suspect anything like that, I'll pack my things and take off without even looking back. I lost enough in my life and I'm not going to lose anymore."

His hands were clenched on the table; his gaze was piercing and fierce.

Lisa opened and closed her mouth in a wild attempt to catch a bit of air. She felt like a fish thrown on the shore, struggling for a breath. A horrid, disgusting shiver overtook her. She was trembling from head to toe. She looked around, desperately trying to find her center, and managed to pull a cigarette from the pack on the table. Somehow, the feel of the cigarette in her hand eased the spasm and she managed to take a few deep breaths. She lit the cigarette and took a couple of heavy, hard drags on it before she felt the now familiar warm and relaxing flow throughout her body.

"Mark, I just wanted to say that whatever happened was meant to happen and therefore it happened for the better. You wouldn't be happy working in such an atmosphere under a self-absorbed boss, so sooner or later it'd end this way or another, equally bad, either way. Let's just say that sooner's better. With your talent, abilities, and experience you'll quickly find even a better job, and a better atmosphere, a place where you'll be appreciated for your skills, hard work, and dedication, where you'll be enjoying each and every minute of your work." She gave him a soft, comforting look. "Life's like a sinusoid; it has its own ups and downs, just like a yellow brick road with bumps and smooth rides. You're on the bumpy part now, but you don't know what's coming up next. Maybe the road will lead you to fortune and will make you forget all your worries."

Mark made a scornful sound. "If you're so smart, Lisa, if you have answers for everything, then tell me what's wrong with me? Why am I not like other people?" His gaze under his slanted eyebrows was hard and helpless all at once. "Why can't I just take things easy like everybody else? Why do I care about the poorly done draft, terrible tool or incompatible machine? What is my interest in this? The draft will be thrown away at a plant, as garbage, the tool and its designer will get condemnation from the workers. Machines will break down before their time and an enormous amount of money will be wasted. So what? It's not like it's my own business running this way, and it's not my money that's being thrown into the air. Why do I even mind those things? I have fairly decent rates. I receive my paychecks no matter what; in fact, I even get bonuses and raises. And all I have to do to maintain my prosperity and have my peace of mind is just to keep my eyes closed and my mouth shut like everybody else does. Right? Then why can't I do that? Tell me, Lisa, why?" He looked at her, pain shadowing his eyes. "Why am I suffering and torturing myself so hard? Why, Lisa?"

Lisa mindlessly ran her hands through her hair and then took another cigarette from the table. She rolled it between her fingers, trying to sort her thoughts out.

Mark reached out and lit the lighter. He held it in front of her for a split second, looking at her through the fire, and then smiled. "I know you can't answer my questions, Lisa. Nobody can. I've tried many sources: doctors, psychologists." He made a gesture with his hand and brought the lighter closer to Lisa's cigarette.

She took a deep drag on it. "Mark, all I know is that you're a great, smart, and intelligent man with a sharp, critical mind who happens to be sincere, responsible, and independent. That's why it's harder for you to relate and fit in sometimes." She ran a comforting hand over his and looked into his eyes. Her expression conveyed tenderness and compassion. "There's no need for a cure, Mark. You don't need a doctor or a pill—it's a part of you. You are who you are: an exceptional man who should be proud of himself." He let out a scornful sigh and drew on his cigarette.

"Mark, what I'm trying to say is that the world isn't perfect, and the people in it aren't perfect, but at the same time it's an amazing and wonderful world; it's life, family, love. It's not worth wasting our nerves, health and energy on unfair bosses or bad circumstances. It's darker today, but it'll be brighter tomorrow. The most important thing is that we have each other and we have Irving. We're a team. Together, we'll conquer the highest mountain peaks, and nothing will frighten us on our way." She grinned at him through the haze of smoke in the kitchen and leaned back in her chair. A sudden headache overwhelmed her and she started to feel dizzy. She felt like a lemon that had just had all of its juice squeezed out.

Mark peered at her through his glasses. His expression was a mixture of passion and indebtedness, and was such a tender vulnerability that Lisa's heart filled with warmth. It was a combination she could never resist. It was the man she loved and cherished. Even in the worst of times, after the ugly and horrifying arguments, the memory of this part of him always helped her to forgive him, bringing an amazing feeling of belonging and unity.

Mark looked at his watch. "It's almost seven." He threw his cigarette into an ashtray. "And it's getting late. I have to go to pick up Irving soon." He grabbed Lisa's shoulder and whispered into her ear, "I see that my dilemma has made you sad. Let's find a better way of spending our time together." His lips gently hovered over her neck. "How about we go lie down and get this load off our chests?" He rose from his chair, one hand around Lisa, pulling her onto her feet and then lifted her into his arms and carried her into the bedroom. She wrapped her arms around his neck. The feeling of his familiar, muscular body made her heart melt. She forgot about everything. Her mind became free from worries and burdens. She no longer felt like a squeezed lemon, but like one full of sweet juices, perfectly ripe, waiting to be picked off a tree. She felt small and fragile in his big, strong arms; she felt safe and secure and she enjoyed every minute of it.

CHAPTER TWENTY

Midterms came much faster than Lisa expected and she became completely absorbed in her studies. Mark, in turn, engaged himself in searching for a job. When Lisa came home during a short break between classes, she found Mark sitting at his computer desk working. He was very happy to see her. He stretched in his chair and yawned deeply.

"I'm so glad to see you, Lisa. I'm so tired of sitting here, browsing through these job sites; it's such dull work. I sent tons of resumes out but got almost nothing in response, except for a few recruiters and their long, pointless questions." He turned toward Lisa and reached his hands out to her.

"Come here. You are my ray of sunshine, my light in the window." He smiled.

Lisa threw her bags on the floor in the hallway and came closer to briefly hug and kiss him. "Mark, I came by on my break to get a bite to eat and have to rush back to school." She threw a brief glance at his table and said, "What are all of those books you have there?"

"Just some boring technical stuff." Mark grabbed her and pulled her onto his lap. "I missed you so much," he said as he nibbled on her neck.

"Mark," Lisa intoned, smiling and pushed herself away from him. "I have just enough time to grab a bite and quickly go over the outline for my test. I have a Sociology test right before my English class!"

"Come on," Mark murmured as he cupped her head between his hands and kissed her lips. "What could you possible learn in those few minutes that you don't already know?"

"Mark." She tried to resist. "It's a very important midterm test, and half of my final grade will depend on it!"

He didn't seem to hear her. He smothered her in hot kisses, pulled her up and over onto the bed. She wrapped her hands around his neck and kissed him. She didn't plan to make love with him at this moment. In fact, she still planned to go over her notes and outlines for the upcoming test. She also hoped to have a little extra time and find her classmates in the cafeteria and have an easygoing chat with a cup of coffee to relax her mind. She was tired and nervous. Sex wasn't anywhere in her schedule for today. But when she looked at Mark, she thought how hard it must be to be home alone, searching for a job nonstop, worrying about their budget, upcoming bills and well-being. It must be a heavy burden for him to bear. She smiled at him and closed her eyes to the sensation of him on her.

Afterwards, Mark pulled out a cigarette from the night stand and offered one to Lisa.

Lisa rushed to put on her clothes as she said, "Mark I don't have time for one. I have to grab some food."

Mark stretched, still lying in bed, "Come to think of it, I could eat too."

"Didn't you eat today?" she asked.

"Well, I didn't wake up that long ago. I decided to start working right away, so I didn't have much time to eat."

Lisa opened the refrigerator and searched for any leftover food. There was a bit of ham, cheese, and veggies.

"How about I make us some sandwiches and coffee?" she asked. "That sounds good."

Mark walked into the kitchen and started helping her make the coffee. "Do we have anything to feed Irving with?" he asked, and then added, "It's okay, don't worry, I'll take care of it."

"Thank you." An appreciative smile came across Lisa's face. "What are your plans for tonight?"

Mark took a drag on his cigarette and shrugged. "I don't know, I feel a bit bummed out so I'll probably take a short nap and then I'll wait for Irving to come home, feed him, and check on his homework. After that, I'm going to stop by my friend's house to pick up some technical drafting books that he's going to bring home from work. They're on the latest technology in the subject and I want to take a look at them."

Lisa laughed. "Wow, Mark, you have your day figured out to the smallest detail. I hope that I can live up to your standards and receive the best grade on my test."

"You're the best student they have, there's no way for you not to have the best grade possible," he said and smiled at her through the haze of smoke.

Lisa ate quickly with Mark, then sped back to school. She rushed through the doors of her college with her mind spinning. She hadn't had time to go over her notes; she felt nervous and lacked confidence. She got into the class five minutes before the test started. The teacher and the majority of the students were already there. Lisa took her seat at her usual desk, pulled a pencil out of her bag and left the bag on the floor.

The professor began passing out the examination sheet together with the Scantron. Getting hers, Lisa briefly looked through it. There were four pages stapled together with print only on the front side of each page. Lisa noticed three different sections: a multiple-choice section, followed by a fill-in-the-blank section, followed by short-essay questions. There were fifty-five questions altogether and the duration of the class was fifty minutes. *Less than a minute per question!* Lisa realized in terror. She looked around to see that people were already scrupulously working and then glanced at the wall clock. Three minutes had passed by and the arrow slowly but steadily moved further with every second. Lisa panicked.

She read the first question. She saw the separate words but she didn't seem to be putting them together into a sentence. She read it over and over in despair but still couldn't comprehend the meaning. Lisa let out a helpless sigh and looked at clock again. Five minutes had now elapsed and the arrow was ready to eat the sixth one.

She closed her eyes. She had to do something before this panic attack completely overtook her. It had already paralyzed her brain and caused her hands to become sweaty. Lisa unconsciously twisted and tossed her pencil on the desk and it rolled onto the floor. She had to get herself together; she had to concentrate and begin to work on the answers. It was only a test, with simple questions on the topics that she had studied hard and knew well. She had to stop looking around and wondering about the time.

She took a deep breath, exhaled and returned to the questions. This time she brought the words on the paper together in her head to form a complete sentence and realized that she knew the correct answer. She filled the appropriate circle in the Scantron and started working her way down the page, question by question, until she had fully completed the Scantron. Then she proceeded with the fill-in-the-blanks section, which was surprisingly easy, and moved on to the essay questions on the last page. She was so absorbed in her work that she didn't see or hear anything around her. She was finishing the last sentence of her essay when the bell signaled the end of the class. The teacher asked them to bring their tests to his desk. He said he was going to punch the Scantrons on his way back to his office and check the essay questions right afterwards so that the grades would be available today. Lisa decided to check hers immediately after her English class.

When English ended, her heart was jumping up and down like she had been running. She walked to the sociology office and opened the door. The teacher smiled at her from his desk.

"Come in, Lisa," he said as he waved with his hand, inviting her in, and then dug into the stack of examination papers.

Lisa got forty-eight questions correct out of fifty on the Scantron, aced all the fill-in-the-blank questions, and the teacher spoke highly of her two essay questions. She had received an 'A' on the test. She could proudly say that she had started this term not badly at all. Her hard work had paid off and she was determined to continue in the same direction.

When she got home, neither Irving nor Mark was there. Lisa stepped into the dark kitchen, recalling that Mark had plans for tonight and had probably taken Irving with him. She was a little worried though, and she wished that Mark had a cell phone. However, he hated cell phones. He said that they were spread around not because of their worth but due to the efforts of giant corporations that make fortunes off them. He thought that friends, relatives, and family members should communicate face-to-face with each other and that the cell phone was just an excuse for people to avoid one another.

Lisa opened the refrigerator. She had cans of chicken soup in there and microwaveable chicken breasts. She decided to make mashed potatoes and add some fresh veggies so that she could have a complete dinner. Not a fully homemade dinner, she thought, but at least a fresh, warm, and tasty one. She felt a little guilty for feeding Mark and Irving some precooked, canned food, but due to her busy schedule, that was the best she could do. She thanked God that her men were kind enough to eat everything that she laid on the table for them, but she was still going to try to make it up to them on her upcoming spring break.

Lisa was studying biology in the bedroom when she heard Mark and Irving come in. They both seemed very preoccupied with a heated discussion. Lisa headed into the hallway. Mark was carrying a few heavy books and Irving had a box covered in wrapping paper.

"I bet it wouldn't work," Irving said to Mark, ignoring Lisa and continuing their conversation.

"What wouldn't work?" Lisa intruded with a smile.

"Mark, it'd be better to buy that other one," Irving said with a slight edification. Mark grinned at him.

"Everything will be all right, Irving," he assured him and started to take his coat off.

"Okay, let's go try it." Irving hopped from one leg to other with impatience.

"Let's take our coats off first, then have dinner and after that you're going to finish your homework like you promised me," Mark said, trying to calm him. "It's really late and you only had a sandwich, and that was more than three hours ago, so you should be starving by now." He brushed his hand through Irving's hair and looked at Lisa. "Do we have anything to eat?"

"Yes, dinner's almost ready." Lisa headed towards the kitchen with Mark behind her. "What's going on?" She asked on the way. "You guys seem to have a few secrets. Do you care to share them with me?" she asked with a smile.

"No secrets." Mark shook his head. "I just took Irving to Subway to grab a sandwich and then he begged me to take him with me to my friend's house."

Mark looked at Irving, who had come into the kitchen and situated himself at the table. Irving's face reflected some disappointment.

"So, we went to my friend's to pick up the books," Mark continued, turning back to Lisa. "We were talking about this and that. Carl is a very big fan of computer games, so it came up in the conversation that he just recently purchased a great video card on sale. So we decided to visit a store and check out this card on the way home," he said, grinning. "It turned out it was still on sale. I checked out all of the specs and this card seemed just as good as the one that Irving wanted, but cheaper, so we bought it." He glanced again at Irving with a smile. "That's why Irving seems a little upset," he added.

"Irving," Lisa placed a pot with heated soup on the table and took Irving's bowl to pour some soup into it. "Expensive doesn't always mean better," she said.

"Well," Irving insisted, "Derek got that one for the game."

"We also bought a new game so we can test the video card," Mark remarked and turned to Irving. "Let's eat, Irving. It's really late and you have some homework left to do. We'll install this card on Saturday and you'll see that what I said will turn out to be correct and that it will work just as good." He turned to his plate, took a spoon and then looked at Lisa. "And how'd your mom do on her test?" he smiled expectantly at her.

The news made both Mark and Irving very excited and happy for her. Mark stood up from his chair, took a bottle of wine from the cabinet and set it on the table to celebrate. After dinner, he sent Irving to his room to finish his homework and instructed him to go to bed right after he was done. He helped Lisa clean up the kitchen, filled two glasses with wine and carried them into the bedroom. As she headed to the bathroom to get ready for bed, she heard him go back to the kitchen and take something out of the cabinets. When Lisa finished in the bathroom and came into the bedroom, she found it lit with white spring aroma candles. Sounds of violins and saxophones along with a piano filled the room. Mark was standing in middle of the room with the two glasses of wine in his hands. He came toward Lisa, hugged her, and handed one of the glasses to her. Everything was so romantic, so inspiring. It was so appealing that he did all of it just in celebration of her accomplishment. Lisa sipped from the glass and gave Mark a warm, compassionate look. She loved him. His lips, his touch; he always made her excited and she always wanted him...but not tonight. She was very appreciative and thrilled with such a romantic gesture, and it meant a lot to her, but at the same time she was still tired and stressed out, and she was worried about her upcoming biology test. She wanted to make sure that she got a good, refreshing sleep to be ready for a full day of studying the next day. But she couldn't turn Mark down. Not tonight. Not after everything he had done for her. After all, it was he who had allowed her to be going to school and taking these tests. It would be like she was rejecting a gift given to her from the bottom of his heart, and it wasn't something that Lisa could do. She closed her eyes and opened her lips to meet his.

CHAPTER TWENTY-ONE

Lisa had two midterm exams left before her spring break. Unfortunately, her break and Irving's didn't match up, as Irving's break was the same as her midterm week. In the past, Lisa would put aside a week a long way in advance by working overtime and changing her shifts so she would be able to spend quality time with Irving on his spring break. They would go to movies or restaurants, read books, and do other fun stuff together. Lisa loved having those days with Irving; they meant so much to her. This year she had been worried about Irving spending his spring break alone, but she soon realized that the silver lining to the cloud of Mark's unemployment was that he was more or less available to take care of Irving. In fact, he was thrilled to do it. He took Irving to the zoo, museums, and exhibitions, teaching Irving about history, animals, and life. They also went to a theme park with a couple of Irving's friends. They went on all the rides, from roller coasters to spinning cups. Irving competed in bumper cars and arcades, and he won a lot of prizes.

They finished upgrading Irving's computer, installed the new video card, and bought another war-strategy computer game. They were really strengthening their bond. Every day they would go to some new place while Lisa was occupied with her studies and exams. They would come back at night, excited, discussing their adventures, talking about how cool it was to see that lion growl or that roller coaster making a vertical loop or seeing the first wooden airplane. Irving started to share his stories with Mark before he retold them to Lisa. He also began to turn to Mark before Lisa when asking for permission. In fact, Mark and Irving became really good buddies and Lisa became a little jealous of them becoming so close. Before, it was she that had all of Irving's attention and all the control; she was the main person in his life. Her jealousy was harmless though, as she was grateful for Mark and happy for Irving. Irving didn't know his father, since he was very young at the time that his father had died, and Mark was becoming a father to him.

The midterm week had started well for Lisa and she intended to finish it that way. She studied biology with Kristina and Sandy. They went through their labs, looking over the cadaver muscles, and quizzed one another on theoretical questions. The group studying turned out to be very helpful, and she felt confident about her work after the test.

On the first day of her spring break, Lisa received her hard-earned grades. The teachers had congratulated her with an A in English and an A in Biology. She was exhausted by the long week, but at the same time she felt like she had grown a pair of wings. She had no doubts about the path she was on anymore and she had a strong incentive to continue.

***

On Saturday morning, Connie and Jerome invited Mark, Lisa, and Irving to their house for dinner. Mark accepted the invitation with enthusiasm. He was still actively looking for a job and so far he didn't seem to have an actual offer. He was stressed out and upset with this fact and looked forward to having some sort of a break. The dinner occasion was appealing to Lisa also. She was happy to have an opportunity for some social interactions outside the college or her own home, even though it would be for the first time in about four months. She was thrilled to finally have a chance to relax and have some fun.

They all got dressed up and showed up at Connie's around six in the evening. The door was unlocked. The three of them walked inside and headed to the living room, surprised to find that the hostess was not there. Instead, they saw Anna standing quietly under the arch in between the dining room and the living room. She was leaning against the wall, staring right at them.

"Irving, this is Anna. Anna, this is Irving," Lisa introduced them to each other. "You're about the same age, so you must have lots in common."

"What's up, Anna?" Irving approached her. "Do you want to go play some computer games?"

Anna said nothing but her eyes lit up and her wide smile answered for her.

"I wondered why a little girl suddenly showed up here a few minutes ago and stood still against the wall," a woman's voice said after Anna and Irving left. "She probably saw you through the window and ran in to meet you."

Startled, Lisa turned in the direction of the voice. A tall, attractive woman with long, brown, wavy hair was sitting on the sofa in front of coffee table. Only a small subtle lamp lit the room, which explained why Lisa hadn't seen her right away. The woman was alone, smoking a very thin and long cigarette, and looking at them with undivided attention. It was obvious that she was well-off. She was wearing tight, black, well-tailored pants and a silk V-neck blouse. Around her neck was a golden chain embedded with small diamonds that sparkled even in the dim lighting.

"Oh, wow. Is that who I think it is?" Mark asked, unable to hide his excitement. At the same time, Connie entered the room escorted by a slim, bald man with a thin mustache and a precisely trimmed beard.

"I assume you guys know each other," Connie said as she smiled towards the woman on the sofa.

Mark just kept standing there, staring at the woman in happy shock. Finally, he managed to utter some words.

"Debra, how long has it been? You look younger than ever! How did you manage to make your age go backwards?" He walked toward the woman. She stood up from the sofa and they hugged.

"Mark, I'm so glad to see you," Debra seemed a bit confused, but happy at the same time. "This is my husband, Nick," she said as she pointed to the bald man who was walking towards them.

Mark turned back toward Lisa and stretched his arm to take her hand. "This is Lisa. Lisa, this is my first girlfriend, and my first love, Debra," he introduced her as he turned to shake Nick's hand. "You must be a lucky guy to get a girl like Debra," Mark said, smiling.

"I sure am." Nick smiled back and looked at Lisa. "And you seem lucky yourself, for having such a gorgeous lady by your side!"

An easy laughter broke the tension of the awkward moment. Connie invited everyone to the dinner table.

During dinner, Mark was very energetic. He kept making jokes and telling funny anecdotes that made everyone laugh. He was a real gentleman and proposed many toasts to all the beautiful women at the table, always making sure everyone's glass was filled. He entertained everybody. He and Debra, who was sitting across the table by her husband's side, spoke effortlessly back and forth, recalling old stories and sharing newer ones. The easygoing conversations floated around the table.

Debra said that they had two children: a six-year-old girl and a boy who was seven. They sent their children to Florida for spring break, where their grandma lived in a condo. Debra explained that usually she and Nick went along with their children, but Nick was opening his own doctor's office so they were too busy with the paper work. Connie interrupted to mention that Nick was an unbelievable dentist and that their entire family goes to him. Nick laughed, joking that Connie was like his own personal marketing agent.

"I'm not saying anything that isn't true; I'm telling them how it is," she objected enthusiastically. "Two other dentists wanted to pull out my tooth but he saved it. The tooth is still alive and healthy, knock on wood," she said as she knocked religiously on the table and then continued to state her point. "And let me tell you how well he works with kids. My Anna and her schoolmates have no problem going to him for their regular checkups. They always leave his office with cute stickers and little toys, right Anna?" she said as she patted her daughter on the head.

"You're so convincing, Connie," Mark said, grinning at her. "You're a great advocate to have at one's side."

"Don't even think about it!" Jerome laughed loudly. "That's only true if you are talking about anyone other than you and me. We are here to get blamed for everything. We don't get praised for anything."

"That's not true," Connie exclaimed with indignation. "I've always thought highly of Mark," she said as she turned in her chair to look toward Nick. "I'm an objective and reasonable person, and I never say what's not there. I always speak the truth bluntly." Jerome just mumbled, but refrained from saying anything. Unlike his usual self, he was acting almost like a real gentleman at the dinner table.

The time flew by. It seemed as though Lisa blinked and the evening was coming to an end. She left the party in a great mood.

"It was a wonderful evening, wasn't it?" she asked Mark on their way home.

He pulled out a cigarette, lit it up and silently blew the smoke through the window. "Irving, what do you think about it, did you have fun playing with Anna?" Lisa asked.

"It was okay," Irving answered from the back seat. He was preoccupied with unwrapping a gift that Connie and Jerome had given to him.

"What a wonderful game they gave you," Lisa said, glancing over at Mark. "It's so inconsiderate that we didn't bring anything for Anna. Next time we have to make sure that we buy her a really nice present."

"Come on Lisa, it's an outdated video game. Irving has newer and better ones," Mark said, his eyes leaving the road to look over at Lisa. "And did you see how stuck up and arrogant that Nick was?" Mark sneered. "Connie needs so little to be impressed. She is very shallow." He smirked. "Just the mentioning of a condo in Florida and a doctor's office is enough to make her bow down in front of them," he said as he tapped his cigarette ash out the window. "I bet she invited that Nick, the so 'significant doctor-friend' just to boast in front of me," he said, scowling.

"He may indeed be a good dentist," Lisa said.

Mark looked at her in astonishment. "Do you know how many dentists are out there?" he asked. "And all of them consider themselves good or even exceptional. But believe me, only a few of them are actually good." He smiled ironically. "And those dentists don't need any advertisement from Connie and they aren't seeking her friendship either." Mark threw his cigarette through the window and lit up another one. "It's obvious that this Nick is just starting his business. He doesn't have that many clients, but he already knows how to act like he's everything, as if he's an extreme pro. Believe me, I know people like that." Mark turned to the window, blowing out the smoke.

Lisa also took out a cigarette and they drove the rest of the way in silence.

CHAPTER TWENTY-TWO

Spring break flew by. Lisa spent most of the time shopping for groceries, cooking, and cleaning. And when she wasn't busy with that, she was making love with Mark. In fact, they were making love every day, and even twice a day some days. And of course, they never missed their legitimate sex at night. It wasn't that Lisa's fire for Mark had died down, but the sex somehow became a burden for her. Not only that, but even the idea of making love more than one time in a row irritated her, if not to say it infuriated her.

All of those emotions accumulated into an angry knot that kept growing and twisting somewhere inside her stomach. She had to work hard not to let the rage explode. It frightened her. What was happening to her? She used to enjoy every minute of Mark's closeness and yet now she was trying to avoid it with any plausible reason. She couldn't stop wondering why she wasn't excited about sex anymore. Was she just losing her libido, or was it simply too much sex, if there was such a thing as too much sex? Lisa felt guilty. She saw herself as a selfish and inconsiderate wife. Mark was working hard, posting his resumes, filling out applications, taking professional tests and going through redundant interviews. Yet, he hadn't gotten any single offer. She knew that he'd been down and depressed because of that, and sex always helped him to ease his nerves. She must indeed be selfish if she wasn't able to make such a "sacrifice" for her husband. "Selfish" was the last word in Lisa's vocabulary and certainly wasn't the word she would normally apply to herself. She loved Mark, and she was willing to do anything for him. So she just kept all of her struggles inside her and went along with his desires.

This spring break hadn't brought Lisa the long-awaited relaxation she desperately needed. She felt herself overwhelmed and stressed and was actually looking forward to her classes starting up again.

Three weeks after her spring break, Lisa had a major exam in Biology. She planned on studying the whole Sunday for this exam.

Sunday afternoon, Mark casually walked into the bedroom, where she had been studying, and told her that they had all just been invited to Nick and Debra's house. Lisa stared at him in confusion.

"What were they thinking, asking us on such a short notice?" she murmured and then shrugged. "It's obvious that we're not going to go." She glanced at Mark briefly, certain that he'd agree with her. However, his posture and his facial expression didn't give her much assurance. "Right?" she asked, puzzled with his silence. Mark shifted uncomfortably on his feet and avoided her gaze.

"I thought maybe we could go, for a couple of hours or so," he said sheepishly.

"But I have a test tomorrow! I have to study, I can't go," Lisa objected heatedly. "You know that!"

Mark shrugged. "Then maybe I'll just go with Irving, and you can stay and study." She stared at him, incredulous.

Mark's left eyebrow went up as he grinned at her, his confidence regained.

"Lisa, do you want Irving and me to sit here, in the apartment all day long, watching you study?" He reached out to put his hand on her shoulder. His eyes were soft as his hand touched her hair.

"You can go see a movie," she said.

Mark's lips curved and his hand slid away from her. She felt a wave of guilt surging through her. At the same time, her heart twanged and her eyes filled with tears. She understood that in Mark's situation, he needed something more than just a movie to lighten his mood. Going to the party with friends might do the thing. She, in turn, couldn't offer much to him, as she had to study. She had to do it if she wanted to succeed in school. But she was doing it not only for herself, but for Mark and for Irving too; she was doing it for all of them. She was sacrificing and beating herself up to make all of their lives better, why couldn't he see that? Why was he so eager to go see his fancy, uptight ex-girlfriend while Lisa wasn't able to go with him?

"Lisa, what's the matter with you? What's wrong?" Mark stood in the middle of the living room with his hands spread wide apart. His posture conveyed a silent disappointment. His eyes bored into her.

"I'm trying my best to make it easier for you. I'm supporting you in all of your endeavors. I'm taking care of everything to make it work for you. I'm going out and taking Irving with me so you can sit here and pursue your studies. What more of me do you want? What else? Just say it and I'll do whatever it takes. Your best interests are the only things that matter to me. If you want me and Irving to sit here so you won't be alone, then just say it and it will be so." He couldn't hide his irritation.

Lisa licked her lips. Certainly, she didn't want them to be tied up at home with her, even though she knew it sounded like she wanted them to. She rubbed her forehead, finding it hard to think. Something wasn't right. It was all jumbled in her head. She couldn't understand exactly what was wrong as now she couldn't remember exactly what the problem was with Mark leaving in the first place. She realized that she had been stubborn and inconsiderate and Mark had every right to be upset with her. She raised her head to him, a confused smile on her lips.

"I didn't know that you were planning on taking Irving with you."

Mark came closer to brush her hair with his fingertips; his eyes were lit with passion. "I know you're a bit stressed out and overwhelmed, but trust me, everything will be all right." He kissed her on the cheek and went to tell Irving to get ready.

After they left, Lisa just stood in the room for a while, mindlessly looking through the window. A vast wave of sadness and darkness enveloped her. She trembled. Her whole body shook with heavy sobs. She threw herself onto the sofa and buried her face in the pillow. In less than a minute it was soaked through with tears. She wasn't able to stop the crying for a long time. Finally she stopped, feeling exhausted as if she'd cried herself dry. She sat up and leaned against the back of the sofa. This sudden breakdown scared her and brought her relief all at once. She slowly stood up, walked over to the kitchen for a cigarette and inhaled the warm smoke.

CHAPTER TWENTY-THREE

After a few more weeks Mark found a new job. It was great news but the greatest was yet to come. Mark had sold his condo and bought a larger and better one in the same building. He broke the news to Lisa that evening during their coffee hour. He was sitting across the table from her with his big, firm hands folded over each other. His eyes were passionate.

"Lisa," he reached over with his hand to cover hers; his expression a mixture of arrogant masculinity and poignant vulnerability, a combination she had always adored. "Will you marry me?" he asked.

Lisa gasped. She thought she had misheard his question. Inexplicably, she didn't respond right away, but stared at him with her mouth open. She must have resembled a deaf old lady who would have to ask to have the words repeated, clearly and loudly.

Mark grinned. "I think this is the perfect time for us to get married. We have a large new condo that we can move into anytime, and I have a job," he said, smiling softly. "So what do you say, Lisa?"

She looked at him for a split second longer, speechless with excitement. "Yes," she said finally. "Of course I'll marry you."

His face showed relief and satisfaction as he bent down to kiss her hand. She folded her arms across her chest and motionlessly watched him light his cigarette and then slowly blow out the grayish rings. With a ridiculous smile floating on her face, she watched the rings grow bigger but thinner and finally break up and turn into wispy, indeterminate figures. She followed them with her eyes until they dissolved in the air. Meanwhile, she was trying to digest what was happening. Everything had happened so suddenly that she couldn't believe the reality of it. Furthermore, she didn't have any evidence to help her comprehend it faster; her finger was still naked. When he saw her glance at her hand, Mark confessed that he didn't know anything about diamonds and was afraid to disappoint her by buying something she wouldn't like. He wanted them to go together during the weekend to the jewelry store to pick out a ring that she liked. With that they decided to get married in a church and have a small reception with just a few of their close friends and relatives, but nothing too fancy since both of them were very busy.

On Saturday they went to the best jewelry store in downtown. Millions of rays of light were being emitted from the ceiling's luminescent chandeliers and were reflected in tall, mirrored columns, throwing light into every nook and cranny of the room, creating an opulent atmosphere. There were big glass showcases that sparkled with diamonds, rubies, and other precious stones. Tall, slim, model-like salesgirls were standing behind the showcases.

Lisa stopped at one of the displays full of beautiful gold and platinum rings loaded with diamonds.

"Would you like to see this one?" The salesgirl, who had been standing attentive and ready until now, approached and pulled out a ring.

Lisa tried it on. The diamond shone immensely on her finger. The salesgirl then calmly said the price and Lisa couldn't withhold her gasp. It was unbelievably high.

"Wow, it was a nice ring though," she said as she took it off.

Mark didn't say anything, but brought her attention to another ring. This time they both checked the price first, but the ring was still too expensive. They began to search and look around more after the salesgirl introduced them to a different section. The prices of the rings were more affordable there, although the rings didn't look as fabulous. Lisa tried one on and it wasn't that bad, but her heart didn't seem to jump out at it. She extended her arm and admired the ring right under the light.

"Remember, once we buy it, I'll insist that you always wear it," Mark said with a smile. Lisa grinned back and took the ring off her finger. She then looked around and stepped to the adjacent showcase while Mark stood still. She heard a voice behind her say, "How about this one?"

She turned her head to the right and saw a salesgirl take a ring out of the display and show it to Mark.

"How about you try it on yourself so that I can see how it looks on your finger," Mark said to the girl, smiling from ear to ear.

The girl obeyed and extended her hand. Her fingernails were long and painted a dazzling shade of red.

"Do you like it?" she asked.

"Oh, yes, I do. It's too bad that I can't take this ring home on such a beautiful hand," he said letting out a deep, if feigned, sigh of regret.

The girl smiled sweetly. "So, do you want me to wrap it?" she asked.

"Lisa!" Mark turned his head to look at her.

A pink color had spread over Lisa's face. *Great,* she thought furiously. *He finally remembered about me.*

132

"No, I don't really like it," she managed to say in a steady voice. "Come on," Mark insisted. "Come over here, you can't even see it well from where you're standing."

She ignored his comment, "I checked everything in here, why don't we go to some other store?" Her eyes were averted and her words came out through clenched teeth.

Mark looked apologetically at the salesgirl. "Well, I guess we have a problem here," he said, letting his voice trail off and giving her a remorseful shrug.

Lisa turned swiftly and as she walked away to the exit she could feel the girl's eyes on her back.

Mark caught up with her outside the store, put his hand on her shoulder, and swung her around toward him. "What's wrong with you?" he asked, anger written all over his face. "You embarrassed me in front of that sales lady. What's the matter? We were about to get you a ring! What, you don't want the ring anymore?"

Lisa looked at him, stunned. "Who were you buying the ring for, me or her?" she cried.

His face looked contorted and filled with rage. "I thought we were past this stage!" He said. "Why do you force me to justify myself every time I look at another woman?"

"You weren't just looking at her." Lisa's eyes quickly filled up with tears and she dabbed them away with her fingers to stop them from falling. "You were giving her compliments. You were flirting with her, you put the ring on her finger!" she spat out intensely.

Mark looked at her in astonishment. "You were busy browsing all the way in another section, so I had her try it on," he said frankly. "I just wanted to see how the ring looked on a woman's hand. Is that a crime?"

He shoved his hands into his pockets for a cigarette, but couldn't find one and made an irritated choppy gesture with his hand.

"I tried to pick out the best ring for you that we can afford," he said. "It seems that no matter what I do, I can't make a woman happy." A sorrowful smile came across his face. He reached again for a cigarette, and frowned in annoyance as he remembered that there wasn't one.

"I left my cigarettes in the car," he said as he took out his keys and spun them around his index finger.

"So, what are we doing next?" he asked. "Please don't hesitate to tell me—I'll do whatever you want." He was curt and his gaze was unwavering, but strained.

Lisa's heart sank. Her blood pulsed in her temples so fast that she almost heard its pounding: boom, boom, boom. She felt horrible and guilty. She tried to sort out her thoughts. As always, there was apparent reasoning in his statements, which made her incapable of justifying her outrageous reaction even in her mind. Everything that had just happened in the store seemed to be unrealistic, like it hadn't happened to her, or to them. She remembered feeling hurt, humiliated and ashamed, but she couldn't understand what had come over her. She laid her hand on Mark's shoulder.

"I guess I was kind of nervous," she said apologetically.

"Ah, Lisa," he murmured, as he let out a tense sigh. "I just want what's best for you." He spoke with less effort in his words. "You know, if you think that our decision was a premature one, then just tell me." He paused, then looked directly at her. "So, what's it going to be, Lisa?"

"What do you mean?" she asked as her heart slowly sunk and her head filled with doubts. *Did Mark still want her?* Her fear must have been reflected on her face. Mark looked thoughtfully at her for a second, and then put his arm around her shoulders, pulling her into his embrace.

"I know a good, cozy restaurant nearby," he muttered as he bent his head and nuzzled his nose with hers. Lisa's heart eased with relief. She felt everything return back to its place again. They stepped into the car and drove to the restaurant, which was only a few blocks away.

The food was delicious, especially the dessert. Lisa had her favorite dessert, tiramisu, with coffee. They ate and talked and had a great time. Right after lunch they drove to a different jewelry store and purchased both the engagement ring and the two wedding rings.

Everything was coming together as never before. Lisa's apartment lease was expiring in two months, and their new home was ready to be occupied by that time. They were in no rush to move and pack since they could do everything gradually during their spare time. Lisa would be done with her finals almost a month prior to that, and would have a short break before her summer semester was due to start, which made it even easier. Best of all, Irving would have an opportunity to finish the school year in his current school, as Lisa hated the thought of him having to transfer in the middle of the school year. Everything was working out perfectly.

They had the ceremony in a small church on Wednesday during Lisa's break in between her classes since all the other days of the week were booked for the next two months. Mark took a half-day off from his new job and picked up Lisa from college. They arrived in the church and helped themselves into the chairs in the lounge area while waiting for the priest. Lisa wore her light blue skirt along with a lacy white Prada blouse, and Mark was clad in his fancy midnight blue suit, the one he had worn on their first date, the one that she liked the most. The priest came about ten minutes later and united them for better or for worse.

After the ceremony they went to a nearby restaurant to celebrate the event. It was just the two of them: two newlyweds sitting across from each other, holding glasses of champagne in their hands, consuming each moment with joy. They were embarking together on a fascinating adventure to a tempting and mysterious destination known as marriage, feeling like they'd never been together, slept together, or shared a life together before.

The wedding party was two weeks after the ceremony. Lisa made a guest list, called everybody and sent out invitations. She booked the flights for her parents and Mark's mother, cleaned her apartment, and did the laundry and the dishes so that everything would be clean and neat. They shopped together with Irving and bought him a new suit along with a white dress shirt and black dress shoes. They also bought a tie, which Lisa carefully knotted under his new shirt when Irving put it on. This small item made such a marvelous difference in Irving; he looked very manly when he examined his reflection in the mirror. She thought he was adorable in his new suit. He looked gorgeous, like a man, her very own little man, her blood, her soul, her baby. Lisa smiled. She knew that Irving would desperately protest if he would find out that she called him "baby" in her head. Since her marriage, Irving had been trying to be very cooperative. He took their wedding very seriously, and snuggled by her side, offering helpful hands. He tried not to create additional problems. He did all of his homework on time without any reminders from Lisa or Mark. He cleaned his room and dusted his computer and desk. He offered help with everything. He was willing to wash the dishes and fold the clothes after they went through the laundry. He kept a very mature attitude, and it seemed that he had notably grown up during the last few weeks.

Mark wanted to adopt him, and Lisa was truly happy with the decision. However, the clerk in the circuit court where they received their marriage certificate explained that it was not a one-minute deal but a long and complicated process that included a lot of paperwork. In the future, Lisa would recall that moment at the circuit court. She would be grateful for the clerk not making Irving's adoption happen. She would thank that woman and thank God! But at the time, they were a little upset for Mark not being able to adopt Irving as quickly and as easily as they had hoped. Nevertheless, that fact didn't spoil their overall mood, as they decided to return to the issue later, when all the paperwork would be complete.

They had to squeeze all the planning into those two weeks between the ceremony and the wedding party, and due to their tight schedule, they had to work to their limits and even past that. They seemed to succeed in their efforts, though, as the wedding party turned out to be beautiful. Mark reserved a lovely banquet hall for small parties just like theirs. The interior was decorated with large colorful balloons that obscured the ceiling. The room was spotted with bright colors from a large disco ball. There were red and blue Picot ribbons hung all around which had Mark and Lisa's names and wedding date on them. Splendid, gilded plates covered the tables in a variety of delicious dishes that ranged from salads to fish to delicacies, along with red and white wines. The room was ready to celebrate the event.

Lisa's parents and Mark's mother came along with Mark and Lisa. Although Lisa's parents were from New York and Mark's mother, Lynn, was from Florida, they all arrived at the same time in the morning with a difference of just ten minutes. It was very convenient for Mark since he had to pick them up from the airport, but of course, Lisa had planned it that way. Other guests started to arrive not long afterward. Mark's friend Carl with his family, Connie with Jerome and Anna, Nora with Steve and their daughter, Nick with Debra and their two children and, of course, Margaret with her husband, Sonya with her husband and their son, a couple of Lisa's other former co-workers including her ex-boss Nancy, and finally, Sandy and Kristina, who were accompanied by their boyfriends.

The band did a great job of entertaining the guests. The waitresses routinely changed the dishes and set more food out on the tables. The party flew by with jokes, merriment, dancing, and laughter. Everyone enjoyed themselves. There were a lot of heartfelt toasts dedicated to the newlyweds. In addition, there were a lot of pictures taken that Lisa later organized into two albums. Albums that she used to like looking through. Except later she kept them at the very bottom of the box in her closet, the box that contains old and unnecessary things, the box that doesn't have any value in it anymore but still serves as a family relic. It was a memory, no matter good or bad, it was her past, it was a part of who she was, of who she is and she can't erase it...

Mark and Lisa decided that it would be better for the parents to stay over in Mark's new condo than in a hotel, while Mark and Lisa would be at Lisa's apartment. Both of Lisa's parents and Mark's mother were more than happy to do so. However, Lisa's parents had to leave the next day after the wedding party because her father had to go back to work. Mark's mother, on the other hand, was retired, so she wasn't in a hurry to get back home. After the wedding party, Mark and Lisa drove Lisa's parents and Mark's mother to his new condo and Lisa gave them a tour of it.

The apartment had more than enough space for all of them. It had three bedrooms, two bathrooms, a large living room and plenty of room for even twice the amount of people that were staying that night. Lisa and Mark decided to pick her parents up early in the morning so they could take them to the airport. Lisa was a bit upset, though, knowing that her parents had to leave so soon. She didn't get to see them very often. The only contact she had with them was over the phone, and with her busy schedule, she was getting fewer and fewer opportunities for even that. She missed them a lot, especially that comforting feeling of gathering together at the big table in their kitchen, with all of them just eating, talking, and joking. Such beautiful, memorable pictures from her childhood. She had been looking forward to this day, hoping that she would have a chance to catch up on things, but unfortunately outcomes don't always reflect the plans made for them. Lisa hadn't had an opportunity to actually sit down and talk with her parents during the wedding. They also regretted not being able to stay longer. However, her dad was still working and there was no way around it. Nevertheless, they were really happy to see the way her life was turning out, especially when they got to hold their grandson, who they hadn't seen since he was a baby. Irving was excited as well. He was very happy to see his grandparents, whom he mostly knew only from talking on the phone.

CHAPTER TWENTY-FOUR

The Monday after their exciting and exhausting wedding party, Lisa and Mark's "honeymoon" began. Mark was off to work that morning, Irving had his school and Lisa had her college classes. She had to leave early though, since she had to bring Mark's mother over. Lynn called in the morning saying that she couldn't bear staying in Mark's condo. She wanted to be around them.

"I didn't come all the way down here just to be left alone," she cried.

It was true. Lynn had come to see Mark and her new daughter-in-law, and to spend quality time with her new grandson, who she liked from the start. She had a strong point, and Lisa willingly drove there to pick her up. Lynn deserved credit also, seeing that after Lisa rang the bell to the apartment, she opened the door, fully dressed, with her bags set on the floor all ready to go. She was a tall, thin woman with short gray hair that framed her finely structured face. There was something aristocratic about the way she looked and presented herself.

"I know you're busy, darling," she said and smiled like a queen to her people. "I don't want to delay you."

Without any apparent reason, Lisa felt odd in the presence of her mother-in-law. She picked up the luggage and they both walked over to the car. Lisa drove quickly on the way back home. Once they arrived, Lisa showed Lynn around the apartment and then led her to Irving's room. She decided that Irving would sleep in the living room during Lynn's stay. She knew that Irving wouldn't be too happy about the idea but there was no way around it. She situated Lynn's belongings by Irving's bed and headed to college soon afterward.

After her classes Lisa drove straight home. The first thing she saw after walking in was Irving proudly waving his hand around with money in it.

"What's that?" Lisa asked. "Where did that money come from?"

"Grandma gave it to me," Irving bragged, swinging his hand around one last time before heading to the kitchen.

Perplexed, Lisa went after him. Lynn was standing by the sink cleaning the dishes.

"We have a dishwasher," Lisa said as she stepped toward the machine to show it to Lynn.

Lynn gave her an odd look, and then said with edification, "There's nothing that cleans dishes better than your own bare hands."

Lisa took a closer look at the dishes in the sink. Her entire dinner set, all her coffee cups and silverware were drying in the rack.

Lynn intercepted Lisa's glance. "I had to redo everything," she said with a condescending smile. "I made a snack for Irving and I was about to serve it on the table, when I found out that there weren't any clean plates in the cabinets!" she said, oddly sounding a bit excited. "See," she pulled out the cup from the sink and showed it to Lisa, pointing at something that could be called a spot, but was most likely just a scratch. Lisa wondered silently whether Lynn had used a magnifying glass when she examined her dishes, or if she had simply assumed that Lisa couldn't wash the dishes properly.

Meanwhile, Lynn walked Lisa over to the table where she had set all the glassware upside down on the fresh tablecloth. The glasses were clean and shiny.

Fine, my mother-in-law has decided to take an inventory of my tableware, Lisa thought sardonically. Considering the fact that Lisa had cleaned and organized everything in her apartment just before the wedding so that everything would look perfect, Lynn's behavior seemed a bit absurd. Lisa really thought that she had done a nice job but obviously her perfectionist mother-in-law had a different opinion. Overall, Lisa was offended and irritated, but she decided to keep her feelings inside.

She looked at Irving, who was already sitting at the table. He hung his head and ate with exaggerated attention toward his food. His ears, however, were straining to catch every single word that was said. Lisa suddenly realized that she was standing in the middle of the kitchen, still wearing her coat. She had come there with the intention of talking to her mother-in-law about the money that she had given Irving, since she didn't feel comfortable with people giving Irving anything, especially money, without consulting her first. She expected to straighten out this matter with Lynn right away. However, after giving it some thought, she hesitated. She made a wise decision to come back to the issue at a better time.

She was on her way out of the kitchen, when she heard Lynn's solicitous question. "Would you care for something to eat, dear?"

Lisa stopped and turned to Lynn. "Actually, I was going to study a little before Mark comes home," she said with a slightly confused smile. She appreciated the offer, though.

"You look tired. It will be a long time before Mark comes home and you shouldn't study on an empty stomach, honey," her mother-in-law insisted.

"Yes, you have to eat something," Irving interrupted with his mouth half-full and a cunning flicker in his eyes. "That's what you always say to me," he added, stretching the words.

Lisa smiled. Her son had a good memory and he definitely knew when to use it. Lisa always made him eat before he started his homework, so there wasn't anything she could say if she wanted to look like an equitable parent, the way she thought that she always was. "Let me change and freshen up a bit first," she said.

When she came back to the kitchen, there was a delicious meal waiting for her and everything was set just right. The napkin was carefully tucked under the fork and knife, and the food smelled great.

"Wow!" was all that Lisa could say as she tried the soft, tender roll. "What's in it?"

Lynn explained that she had mixed vegetables with chicken strips, soaked in her special sauce and spices, and wrapped it all in a thin pastry that she made from scratch. She stood there with her hands on her hips, proud at Lisa's amazement at her cooking.

"Let me make you some tea," she offered when Lisa finished eating. Her tone didn't leave any room for a rejection. "I also made some white chocolate Macadamia nut cookies," she added. "Even though some people may consider them as a source of weight gain," she said, pursing her lips, "the calories, taken in a reasonable amount, are essential for the body's energy."

Lisa glanced over and noticed her big ceramic bowl on the table, full of soft, tasty-looking cookies. *Lynn probably re-washed the bowl a couple of times before she put her cookies in it,* she thought wryly. However, she didn't have any hard feelings about the matter. After all, her mother-in-law wasn't as thorny as she might have seemed at first. She was indeed an old-fashioned woman with her own peculiarities, but who could claim perfect normalcy nowadays? Especially at Lynn's age. Lisa would be thrilled to look and feel and do things the way Lynn did when she reached that age.

"I usually drink coffee," she said with a smile of appreciation. "We have a coffee machine, so I can make us some really fast." She stood up from her chair.

Lynn stopped her with an indisputable gesture. "Coffee's not beneficial at all, dear. It might boost your energy for a short period of time, but then you actually feel weaker afterwards, and in return you drink more and more coffee. It's a never-ending cycle," she said, smiling as she poured some hot, aromatic liquid into two cups. "I exclusively drink herbal tea."

She settled into the chair next to Lisa. "Try this; it's a mixture of chamomile, mint, and a pinch of orange citrus. It refreshes and relaxes you at the same time," she said while sipping the tea from her teaspoon. "You can make different flavored teas by mixing the leaves together, or you can just make it from a single type of leaf. You can try adding different sweeteners like honey or strawberry jam to achieve the taste you desire," she said in between sips.

Lisa took a mouthful of tea from her cup and closed her eyes. The liquid spread through her system, relaxing her muscles and nerves. *Not bad*, she admitted. *Not bad at all.* She smiled, stretching in her chair.

It turned out that her mother-in-law had actually brought along some extra boxes of tea. Lynn put her tall, round, precisely-labeled boxes on the shelf of one of the cabinets. Right next to it she placed honey and jam jars that she had brought all the way from her home. Although Lynn seemed to do whatever she wanted in Lisa's own kitchen without asking, it didn't bother Lisa. She smiled, giving her mother in-law a warm look. Afterwards, they both cleaned the table and washed dishes while Lynn shared her stories with Lisa. She spoke about her youth and the wonderful times back when the world was full of tradition and custom, when children respected their parents, when there was no violence or sex on television. She shared her memories of ambition and hope that had died with her marriage. She poured out her stories of how she struggled, being a single parent and raising Mark all by herself. She also relayed what a great son Mark was, so smart and handsome. The time flew by. Lisa didn't even notice when Mark came home.

Later that night, Lisa shared her thoughts about his mother with him. Mark's outlook wasn't as optimistic.

"Try not to argue with her. Let her do whatever she wants. She's a hard-working woman who can't stand a minute of her hands being idle," he told her with an odd smile. "Disputes built a thick barrier between my mother and my ex-wife. Last time that she visited us, she was really unsatisfied and furious. She even cut her stay down to a week, instead of a month as it was originally planned. She claimed that she wanted to visit her old girlfriend, but it was just an excuse. She hated my wife, who tried to treat her as a guest. She'd show her to the living room to watch TV every time my mother intended to wash the dishes or do the laundry. My wife complained to me about my mother being stubborn and mad. She said that my mother drove her crazy and criticized her every move, redoing everything after her. My mother, in turn, complained about my wife being a lousy housekeeper and an unskilled parent. She also nagged about my children being badly behaved and poorly taken care of. It was complete Hell with my mother there. I was honestly relieved when she left early." Mark let out a deep sigh and made a helpless gesture with his hands. "I become more depressed around my mother. I don't know how it works, but it seems like all the memories from my childhood rise to the surface. And I feel again like that small, unconfident boy who tried his best to please his mother but was never good enough at anything. Do you know what she used to tell me?" Mark went on. "She'd stand in front of me with her hands on her hips, and say, 'I bought you a beautiful present.' Then she'd pause and look directly into my eyes, waiting for me to become impatient for the present. And after I did, she would scowl and say, 'But I saw that you didn't work hard enough in school so I returned it.'" Mark lit a cigarette and heavily drew on it. "Can you believe that?"

Lisa looked at him, stunned. She couldn't imagine such a thing. She was shocked and her heart was filled with remorse for him. She felt goose bumps all over her body as she imagined being told anything like that by her parents. She clearly saw that Mark's mother was a domineering and stubborn woman who had sprained her child's soul. But despite everything, Lisa got along with Lynn pretty well, and most importantly she was pleased to see how Lynn and Irving got along well and simply enjoyed each other's company.

For the next few weeks Lisa found herself stretched thin between hosting her mother-in-law and keeping on top of her studies. Lynn required a lot of attention and she knew exactly how to get it. One day Lisa came home after school and found Lynn washing the floor. The woman was standing in the middle of the living room, trying to squeeze out the mop. She groaned and held her hand on her lower back with a painful expression on her face.

"It's so sad to be old, like me," she said with a wan smile. "Nothing seemed to be hard for me when I was young." She let out a deep sigh. "But I'm not complaining. I got used to hard work all throughout my life. I'm just grateful for God that I am still alive and can take care of myself," she declared dramatically and attempted to proceed with her work.

Lisa wondered sometimes why her mother-in-law never started cleaning anything until she knew Lisa would be home. Was it just simple coincidence or a smart tactic? Lisa didn't care enough to figure it out, though. She acknowledged that Lynn was an old and lonely woman. Sometimes elders act like children and demand attention by any means possible. So, without further consideration, she ended up spending her after-school hours by washing the floors, vacuuming the carpets, dusting, cleaning, and entertaining Lynn by being a good listener to her never-ending stories. And while keeping her face sober and thoughtful, Lisa contemplated any excuse she could think of to leave and study. To her disappointment though, it was almost impossible to have any solitude with her books while Lynn was there. Lisa even started to fear that she would fail her finals if things continued this way, when her friend Kristina came to the rescue. At her smart advice, for the rest of Lynn's visit, Lisa didn't rush home, but went straight to the library where she could dig into her studies undisturbed. When Lynn finally left, Lisa was relieved.

Chapter Twenty-Five

They moved into the new condo in the beginning of June. Irving had one more week left in his school year. Although this last week didn't seem to affect much of his education, Lisa didn't want him to skip his last school days, especially now that she had time to drive him there. She was done with her finals and had a couple of weeks to relax before her summer semester. She was proud of the final outcome of her first year. She finished with all A's, and only God knew how hard it had been for her. She felt satisfied with herself. She was registered for two classes in the summer semester and was ready for the upcoming challenges. The challenges, however, were the complete opposite of what she expected.

On the Saturday after Irving's last day of school, Lisa and Mark were relaxing in the living room while Irving played on his computer in his room.

"I'm excited about my summer classes. I signed up for two," Lisa confided to Mark.

"You're studying over the summer?" Mark asked tersely.

"Of course," Lisa replied, a bit surprised that Mark hadn't realized she would be. "I need to get my classes done as soon as possible, so I can start the Physical Therapy program. I don't want to waste a summer being idle."

Mark forced out a deep sigh. "I can't believe you didn't talk to me about this. I've been desperately waiting for the summer so that all of us could get a break," he said, words dripping with annoyance.

"What do you mean?" Lisa asked.

"Even though you may not realize it, Irving and I have been deprived because of your studies. We may be even more deprived than you think you've been. You've been gone as a wife and mother. During the rare times you're home, you're in another dimension! You're swallowed by your books. Your son hasn't been resting properly or eating properly. He needs nutritious food, but you're feeding him microwave meals and canned food." The disgust in Mark's voice was evident and Lisa couldn't think how to defend herself as he continued.

"Don't you remember the other night when we found out at dinner that Irving had been playing computer games and hadn't done his homework? And that wasn't the first time. Irving only starts his homework when I get home. He'd have failed his classes if I didn't help him every evening. But I'm not a machine. I can't keep going like this. I'd at least like a shoulder to lean on, but I don't even get that. My job is demanding and competitive, have you considered that? I've been spending all my money on your education and I haven't been able to save a single dime in case a rainy day comes along. I'm making good money. The average family of four with two working adults, would be pleased to have my gross income." Lisa stared, open-mouthed, unable to respond.

"But I don't care about the money, that's not the point. I've been doing everything I can to make your life easier, and to unload your stress. Every weekend we go out so you don't have to cook. I take my shirts to the cleaners so you don't have to do laundry. In case you didn't know it, other wives clean and cook. Connie pulls the whole household weight on her shoulders without any help. She keeps her house spotless and the food she serves is full of nutrition and the love she puts into making it. Her husband doesn't help out at all and she has a job. I've closed my eyes to the floors going unwashed, the dirty carpets, and the canned chicken soup in my bowl that makes me nauseous." Pain stabbed through Lisa, but still she said nothing.

"I don't ask much from you. I know you're not Connie. You're more intellectual and more fragile. That's why I try to carry everything on my own shoulders. All I've wanted in return was to come home to a house that's a real home. A clean house where my wife greets me with a homemade meal that was made from the heart. A home that I can enter and forget all the troubles I have outside. I want a home where I can be myself, where I can relax and enjoy talking to my real wife. Not a shell of a wife, a woman who perceives nothing except for her books. And, shame on me, I want to make love to my wife and not feel guilty afterward because she has a headache, or has to study for her midterms and other crap like that." Mark scowled and his dark gaze froze with its intensity. "The bottom line is that Irving and I need you to be here for us and it alarms me that you can't see that for yourself."

His words hurt. The way he said them simply knocked her down. It slapped her in the face, stabbed her right in the heart, making it bleed from invisible wounds. His lips were twisted in a scowl; his glance was scornful and estranged. His gestures were neglectful and insolent. His steady voice echoed in her mind. His pose, his appearance, his attitude were all a mixture of disappointment and a sneer of extreme arrogance.

It smacked her down. Lisa stood before him, her face pale, her mouth dry. She tried to think straight, unable to say a word.

It wasn't that what he said didn't have some rationale about it, because it did. It was just that he had presented the facts from his own perspective only. Everything would look different when taken apart from her angle. First, she didn't choose her path on her own; in fact, it was Mark's idea for her to quit her job and start college. She was well-off with her previous job and never would have dreamed of changing it, or better yet, of going back to college. Although, that wasn't exactly correct because although Mark had demanded she demonstrate her trust in him by quitting her job and going back to college, he actually hadn't dragged her on a leash.

She acted in good conscious and of her own free will knowing exactly what she was getting herself into. Besides, he had her best interests at heart and wanted her to fulfill her potential, to make her unspoken dreams come true. But the point was that her dreams had always been in her family's best interests and it was a matter of fact that her family would benefit with her having a more independent and higher-paying job in the future. Otherwise, why flip everything upside-down if not to ultimately benefit all of them? So what was Mark thinking when he lured her into this ambitious venture? What could he possibly expect, sending her back to college? That everything would somehow blow over on its own and have no significant effect upon their lives? How it could be possible? Didn't he fully realize that there would be a certain price for all of them to pay? Worse yet, did he care at all? Or did he think that his mission was completed with his generous offer and now it was Lisa's exclusive prerogative to have all the ends meet and be grateful for him until the end of her life? And she was grateful, wasn't she? At least she thought she was. But obviously it wasn't good enough for Mark. He had clearly conveyed to her that she was a bad mother, an inept wife and a lazy housekeeper, who didn't do her part but rather just spent most of the money. He had talked to her like she was his maid or property. Lisa felt immaterial and trivial, as if she were someone who had groundlessly gone too far and simply had to be shown her place.

She stood there speechless, gasping for air like something had just pulled her underneath the surface of the ocean. Her face burned; she bit her lips in humiliation. She was trying to hold back her tears but still they poured down her cheeks.

Lisa didn't know what she could say. She couldn't object, nor could she defend herself. All her thoughts were running in circles and she couldn't focus or know how to respond. *This shouldn't be happening, not to me.* The sorrow she felt was overwhelming. The pain and disgrace burned her heart. Lisa felt as if she were suffocating. She was full of humiliation and shame. She couldn't handle it. She didn't deserve it, any of it. Wasn't it she who sacrificed herself for her family? Who deprived herself from sleep, rest, her friends, from the whole outside world? Who for months had been engaged in a continuous circuit between her home and her college with a grocery store in the center, torn between her family and her studies? Her working day was far beyond normal. She cooked and cleaned and washed and dusted. She cheered and comforted, soothed and cuddled. Her whole world, her every thought was concentrated on Irving and Mark. She studied and did homework, yes, but even that was ultimately for them. She loved them, both of them, with all her heart; this love nourished, strengthened her; kept her going. It was the source of her motivation and energy. She wouldn't have survived this marathon; she wouldn't have survived any of it, if it hadn't been for that love. Why couldn't he see that? How could he humiliate her in this way? She could never do it to him. Why would he?

As she stood there, frozen, Mark left the room. She couldn't hold it in anymore. Stifled sobs tore her apart. Tears fell from her eyes accompanied by long moans. She screamed like a wild animal that had just been wounded by a hunter. She threw herself on the couch and buried her face in the pillow. But it didn't help stop the screaming.

Mark quickly returned. "What's going on?" he asked, then froze in the middle of the room with a cigarette still in his hand. She continued to cry.

He headed to the kitchen and returned with a glass of water, sat on the couch next to Lisa, and placed his hand on her shoulder.

"Lisa, what's going on?" he asked again, then touched her hair. He moved gently, like a nurse or a doctor would behave at the bed of a terminally ill patient. And somehow, this thought sobered her. She fitfully drew air in until her scream stopped. She sat up and wiped her face with the palms of her hands. Her cheeks glowed and her eyes hurt under the bright daylight. She rubbed them with her hands, took the glass from Mark and sipped the water, then looked around. Mark was sitting beside her: big, strong, and muscular.

"What was that all about?" he asked. "You scared the hell out of us!"

All at once Lisa noticed Irving standing in the doorway. His precious face was pale. He looked frightened. Lisa lifted herself up from the couch and headed toward her son to hug him. She felt dizzy; her legs were wobbly and she had to lean against the wall for support. She pulled Irving closer to her, locked her arms around him, and kissed his head. Unlike his usual demeanor, he didn't resist her smothering embrace. Her son might have somehow sensed, instinctively, that something bad had happened and that his mother needed him, needed his warmth, his sympathy, and his support. He put his arms around her, and buried his face in her chest, in the same way he used to do when he had been a very little boy looking for comfort in his mom's arms. Only this time, it turned out that she was on the receiving end. They stood there for a moment clinging to each other.

"I am so sorry, sonny," she said as she softly pulled away from Irving.

"Are you okay?" he asked. "Did you fall? Were you hurt?"

His worries for her made Lisa's eyes water even more but she quickly controlled herself. "I'm fine, sonny," she said smiling and bent her head to kiss him on the cheek. "I just feel tired, that's all." He looked at her, suspicious.

Lisa smiled. "I'm fine, honey. Let's go play. Everything's under control now." She moved her hand through his hair and turned him around, pushing him toward his room, and then headed to the kitchen.

"Or you can call Billy, if he'd like to come over, so you can play together," she added over her shoulder.

She saw that Irving was still standing there and watching her. She turned around and blew a kiss to him, with a wide smile. Irving grinned back and rushed to call Billy.

In the kitchen, she occupied herself making coffee. Her head felt heavy. Not a single thought seemed to gather in there, except for one. And this one thought stretched through her brain. Small hammers knocked about in her head in constant intervals. You don't need his money. You don't need his charity. You should throw it in his face. You should throw it in his face and turn your back on him with your chin held high. You don't need him and you should leave him; you should leave him immediately, right away. Take your son, your books, and slam the door shut behind you. Slam the door shut behind you. Slam the door shut behind you. Slam the door shut and–

And then what? What was she supposed to do then? Where was she supposed to go, where was she supposed to take her son and her books? And what in the world would she need her books for then? Her old apartment was gone. She didn't have any place to live, and no money to survive on. She wasn't even entitled to some alimony, she thought, as Irving wasn't Mark's biological father. He had wanted to adopt him but because of the time-consuming bureaucracy involved, they hadn't done it yet. Plus, Lisa would never sue Mark for any money. How could she? He had done everything he could in her and Irving's best interest and it wasn't his fault that she couldn't make this marriage work. Lisa dragged a hand through her hair, staring ahead blindly.

Mark hugged her from behind. She hadn't heard him come in and was startled. He nudged her closely and bent his head to nuzzle his nose at her cheek. Such a familiar gesture of guilt and apology. Such familiar warm arms, masculine scent; such an invigorating feeling of unity. His shoulders covering hers were like a canopy of protection and security; his body entirely melded with hers. She was wrapped up in comfort and peace. Everything that just moments before had seemed so hideous and miserable looked so small and unrealistic now. She had been too sensitive, too selfish. She had simply overreacted, exaggerated things.

"I let Irving go to Billy's. Why don't we take a nap and dissolve into one another's arms," Mark whispered into her ear.

She tilted her head to rub her cheek against his chest. Everything was returning to normal. She turned around to bring her arms up to his neck, and turned her face up to look at him. He bent toward her gently as if she were fragile. His gaze was soft and apologetic and yet he remained masculine. It was an inexplicable combination, and yet a mixture that acted upon her in a powerful way. It evoked in her some primary instincts, seduced her senses, hypnotized and shrouded her in some fog of love and passion. She smiled. She must have known him from a past life. They must have been somehow related or connected over the centuries by some mystifying bond. He lifted her off her feet and carried her to the bedroom. This time she was eager to make love with him, to feel his hands and body over her, to totally dissolve, and meld with him, body to body, soul to soul.

Chapter Twenty-Six

They both decided that Lisa should take just one summer class out of the two that she had in mind. She chose Microbiology. She had heard from junior students that this four-credit class, which also included a lab, was fairly complex and as such it was wise to finish it off in a short summer session instead of dragging it out through the fall. Lisa had about a week left before her class began and she spent it devoting herself to her family. She made delicious meals, special sauces; she baked cookies and sweets; she gathered together with Irving after school and with Mark at night. Mark worked late those days, and they usually stayed awake long into the night drinking coffee, smoking and talking in the kitchen before going to bed. Everything went smoothly. There was love, mutual understanding and peace in the family.

There was also something else, something so subtle and elusive that Lisa couldn't clearly define it, couldn't think it over. By all obvious reasoning, her life was great. She had a loving and caring husband, a precious son, and a great career in front of her. She lived in a beautiful condo; her son had everything that a boy his age could possibly have, including a computer and tons of games and fancy school clothes. Not to mention the crucial and significant fact that for the first time in his memory, Irving had a full family. Lisa didn't have to worry about rent, bills, or her budget. She had everything she could need. Everything that had happened to her was like a fairy tale, a miracle. She was lucky and she was blissful. She was both admired and envied by less-advantaged women. She should be happy and grateful. For many reasons and for her sanity, she should look to the future and be grateful to God.

Instead, an inexplicable fear would often shock her awake in her bed. She found herself waking up in the middle of the night; her heart jumping out of her chest and sweat rolling down her forehead. She would be shaking and covering her mouth so as not to scream. She didn't know what it was. It seemed like some dark force that came from nowhere and overpowered her, hunting her down while asleep in her bed. Sometimes Mark would wake up and hold her in his arms, kissing and cuddling her, and she would fall asleep like a baby in the shelter of his arms. She couldn't comprehend how she had lived without him all these past years. She couldn't even imagine how life would be if she hadn't met him.

Mark became very busy at work. He was preoccupied and concerned with how things were going there because some problems had arisen. There was a growing tension between him and his eldest co-worker who had worked for the company for over twenty years. At every meeting, to his face and behind Mark's back, this guy promoted and justified his own ideas and undermined Mark's using the simple reasoning of his seniority at the company.

Mark would come home angry and depressed, and despite loving the job, he was determined to quit. For long hours, he and Lisa discussed his situation at work, making various plans and developing strategies on how to turn things around and transform that unhealthy competition into a civilized and productive work environment. Eventually, she suggested that Mark invite the guy to lunch where they could talk openly. It could be that his coworker acted aggressively out of frustration at losing his job to such a younger and more capable employee as Mark. The lunch turned out to be a great idea and Mark and his co-worker were able to straighten everything out during it. Because of its success, Mark jokingly called his and Lisa's time spent together in the evenings his therapy sessions and Lisa his little shrink and they continued the sessions. There was lots of coffee and cigarettes during those hours.

The semester had started and in an instant Lisa's every day became a whirlwind. She was glad that she only took one class in the summer. This class turned out to be a tough one with its extensive labs. There was a lot of information to memorize and there were pop-quizzes and tests to take. And of course it was summer with its beautiful, hot weather, the relaxing sun, and the alluring lake with its wonderful sandy beaches. This made Lisa's life even harder since she had to keep herself on track, keep going and resist the temptation to give everything up and find herself on the beach with Irving and Mark, instead of studying the books in the library or visiting the lab over the weekend. The only luxury she would allow herself—and what reminded her that it was indeed summer—was the delicious fresh fruits and vegetables that she purchased at a local farm every Sunday. She prepared a delicious, country-style, home-cooked meal for her family and they all enjoyed eating it on the balcony.

But even those marvelous dinner hours didn't seem to be enough for her to have a break, to rejuvenate. She felt exhausted and overworked most of the time. She felt like everything was on her shoulders; she was working beyond her ability. It was like she had shifted into high gear and had to do everything faster and better. Only the harmony and peace in their house gave her strength.

Unfortunately this didn't last long. One day, Lisa was running low on fuel. She pulled into a gas station on the way home from class. She took out the hose and put it in her car and was ready to fuel her car up until she noticed that she had no cash. Mark gave her money for her expenses and she used to ask him for cash every time she ran out of it. Yesterday, she had forgotten to check her purse and ended up without a penny in her pocket, in the middle of the gas station. She noticed a few people watching as she replaced the nozzle and drove away, feeling humiliated. She arrived home and told Mark about her situation. Mark suggested that next time Lisa not forget to ask for cash on time. Lisa asked him why they couldn't have a joint account or at least a credit card so she could have something in reserve. Mark gave her an odd look. There was a silence for a split second during which Lisa felt color wash up into her face. She didn't work, she didn't contribute to the account, she just consumed—she read it on his face.

"I'm an old-fashioned guy, Lisa," Mark said after a pause. "I'm a provider, a supporter. I'm the man of this house." He focused his direct stare on Lisa. "Is there anything that you're in need of? Is there something that isn't enough for you?"

Lisa shook her head. Of course she had enough; she couldn't complain about anything. She was thankful for everything he did for her.

Mark continued. "I believe that money needs to be kept in one hand. It has to be well-managed and under control. I think it's a man's job to see that the budget stays fit, and that money doesn't fly around unknowingly. That's how it was in the house of my grandfather, and my dad, and that's how it will be in my house." He smiled and reached out his arm to hug her. "You're the woman of the house. A man is the head, a woman is the neck, and the neck turns the head. All women know this axiom and use it profoundly. Women are smarter than guys and they always like to be in control." He smiled broadly at Lisa.

His reasoning, as always, was bulletproof. And Lisa had nothing left but to agree with him. It wasn't that she considered his decision unfair or outrageous but something about it made her mood plummet.

During the rest of their married life together, the two never had a mutual account. Lisa got accustomed to asking Mark for money and for his permission on all of her expenses.

CHAPTER TWENTY-SEVEN

There was something collapsing, falling apart inside of her. Lisa stared into the mirror, thoughtfully studying her reflection. A strangely sad and unfamiliar face looked back at her. Drab, lusterless gaze; pale face; dull hair. She tossed her hair off her forehead and her lips twitched. She recalled the conversation she'd just had with Mark. They were sitting in the kitchen, drinking coffee and smoking.

"You look like my mother," Mark had said suddenly, smiling through the haze of the smoke. Lisa remembered that a wave of frustration had come over her. If she understood him correctly, he had implied that she looked as old as his mother and wasn't as pretty or attractive for him as she used to be. She felt too confused and embarrassed to request an explanation from him; she knew that it was exactly what he meant, anyway. In an instant, her face burned red and her eyes filled with tears. She whimpered like a dog and turned her face away. Mark seemed not to notice her reaction. He took another drag on his cigarette and turned to the window. "Such a dark sky outside. Most likely it will rain tomorrow," he said casually.

Lisa wiped her eyes with the back of her hand and reached out to grab the cigarette pack. Trying to regain control of herself, she pulled a cigarette out, took a lighter, paused pensively, looking at it, and then lit up the cigarette. She was preoccupied with her routine until she finally felt the hit of the cigarette and let out the smoke. Only then was she able to look up at Mark. To her relief, all of Mark's attention was focused on determining tomorrow's forecast rather than on her.

Lisa sighed and pulled herself closer to the mirror. There was not a hint of vitality or strength left. The woman in the mirror looked tired and old. She hardly resembled the former Lisa. A sad smile came across her face. What did she expect? She stayed at home or at the college every day. She drove her car to places that she could easily walk to if she had the time.

Her schedule was intense and she was under constant stress, worrying about her tests and acceptance into the physical therapy program. She ate here and there, grabbing snacks in between her classes, and other days she'd go without food all day long. She'd drink too much coffee and smoke too many cigarettes. She needed a break and she knew that now. Lisa turned away from the mirror and left the room.

In the kitchen she opened the refrigerator and took out some potatoes, carrots and onions. She placed the skillet on the stove, poured in some olive oil and began to shred vegetables.

Mark came home from work just as Lisa was stirring the vegetables in the skillet.

"What's cooking?" he asked from behind her.

"Some vegetables," she answered as she turned to him.

"Must be a lot to fill me up." The sarcasm in his voice made Lisa jerk.

"I'm also going to make chicken noodle soup and chicken fajitas," she said as she gathered all her patience.

"Oh, my favorite: canned soup," Mark exclaimed, his voice full of scorn.

"Today's Friday, and we ran out of the meat I bought last Sunday at the grocery store. I'll be doing shopping this Sunday again," she replied.

"Are the stores open on Sundays only now?" he asked, his eyes widened in an innocent expression.

Lisa stiffened and turned back to her routine of stirring the vegetables. "I was very busy this week."

"You always find a good excuse." She could hear the burst of irritation in his voice.

A sudden rage took over her. She scraped the spoon angrily against the bottom of the skillet and it crashed off the burner and onto the countertop.

"What has gotten into you?" Mark asked, his voice condescending.

Lisa grabbed the skillet and slammed it back on the stove. The oil and vegetables flew about the kitchen. Mark turned bright red.

"What can you expect from me? I'm as old as your mother!" Lisa turned to face him.

"You're nothing compared to my mother," Mark said, sneering. "She cooked and cleaned and worked two jobs while raising her child alone."

"Don't I work enough?" Lisa asked.

"Lisa, I told you many times, I want to come home and have a decent meal, a clean house and a smile from my wife." He lit a cigarette.

Lisa felt a rush of heat run up to her face. Her lips trembled and her eyes filled with tears.

"You're describing a maid, not a wife!" she cried.

"So, I guess you have a misunderstanding of a wife. Look around you, look at other women. Look at Connie. She has a job, she has two kids, a whole house to take care of and she's always around for Jerome. Her house shines with cleanliness, their table is full of fresh, homemade food every day." Mark exhaled a stream of smoke forcefully.

So now Connie is the perfect wife, but not too long ago she was shallow and simple. And so what if Connie works, Lisa thought in despair. *I work, too, and Connie only works part-time. The only difference is that Connie gets paid for her work. Maybe that's it, maybe that's what it's all about? The money?*

These thoughts spun around in her head; her lips twitched with unspoken words. She wanted to scream out loud but she couldn't. She was shaking from head to toe.

"If you think that you can get something out of me with your hysteria, you're very wrong," Mark said viciously as he smashed his cigarette into an ashtray. He immediately withdrew another one. "I'm not the kind of guy that can easily be fooled around with."

Her hands flew up to cover her face. Sobs poured out. Mark smashed the cigarette into an ashtray.

"I don't have to take this crap," he said. "I don't think it was a good idea for us to get married in the first place." He walked out of the room. A dense silence filled up the kitchen. The last sound she heard was the sound of the front door being slammed shut.

Her sobbing suddenly stopped. She took a deep breath and then felt strangely relaxed. She stood up from her chair, opened the cabinet and pulled out a bottle of chardonnay. She placed the bottle on the table and looked pensively at it for a second. Then she opened another cabinet and pulled out a tall crystal glass. She stood there for a while more, then turned around and opened a drawer to get a corkscrew. With a screw in her right hand and a bottle in the left hand, she situated herself at a chair by the window. Then she opened the bottle, filled the glass with the sparkling, golden liquid, and emptied it in a few, heavy gulps. The warm fluid spread pleasantly throughout her body. She pulled out a cigarette from a pack and drew in smoke.

So that was it. Her marriage was over. Mark had said it and she had heard it. He was sorry that he had married her. She wasn't good enough for him. Well, she didn't want to be a burden. She should pack her things, leave and let him be free. For good.

Lisa lifted the bottle and poured the glass full of wine again, then set the bottle back on the table. She looked at her left hand and studied her wedding ring. She touched it with her right hand, twisting it around the ring finger, then slowly pushed it up. She moved her hand above the glass, then studied it for a split second in the sparkle of the wine. Slowly, she spread her fingers apart. The ring made a swift splash and then sunk to the bottom. Lisa calmly lifted the glass and drank it all at once, leaving the ring in the empty glass.

"Mom, are you okay?"

She lifted her head to see Irving standing over the threshold of the kitchen.

"How long ago did you get home?" she asked, pulling out her cigarette.

"I just came from Billy's house." Irving's immobile look was focused on her. "Why are you sitting in the dark?"

Lisa raked her fingers through her hair. "Are you hungry?"

"I ate at Billy's."

"It's time for bed, go brush your teeth. Go to sleep sonny," she said.

Irving said nothing. He just looked at her, then turned around and silently headed to the bathroom.

My dearest, precious son, she thought. He understood everything, and didn't blame her. He loved her and accepted her as she was. And what did she give him in return? Broken dreams.

Lisa grabbed the bottle swiftly, filled the glass again and drank it down.

She had messed up. Failed them. She didn't deserve Mark's love. She didn't deserve to be his wife. He had left for good, and nobody could blame him.

A wave of fear spread over her. She grabbed her head with her hands and dreadful sobs escaped her mouth. She picked up the bottle and drank it to the bottom, not bothering with the glass. Then she lit a cigarette up, and took a deep drag on it. Suddenly her head started spinning and her hand dropped to the table. The only thought that she had enough strength for was to put out the cigarette so that something wouldn't be catch on fire. She smashed it.

Next thing she knew, she was awakened in her bed by Mark's soft kisses. He was lying down next to her. His masculine scent was so familiar and invigorating. His strong, warm arms were comforting and secure, as always. *How blessed and lucky she was to feel him next to her!*

She had a terrible headache the next morning. She got off the bed, put on her robe and walked to the washroom. She took a nice hot shower, then wrapped a towel around her hair, threw on her robe, and went into the kitchen for a cup of coffee.

Mark was already there, talking on the phone with someone. He spoke loudly, with some irritation in his voice. Lisa just heard a name. Sharon.

Wasn't that the name of his ex-wife? She poured the freshly-brewed coffee into a cup and sat at the table across from Mark.

"You're the same old you," he said into the mouthpiece heatedly and slammed the phone down.

"I had a talk with my ex-wife," he announced as he lit his cigarette.

"I kind of figured that out," Lisa said, helping herself to a cigarette as well.

"I tried to convince her to give the children to me for full custody. I thought that enough time has passed for her to cool down and start to think straight. I figured she could understand that she's inept and incapable of raising the kids, and that it would be in the children's best interest to have them grow up with me."

Mark waved his hand in the air. "Nothing helped; it's still hopeless. What did I expect? People don't change." He looked directly at Lisa with a wry smile.

"Do you know what she told me? She told me that I'm a sadist." A sad irony lit up in his eyes. "She said that the kids shouldn't be let within a mile of me because I would crush them." He heavily drew on the cigarette and looked out the window.

Lisa watched him, her eyes wide. A thought occurred to her. He was a sadist. It all made sense now. That's what he was doing to her. He would torture her, intentionally, in some twisted, sick way, and then he would comfort her. He was trying to make a masochist out of her and that's what she was becoming. A masochist!

Lisa raked her fingers through her hair and looked up at Mark. He was still smoking pensively and looking out the window. His face was tired. He had a gloomy stare. Her heart filled with sympathy and some guilt. How could she think of such a thing? She reached out to touch his arm with a comforting hand. Mark turned to her. A wary smile came across his face, but she could see pain in his eyes.

"Is Irving still sleeping?" He looked at his watch. "Wow, it's already time for breakfast. How about we relax and go out this morning?" He grinned at Lisa.

It was a beautiful idea. Lisa headed to Irving's room to wake him up. They went straight to the pancake house. Mark had an omelet with bacon and sausage on the side; Irving and Lisa both had Belgian waffles with strawberry jam. After breakfast they stopped at a computer store to shop for a new action game for Irving. Then they went to the movies and drove home for dinner. After dinner Irving went to play his new game. Mark watched television, and Lisa went to her books. The rest of the day was quiet.

CHAPTER TWENTY-EIGHT

Red, green and ochre colored the trees in all the shades of fall. It was a warm afternoon. The sun beamed from the bright sky and caressed Lisa with its gentle heat. She rolled her car window all the way down and inhaled the fresh scent of fall. The weather was idyllic, just like it was on the day that she first met Mark. Lisa couldn't believe how fast time flew by. It was September already. Exactly one year since their first date. So much had happened in that short period of time that it was hard to believe it had only been just a year. It seemed like an eternity.

She made a right turn into the college parking lot and found a free spot in the second lot. She turned off the engine, opened the back door, and took out her bag. The bag was really heavy, full of books and notebooks. Lisa took one book out of it to hold in her arms and hung the bag over her shoulders. She had only seven prerequisites left— seven classes to take and three more semesters to survive, and then she would be ready to apply for her physical therapy program. She was taking three classes this fall semester, two Biology classes and one Psychology class, and planned on taking the last four classes in the spring and summer. It was so exciting to think about that. She was on the right track; she had worked hard and her hard work would finally pay off. She inhaled deeply, took another book out of the bag and carried them across her chest, heading towards the campus.

Just seven prerequisites. She planned everything out and thought everything over. If everything would go as planned, in the summer she would send out applications to a couple of physical therapy schools that she had chosen together with her counselor. She had a 4.0 GPA so far, she would have great references from the hospital where she was volunteering, and the acceptance into the program would be a natural next step for her. The only thing left was to revive her plans. Ironically enough, she wasn't sure if she would have the strength or the ability to live out her plans, considering the way her life was unfolding. Her worries and fears were getting worse and worse, despite her evident stability. She loved Mark with all her heart and she knew that he loved her and supported her. The truth was, she wasn't sure anymore if she could give him everything that he expected of her. Evidently, Mark needed and wanted a woman like Connie, whose only interests were homemade food, a clean house, church on Sunday, and always being available for her husband. In fact, Mark was making enough money to support his family and even have his wife be a stay-at-home mom. The twist was that such a life wasn't for Lisa. Not because there was something wrong with stay-at-home moms or women like Connie. It was nothing like that. She respected Connie and even admired someone who managed to keep such an uneasy household as hers together. Simply put, however, Lisa wasn't Connie, and she had her own vision of happiness and fulfillment, which now included her being a physical therapist.

Lisa tried to fit it all in, she tried to give Mark everything he needed and at the same time keep her own spirit intact. The sad fact was, she wasn't sure anymore that it was realistically possible for her to combine the two and continue much longer. She was thankful to Mark for everything that he did for her and continued doing. She did her best and even more to demonstrate her love and gratitude to him. But she wasn't completely sure that was enough for him. She was becoming less and less confident. She was getting overly sensitive and melodramatic, and she wasn't sure if she had enough strength left in her. She felt unable to give any attention to Irving in the way she wanted to, or in the way she used to. They were slowly drifting apart. Their strong bond was in jeopardy. She blamed herself a lot for it. Sometimes she couldn't help but wonder whether this condo of Mark's was actually cursed, or maybe the building was built on cemetery grounds or something.

***

It was a beautiful Saturday morning in October. The sky was clear and the sun was shining. Nothing portended of a storm as the weather forecast had predicted. It seemed to be wrong as usual. Lisa walked out of the bathroom and made her bed. They had planned to go out for breakfast at a pancake house, and then stop by a computer store to buy a new game for Irving.

"Mom, when are we leaving?" Irving asked when he appeared at the door, all dressed up, impatient to go.

"In a couple of minutes, sonny. Let me change my clothes." She smiled at him.

Mark looked at her through his designer glasses. He wore blue jeans and his favorite blue shirt. He looked somewhat tired and disappointed.

"Do you want to redo the bed before we leave?" he asked. She looked at him, puzzled. "The bed is a mess," he said, sounding irritated. She felt her face turn red.

"I just made this bed, it looks fine to me," she answered. With a sidelong glance she saw Irving still standing in the doorway.

"It's not fine," Mark said through clenched teeth. "You do everything carelessly. Everything you do in the house you do it with your left hand and you stop as soon as it looks like it's done. Your studies and your interests are all that you care about." He looked directly at her. "We aren't going anywhere until you redo this bed."

Lisa stood still, her face burning.

"I'll do it." Irving ran towards the bed.

"Get away from there," Mark said, waving his hand. "Let your mom learn how to do it. We're not walking out of this room until your mom can do it."

"Do you have any idea what you're saying? How dare you talk to me like that!" Lisa shook with rage. "I'm not a teenage girl–I'm your wife for crying out loud!"

"I'm supporting you, I'm providing for you. I put food on the table, and I put a roof over your head. I'll say whatever I please. Just calm down and do as you're told."

"Screw your money and your charity!" she cried. She was trembling, covered in sweat, tears streaming from her eyes. "I don't need your money, I don't need your food, and I don't need you!"

"Well then," Mark said flatly. "I'm going to make an appointment with my lawyer and start filing the divorce papers." He left the room. Lisa heard him dialing the phone in the kitchen and then discussing something with someone. Then she heard the door slam shut behind him.

Panic flooded through her body. She sank down to the floor and started rocking back and forth holding her knees. Her sobs carried through the condo. Irving stood there, looking at her in horror, but she barely noticed him.

What was she going to do? She was halfway through her semester and had planned on taking two more before moving on to Physical Therapy school. What was going to happen to all of her plans now? Where was she to take Irving? Her son finally had a family; he had a man who had taken the place of his father, who took care of him. He had a beautiful home to live in; he had a computer, he went to a great school. She had just deprived him of everything, in a heartbeat. Lisa hit the bed with one fist, and then with the other one.

What had she done? God! What had she done? Didn't she know that Mark had a very difficult time at work? That he had worked a lot of overtime hours in the past few weeks? She knew how hard he had worked. Everything he said, he didn't mean it. He didn't mean to humiliate her. He was just tired and depressed. That was all. She should have understood that. She should have let it go, turned it into a joke, or just made that bed.

It was too late now, too late to do anything about it. Lisa climbed into bed, laid flat, and grabbed a pillow. She was squeezing, clutching, wringing the pillow with her hands, and crying out her soul into it. She didn't know how much time had passed by the time she let it go. She rose from the bed and went to the kitchen.

In the kitchen, she opened a window, pulled out a cigarette, lit it up, and blew the smoke out the window.

It's over. I've ended it all for good now, she thought. She sat there, smoking cigarettes, mindless and listless. She didn't know how many cigarettes she smoked; she didn't know how long she sat there either.

She was nothing. She was an arrogant little nothing. Mark showed it to her; he had to. Everything she'd achieved and everything she'd been proud of, was all because of him. She had taken everything for granted. She had worn out his patience and abused his kindness. She deserved the punishment and its consequences.

Lisa smashed the next cigarette into an ashtray, brushed her hair off her forehead, and rose from the chair. She was dizzy. There was not a single thought in her mind. She moved automatically, like a machine. All she remembered was that Irving hadn't eaten anything since that morning.

She opened the refrigerator, took out some bread, cheese, ham and lettuce and set it all on the table. She stood still for a moment, blindly looking at the table. Then she turned around, opened the refrigerator again and took out the mayonnaise. She prepared a sandwich and went into the living room.

Irving was sitting quietly in the living room, playing Nintendo. She placed the food on the coffee table in front of him, walked to the bedroom, and fell down on the bed. Fatigue overwhelmed her and smothered her into a deep sleep.

Lisa opened her eyes. The sun shone through the blinds of the window. It was quiet and only the sounds of the ticking clock pierced the silence. The clock showed 3:00 p.m. Lisa jumped out of bed. Her head was pounding. Her face and her eyes were puffed up. Her whole body was aching. She walked out of the bedroom and headed towards the living room. Irving was still sitting on the floor playing his video games. Half of the sandwich was eaten, and half of it remained on the plate. His glass was still full. She sank onto the floor next to him and hugged him.

"Why haven't you eaten, sonny?"

"I'm not hungry," he said, continuing to play his game, forcefully hitting the controller.

"I'm sorry son, I'm just so sorry." She hugged him more closely, falling into sobs.

"Mom, stop crying. Why are you crying?" Irving struggled out of her grasp.

She wrapped her arms around her legs and began to rock back and forth, trying to stop weeping.

Irving got up to his feet, and patted her on the head. "Mom, don't cry. Don't cry, please," he said, his voice trembling.

Lisa pulled together all her strength and wiped her eyes with her palms. She reached out to hug Irving.

"Everything will be all right sonny. Everything will be great," she whispered. More to herself than to him.

They sat there for a bit longer holding each other. Then Lisa rose and headed toward the kitchen.

"Mom, are you going to smoke?" Irving asked from behind her. She paused, then said, "I'll go make some coffee, son."

Mark came home around eight in the evening. It was getting dark outside. Lisa was sitting in the kitchen, looking out the window. A white moon shone on the night's horizon and gleamed into the room.

"Why are you sitting in the dark?" he asked as he stepped over to turn on the light. Lisa fiercely pulled out a cigarette and lit it up.

"I filed the divorce papers," Mark said flatly and then walked out of the kitchen.

The tears came again and a dreadful panic tugged at her heart. But crying wouldn't help; it would only cause more harm. Lisa hastily drew on her cigarette, trying to compose herself.

"What's the matter, Irving, have you been crying?" she heard Mark say from over by the couch. Then there was a deep sigh of regret. "I know that you want to stay with me. I want you to live with me, too. But as you can see, it's impossible now. Your mom and I will be divorced soon, and by law, they'll make you live with your mother."

Lisa heard him sit down next to Irving.

"Unless we persuade your mother into letting you stay with me, there's no other way for us to be together," he said as the couch creaked under him. "But no matter what, no matter how things unravel, you must know that I will always love you. The problems we are having are just between your mom and me; it has nothing to do with you..."

Lisa didn't hear any more; she couldn't keep listening. She smashed her cigarette into the ashtray, her body shaking from horror. She bit her lip to stop from screaming.

Mark is right, she thought. Irving would be better off with him. He would have a supportive and loving father in Mark. Irving would live in a wonderful home, have his computers, and games, and go to a great school in a wealthy and safe neighborhood, and not be in need of anything. There would be a great future there for him. She had to admit to herself, she was a failure, a loser. She was nothing. She wasn't able to provide for Irving in the way he had become accustomed to. She wasn't sure she would be able to provide for him at all now. However, she knew somehow that despite all those advantages of living with Mark, Irving wouldn't be happy with him. And she would die without Irving. She wrapped her arms around her legs and stared silently out the window.

Mark walked into the kitchen and touched her shoulder with his hand.

"I put Irving to bed." He pulled her closer to him, and with his hand brushed the hair off her forehead. "It's kind of late, let's go to bed," he said.

There was hope. He wasn't leaving yet. He still desired her. He wanted her to go to bed with him. They'd sleep together, make wonderful love and everything would dissolve and disappear in their hot embraces. Everything would be different tomorrow. Everything would be back to normal.

They went to the bedroom. Mark hugged her, reached down and kissed her. She wrapped her hands around his neck. The feeling of such familiar arms and his well-known, gentle lips invigorated her.

"Mark," she said afterwards, as they were lying in bed in each other's arms, her voice quiet. "I'm sorry for what happened earlier. I love you. I want to be with you, forever. Reconsider. Give me another chance. We can start everything all over."

Mark sat up on the bed, dropped his feet to the floor and searched around on the night stand cabinet. He took out a cigarette and lit it up. Under the moon's light Lisa saw his strong back and broad shoulders. She raked her fingers through her hair. She had no shame. She didn't feel anything but love for him. She lifted herself up and clung to his back.

"Mark, please. I love you, I can't live without you."

He jerked her off his back and moved further to the edge of the bed. "Don't you understand, there's nothing left between us anymore. You irritate and annoy me. The only thing that's left in my heart for you is pity and great sadness that Irving has to be left with you."

Lisa fell back down on the bed. "Did you get a date for the divorce?" she asked.

"Yes, our divorce should be very quick because we don't have anything to divide. We don't have mutual accounts or shared belongings. You can of course get your own lawyer, but I don't think you have the money. There's no point for you to really even get one; we haven't been married that long. My lawyer will present the papers in court in a few weeks. Then we'll part."

A sudden thought struck her mind. *Mark wasn't the person she thought he was—keen, strong, generous.* Trying to comprehend this thought, she asked. "Do you want us to be out of your house by then?"

"Lisa, I told you many times, you don't have to take Irving, you can leave him with me. I'm sure you understand that Irving will be better off with me. And I think that you know how much Irving wants to be with me."

"Irving will stay with me, Mark," she said.

"I didn't expect anything else from you." He let out a deep sigh of regret. "You're too stubborn to act wisely." He turned to her to touch her shoulder.

"Do you know where are you're going to live and how you're going to live?" He sounded sympathetic.

No, Lisa didn't know. She didn't know what she was going to do or how she was going to live. But she knew for certain that Irving would stay with her.

"Mark," she said. "I just need one favor." He blew out cigarette smoke and stared at her in silence. "Let us stay with you for a short while. I need time to find a job and an apartment. Let us stay here a bit longer, please."

"Lisa, you can stay here as long as you need. We can even continue to make love together. There's no harm in enjoying our sex life, we seem to have some sort of chemistry with it. You know that I don't have anything against you, Lisa. We're just not meant for each other." He put out his cigarette and turned off the light. Then kissed her on the cheek, and went to sleep.

CHAPTER TWENTY-NINE

Lisa forced herself to wake up early in the morning. She took a quick shower, got dressed, and went to the kitchen. Mark was already there. The smell of the freshly brewed coffee tickled her nostrils. Lisa poured herself some coffee and sat across from him at the table. Mark was skimming the morning paper.

"Oh, wow, the economy's going down again," he blurted and looked at Lisa. "Ah, well, whatever, it looks like it's going to be a gorgeous day outside," he said, then set the newspaper aside. "Cigarette?" he offered.

They smoked a few cigarettes together, finished the rest of their coffee, and then Mark left for work. Lisa emptied the ashtray into the garbage, washed the two cups, and woke up Irving to get him ready for school. It was a typical morning. Everything was the way it had always been, like nothing had happened and nothing had changed. *We look like a typical American family*, she thought sadly. A beautiful home, a happy marriage and a lovely child. Wasn't this her dream? Wasn't this her understanding of happiness?

Lisa saw Irving to the school bus, then went to the bedroom, put her books into her bag, and went to college. This didn't mean that she had made up her mind on college, but she couldn't just drop it. She had lost so much in this short period of time that losing the habitual routine of going to school would kill her. On her break, she called her ex-boss at work.

"Lisa! How are things going? Are you accepting new patients already?" Nancy sounded very excited.

"No, I'm...umm...not..." Lisa mumbled. "In fact, I'm looking for a job right now. Some sort of a part-time work," she slid it out fast, trying to overcome her embarrassment. There was a pause on the other side of the wire.

"Is everything all right, dear?" Nancy asked.

Lisa's lips tightened; she felt tears coming on.

"Everything's fine, it's just...it's a bit rough recently," she said finally. There was a deep sigh on the other end of the phone.

"You know how highly I think of you, Lisa. How I appreciate you as a person and as a professional." Her ex-boss sighed again. "I'd love to offer you a position. You know I would if I could. The thing is that we have your position filled already. You know you left us in a very bad situation. For a long time we couldn't find a person of your caliber to fulfill the job. We tried two different massage therapists, but ended up having to let them go. After you left, Lisa, our clients weren't satisfied with anyone else. We lost a lot of our clients for that reason. Thankfully, we're getting back on track now and are almost up to where we used to be with this third massage therapist. You know how hard it is to find a good professional who fits into our work environment."

She paused and then continued. "When Margaret left she left us in a jam too. I wouldn't be completely honest with you if I said that I wasn't angry at her for that. But I have to be fair, she needed to follow her husband. It's understandable, I can't blame her; it's just life. We all do what we have to do."

Lisa knew that Margaret had left. Her husband received a great offer in San Diego that he couldn't refuse and they ended up moving to California.

"It's okay, don't worry, I'll be fine." There was an exaggerated cheer in Lisa's voice.

"It was nice talking to you, Lisa."

"It was nice talking to you, Nancy. Say hello to everybody for me." Lisa hung up the phone.

On her second break she drove to a gas station and bought the local newspaper. Then she went to the cafeteria and opened it. She turned to the classified section and started to look through the job opening ads. The third ad was exactly what she was in search of. A large beauty salon had part-time openings for a massage therapist and the conditions were very satisfying. It offered flexible hours for qualified candidates. Lisa cut out the ad and stuck it in her purse. She made a call the first chance she got.

A quiet woman's voice asked her name, her credentials, and set a date for an interview.

Lisa broke the news to Mark right after he came home from work. He looked at her through his designer glasses. His stare was intent. It had either some interest or wonder. She couldn't exactly make his face out.

"You're not wasting any time," was all he said.

"I'm not hired yet, but I was invited for an interview," she said.

Mark sat down on a chair and lit up a cigarette. "Don't do anything that you'll end up regretting later." He looked directly at her. "I'm not kicking you out, you know that Lisa, right?"

Lisa slowly reached her arm to pull out a cigarette; her hands were trembling.

"I have to learn to live on my own, don't I?" she said, forcing a smile.

"Hmm, you're all grown up. Let's hope you know what you're doing." His arms spread wide open in a helpless gesture. "Anything for dinner? I'm starving," he said, changing the subject.

The divorce papers came in December. Lisa had just arrived home from school and was in the kitchen making coffee when the doorbell rang. She opened the door and saw the mailman. He handed her a big orange envelope and asked her to sign for it. Lisa noticed that the envelope was addressed to her. Curious, she opened it and carefully took the printed papers out. "In the order to...," she started to read and the letters began to blur out with her tears. She threw the papers on the table and helplessly dropped into a chair. The bitter reality hit her. It wasn't just a mean prank and it wasn't a nightmare. Nothing magically dissolved and took care of itself. This was the end of her married life, the end of her hopes and dreams.

She hung her head in her hands and closed her eyes. It wasn't like she found out about the divorce today. Mark had announced it to her a while ago. He had said in a straightforward way that he didn't love her. But then again, nothing in their life had changed since he'd said that. They continued to live together and sleep together. They gathered at the dinner table, went to the movies and spent long hours in the kitchen talking, drinking coffee and smoking. Plus, Mark and Irving's relationship hadn't changed at all.

Lisa had somehow felt that their relationship was growing stronger when, in fact, it was inevitably coming to an end. The divorce papers had suddenly splashed cold water in her face.

Lisa didn't read the paper. She didn't want to; she couldn't. She just briefly mentioned them to Mark during their coffee hour in the evening. Mark walked over to the living room and returned with the documents.

"You have to sign and date them." He handed the papers and a pen over to her.

Lisa's face turned pale as she took the pen and started signing the documents.

"You should read everything to see if you find it satisfactory and fair," Mark instructed.

"I'm sure everything is fine," she said, signing and dating the last page.

Mark let out a deep sigh, lit a cigarette, and drew in smoke. "Oh Lisa, even though it's over between us, I still feel sympathy towards you. I don't want you to fail in life."

Then why are you divorcing me? She wanted to scream, but managed to smile bravely. "I'll survive, Mark. I'll be fine."

"Fine? What do you mean fine?" Mark cut her off angrily. "Look at yourself; my old mother looks better than you do. You're irrational." He smashed his cigarette into the ashtray and immediately lit up another. "You're pathetic, you're neurotic and jittery. Without me you won't be able to take care of yourself, not to mention your son. The only advice that I can give you, and you better listen to it, is to leave Irving with me. He'll be much better off in this condo, and in this neighborhood. Plus, this'll give you a chance to stand back up on your feet. Otherwise you'll end up on the street, homeless and sick." He paused and focused his direct stare on her. "Did anything that I just said make any sense at all to you?"

Lisa didn't say a word. She just sat there, her face burned. She couldn't find the strength to get up from the chair.

He's right, she thought, dazed. She was indeed pathetic, brash, and poor. Nobody was there to take care of her. She was all alone in the world. There wasn't anyone who would give her a hand. The shocking fear paralyzed her. *Why couldn't Mark just understand her frustration? How could he lose his love for her this fast?* She couldn't comprehend it and she refused to believe it. She still loved him. He was her husband, her lover; he was a part of her. Life without him was not imaginable. She needed him. She needed him now more than ever. While she wanted to scream and beg him for forgiveness, nothing came out from her mouth. She remained motionless, her face pale. Mark's eyebrows went up as he looked at her.

"I'm your friend. I wish you and Irving only the best. However, the decision is yours. I can't make up your mind for you." He rose from his chair and looked at his watch. "I have to stop by my friend's house to take care of some business." He put out his cigarette and left.

Lisa pulled a cigarette out of the pack but made no move to light it, and continued sitting at the table simply rolling it in between her fingers.

CHAPTER THIRTY

The beauty salon where Lisa was hoping to work at was located in a big, busy plaza. Lisa easily found the place with the directions the receptionist had given her and pushed open the glass front door. Right from the threshold she felt the coziness and warmth of the place. She looked around. To the right she noticed the hair dressing area. It looked very busy; all eight of the booths were occupied. Adjacent to this area was a spacious waiting room filled with a couple of coffee tables surrounded by maroon armchairs and two couches of the same fabric and color. Groups of ladies were sitting there talking, drinking coffee, and eating some muffins. Lisa stepped to the front desk and introduced herself.

A youthful receptionist with thick brown hair rose from her chair and extended her hand to Lisa.

"Vicky," she said, smiling at Lisa and shaking her hand. "It's so nice to meet you, Lisa. Let me introduce you to our boss, Marcy. She's expecting you." She walked over to Lisa to show her to the owner's office. They proceeded to the adjacent area, and as soon as they stepped over the threshold and closed the door behind them, soft, gentle music streamed into Lisa's ears.

"This is our spa area," Vicky said proudly. Lisa noticed how lovingly Vicky talked about the place. They walked through the hallway, passing many doors until they reached the right one.

Vicky opened the door and let them in. "Marcy, this is Lisa, the massage therapist." She introduced Lisa with a smile and walked out of the room.

"Nice to meet you, Lisa, please come in, have a seat," Marcy invited her to the chair across the table from her. She was in her late forties and looked very casual and friendly. She asked Lisa a few general questions about her education, license and professional background and then asked Lisa to demonstrate some techniques on her. They went back to the hall and proceeded into the massage room, which was to the left from Marcy's office.

"Our massage therapist who worked in this room just left," Marcy said while opening the cabinets and showing Lisa the products.

The cabinets were located around the massage table, which was in the center, making everything easily accessible. Lisa noticed that this room was very well spaced and that it was a bit larger than her previous massage room. She already loved this spa, the room and the atmosphere.

She performed her massage and Marcy was very pleased. They returned to the office and briefly went over all of the details. Lisa was excited. She was going to work three days a week, Friday, Saturday, and Sunday. She didn't have classes on those particular days and now with her new job it gave her hope that she would be able to pull it off.

She left the salon in an upbeat mood and decided to drive around the area. Marcy mentioned that the spa was located in a very quiet and safe middle-class neighborhood. Lisa turned onto a side street and headed toward an intersection. On her left-hand side, she noticed a big sign that stated "Apartment for Rent." She followed the directions on the sign and arrived at an apartment complex. She parked her car in front of a large one-story office building and wandered through the main door.

As she walked in she saw a middle-aged man with gray hair sitting at a big wooden table next to the window. He seemed to be occupied with some papers, but looked up when Lisa entered. "Are you looking for an apartment?" he asked Lisa. "I'm John, the complex manager."

"Yes, I was actually driving around, looking at the area, and noticed your sign."

"Say no more," John said, smiling as he stepped away from his table, heading to a glass cabinet on the wall. "It's a very good area. It's quiet, safe, and has great schools," he shared while opening the cabinet and pulling out some keys. "Do you have any children?" he asked.

"Yes, I have a son. He is almost nine years old," Lisa replied.

"Then I'm sure this is the place you're looking for," John said, smiling. He took a folder from the table and headed to the door. "Shall we?" he opened the door to let Lisa out. "Let me show you the building."

He escorted Lisa to a light-brown four-story building. As she had already noticed, the building looked well-kept. It was surrounded by several trees and open spaces, making it seem secluded and private. They headed inside the building and walked up three flights of stairs to enter into a wide, well-lit hallway. They walked about halfway down the hallway before John stopped at one of the doors and opened it. They stepped into the living room. The apartment was small and, to Lisa's surprise, was furnished, making it seem very cozy.

"Our previous tenant had to suddenly move to another state and left most of his furniture," John explained. "If you want, you can use the furniture, but if not we can take it all out," he said.

"Oh, no, I really like it!" Lisa exclaimed. She had sold most of the larger furniture items from her apartment when she moved in with Mark. She looked around. To the right of the front door there was a small kitchen with a refrigerator, a stove and a small table with four stools. Straight ahead was the living room. A black leather sleeper sofa stood in startling contrast to the white wall while a maroon Italian dresser made an excellent counterpoint across from it. On the dresser there was a 27-inch round tube television. The right wall in the living room had three doors in it. One of the three doors led to a small closet, the other, which was the middle door, led to the bathroom. John opened the door and Lisa saw a white bathtub, a white sink, and a white bathroom rug on the floor. It was a tight space but it looked recently remodeled and was clean. Lisa was excited. She already liked this apartment.

John continued with the tour, opening the left and final door, which led to the bedroom. The room was very bright. A queen-sized bed dominated with a dresser and a big mirror in front of it and two night stands flanked the bed.

"How much is the rent?" Lisa asked.

"$600," John replied. "All is included – gas, heat, water, except for electricity. You'll need to pay your electrical bills." Lisa nodded in understanding. "You can fill out the application and I'll let you know if you're accepted by the end of this week. We've already had a few inquiries, so get the application in soon." John pulled out some papers from the folder and invited Lisa to the chair at the table in the kitchen. He handed the papers over to Lisa.

Lisa panicked. She loved this place. She already had grown accustomed to it. This apartment had to be hers and only hers. The rent was similar to what she used to pay in her old apartment, though now she would only be working part-time. However, with the apartment's furniture, location, and school, Lisa knew that the rent wasn't just reasonable—it was a great deal. It was perfect for Irving and her and she had to do something; she had to convince John to give this apartment to her.

"I'm a very reliable and a responsible person," she said wholeheartedly. "I'm working; I just got an offer from a beauty salon right around here and I'm studying to become a physical therapist. My son's a very smart and dependable boy."

"What's the name of this beauty salon?" John inquired.

"'Paradise; it's located not far from here."

A wide smile came across John's face. "Is Marcy your new boss?" he asked.

"Yes." Lisa's eyes filled with hope. "Do you know her?"

"I'm a good buddy with Marcy's husband. We get together with our families very often." John looked at Lisa thoughtfully and paused. "Well, you're in, girl," he said finally, then pulled out another paper from his folder and put it on the table in front of her.

"It's an apartment lease. Read it, and sign it," John instructed. Lisa took the pen and quickly signed and dated the paper before John had the chance to change his mind.

John also signed the document, then gave Lisa a copy and carefully returned the original back to his folder.

"You can move in two weeks from now. January first. Are you ready to pay your deposit and your first month's rent today?" he then asked.

Lisa hesitated. She'd forgotten that most apartments require the security deposit and the first month's rent in advance. She started to desperately think where she could borrow the money until her first paycheck.

"Will you be ready to bring in the money on the first day you move here?" John seemed to read her thoughts.

"Of course, I definitely will," Lisa assured him. "Thank you. I appreciate your generosity," she said as they proceeded outside. "No problem," John said as he waved his hand.

Lisa walked out of the apartment and got in her car. She drove home wondering how she would break the news to Mark.

Mark came home around seven that night. While Lisa was warming up dinner, he made some coffee, lit a cigarette and helped himself to the chair at the table. Tiny, gray circles of the smoke were floating to the ceiling. The sudden thought of quitting smoking occurred to her.

"Mark, I found an apartment. Irving and I are moving out in January," she said quietly.

Mark looked at her for a split second, a combination of wonder and surprise on his face.

"Good, finally I'll be a free man again." He smiled broadly and waved his hand in a careless gesture. "Hopefully, I'll find a woman that will love me for who I am and I'll keep her."

Lisa's heart sank. That was it; a simple and causal ending of her love and her dreams. He was letting her go just like that, like there was never anything between them. No love, no bond, no past, and no future.

Lisa smiled to herself. What did she expect? That he'd realize what he had done and then fall onto his knees and beg her for forgiveness? She was such a naïve girl.

She glanced at Mark. He was sitting in the chair – strong, muscular, and confident as always. Her heart squeezed. She so desperately wanted to lean over to him, and cuddle under the shelter of his big strong arms, to feel his body, and his warmth. . . but she knew she couldn't.

Her lips quivered. She lit up a cigarette, took a deep drag on it and looked out the window. Heavy crimson clouds burned alongside the horizon by the rays of setting sun. The picture was astonishing and fearful at the same time.

CHAPTER THIRTY-ONE

Winter break had started and in a way, the timing for it was perfect. Lisa had two weeks left before she was going to move out. She had only two weeks left before her married life, her hopes and her dreams would be gone for good. Only two weeks left for some miracle to change everything back to normal with her and Mark.

She kept herself busy with packing and cleaning, and she did her tasks as scrupulously as she possibly could. She wrapped every single item individually, no matter whether it was a fragile ceramic cup or a plastic cup that she used in the kitchen. She wrapped these items, one by one, then labeled them with a red marker, and packed them into the labeled cardboard boxes. She was desperate to keep her mind busy with these simple tasks so there would be no space left in it for worrying how she would live without Mark. She couldn't imagine her life without him.

Mark observed her from the side. He wasn't involved, and up until their last night together he acted as if nothing was happening.

"So you're moving out tomorrow?" he said when they were in bed.

"Yes, we are," she said. A silly thought of hope came into her head. What if he would start laughing and say that everything was just a joke? That he was just kidding and that he loved her and Irving with all his heart. They were his family; he couldn't just throw them out.

"Well, I hope you know what you're doing." Mark reached out to brush his hand through her hair. His gesture seemed sympathetic. "I want Irving to take the computer and all of his games and software that I bought him," Mark said. Then he took something out from his night stand and reached over to set it on Lisa's.

"It's a one thousand dollar check. I want you to have it," he said as he laid back down on his pillow.

"I don't understand," Lisa said, her face turning red. She was glad Mark couldn't notice it in the dark.

"Lisa, I know that you might want to throw this money into my face because of your stubborn and proud personality. But for once think wisely and think about Irving. This money is more for him than it is for you," Mark said as he gave her a good-night kiss and turned around to go to sleep.

In the morning, Lisa glanced at her night stand. It now looked strangely empty without all her books and notes. Mark's check was laying there all lonely, right in the middle. A small blue bump on a smooth, cherry wood surface. A sad smile came across Lisa's face. What did Mark say about her being proud? She thought that she showed him lately that she was everything but proud. Lisa hesitated, then picked up the check from her night stand and put it in her purse. If she was ever proud in her life, then today she had to forget it. She couldn't allow herself to have such a luxury. She needed this money. She had to take it for her and Irving's own sake.

The moving crew came at around eleven in the morning. They quickly loaded everything into the truck and left. Lisa and Irving followed the truck in their car and soon after arrived at their new place. The movers brought in all of their belongings and the small apartment quickly filled up with boxes. Lisa paid the men, closed the door behind them, and looked around. This small, messy place was now her new home, her new life. A sudden feeling of loneliness gave her a shiver. She crossed her arms over her chest and lowered onto the one of the boxes. It occurred to her that Irving must be as scared and terrified as she was. For God's sake, he was just a child, a brave and courageous boy, but still just a child. Lisa combed her hand through her hair. Poor Irving, she had never even spoken to him about what had happened between her and Mark. She never gave him a chance to choose, but instead just dragged him down into the pit with her.

"Irving," she called him quietly, "Come here, son, I need to speak with you."

Irving slowly walked into the living room and stopped at the box next to her. He was silent; his expression was serious although it didn't show any emotion. Lisa's heart felt pity for her son.

"Have a seat sonny," she said as she pulled him by his shirt to take a seat upon a box. "Irving," she started and reached out to pat his hand. "Mark and I are divorced."

"I know, Mom," he said.

She paused. "Sonny, what happened between Mark and I has nothing to do with you. Mark loved you and cared about you. He wanted you to have the computer and all of its games," she gestured toward the bedroom where the movers had put the boxes with Irving's stuff. "I'll help you unpack it tomorrow and set it up in your bedroom."

"It's okay, Mom."

A hot wave of guilt came over her. She tried to push it away but failed. Tears streamed from her eyes. She wiped them with the back of her hand. She was mortified. She didn't know what to say to her son or how

175

to explain to him that her failure in life wasn't his fault. Even if she did find the words, how would they help Irving live the life she was about to put him through?

"I know that your new bedroom is much smaller than the one you had. But on the bright side, it's very cozy, and you still have enough space to wrestle with your new friends," she said, forcing a smile through the tears in her eyes. Irving stared at her silently.

"Sonny, for a while our life won't be the way it used to be. We won't be able to go out for dinner, buy many new things, or go to the movies as often."

He kept looking at her, his face pale. His young, innocent and helpless image blurred in her eyes. It raised unbearable guilt in her.

"Irving, I'm so sorry, I didn't mean to put you through any of this. I only wanted the best for you. I wanted the best for all of us. I don't know if you'll ever be able to forgive me," Lisa buried her face into her hands.

Irving jumped up from his box and rubbed her shoulder. "We'll be fine, Mom, we'll be fine. I'm with you. I love you. We are a team, we can do it. We'll be just fine, Mom."

Lisa lifted her head up to look at her son. She pulled him closer to her, and hugged him, smothering his head in kisses.

"What would I do without you, sonny?" she said, smiling at him through the tears. She kissed her son again, patted his hair and then rose from her box.

"Let's go unpack our bed sheets and go to sleep. It's really late." She made Irving's bed and tucked him under the blanket. "Good night, sonny. Everything will be better tomorrow," she said with a smile. And although she said it to Irving, she didn't believe it. She knew that her life would now be miserable.

Lisa closed Irving's door and returned to the living room. It was so cluttered with boxes she had no room to make up the bed. She threw the bed sheets on top of it, lay down and closed her eyes.

The dreadful dark forces seemed to wait until this very moment to fall onto Lisa with their demolishing power. Panic, loneliness and fear swept over her body, filling her heart with terror and despair. She was alone. She was all alone in the world. There was nobody there for her. Nobody, except her brave little son. But she wasn't supposed to dump all of her problems on him. She shouldn't make him pay for her failure. She was his mother; she had to support and nurture him. That's the way it should be, not the other way around.

But the horrifying truth was that she didn't know if she had the strength to live that way. She was nearing empty and she had no energy, nor a will to keep on living. She only wanted to go to sleep and never wake up.

Through the Clouds

Exhausted, she fell into heavy dreams.

CHAPTER THIRTY-TWO

A sudden invisible wave came over her. Lisa opened her eyes and sat up on her couch. The alarm clock showed 3:15 a.m. This was the exact same time that she'd been waking up for the past two weeks. Lisa looked around. The moonlight shone through the window, filling her heart with fear and misery. She pulled her knees up to her chest and wrapped her arms around her legs. Blankly, she stared into the space in front of her. She didn't see anything but darkness. Dreadful, deep darkness that pressed and squeezed around her from every side. Fear, loneliness and terror pierced her heart like a sharp knife. Overcome with terror, she touched her mouth with a clenched fist to hinder dreadful moans. She was alone in the world; no one was there for her. What was she supposed to do? How was she supposed to survive? Horrifying, hopeless thoughts crept into her mind and as soon as she battled one out, another came rushing in. She stiffened. Her eyes filled with tears. She began rocking back and forth. *Why me, God, why me? What have I done, how have I failed you?* Fear and despair overwhelmed her. She couldn't stand her life anymore. She couldn't survive. She didn't want to.

Her whole body was sweating and shaking. There was no reason for her to live anymore, no reason at all. She grabbed the pillow and cried her tears into it. Her soul was torn apart. "Oh, God! Dear God!" she groaned. "Please let me die, just let me die!"

She jumped off her bed and started to pace throughout the room, kicking the boxes out of her way. She bit into her fists and didn't feel any pain. She started thinking. She had to end her life. She had to find a way. She must have committed some awful crime in her previous life and now deserved to die. She had to simply accept this fact. Lisa bit deeper into her fist. How should she do it? How should she end her life? She had no doubts about ending her life but she needed to plan everything out carefully. She couldn't just abandon her son. Irving didn't deserve to be poor, he didn't deserve to suffer. She had to make sure he was taken care of when she was gone. There had to be a way to protect him until he would be able to survive on his own.

Lisa paced through the room faster and faster. A perfect idea popped into her head. She would die and make it look like an accident. From this moment everything clicked. She would send Irving to his grandparents and have the life insurance money secure him.

She stopped in the middle of the room and pressed her nails to her forehead. She knew how to do it. She would drive her car at night at its highest speed. She imagined the intensity of the speed. Seventy, eighty, hundred, one twenty. The road was empty. It was just her, the car, and a bridge. The bridge came closer and closer; a hundred feet, fifty, then thirty, twenty—then only the sound of the car smashing through the bridge's fence was heard. The car halted in midair and then swiftly fell down into the river. There was just a large loud splash and then there was only silence. A blissful silence. Finally, there was peace in her distorted mind and soul.

Lisa felt sudden relief. Everything was planned out. She approached her bed, crawled under the blankets and instantly fell into a deep sleep.

She woke up to the sound of the telephone. Rolling over on the bed, she searched around, found the telephone on the floor and picked it up. It was Margaret.

"I know what happened. Why haven't you called me?"

Lisa shifted and pushed herself up to a sitting position.

"I'm so happy to hear from you, Margaret," she said.

"Lisa, dear, how are you? Where are you? I didn't know you'd moved. I called your old number and talked to Mark. He told me that you moved out and gave me this number. Tell me, what happened?"

Lisa felt a knot in her throat, it was hard to speak. She swallowed hard and pushed it down.

"We are divorced," she managed to say. "I rented an apartment; it's small and it's full of boxes."

"That doesn't matter!" Margaret exclaimed. "The good thing is that it's your very own apartment."

"I don't want it. I can't live here. I can't live anywhere!" Lisa couldn't help her screaming. "I'm a loser. I'm a failure. I don't know how to live, and I don't want to."

"What's the matter with you? What's wrong with you, Lisa?" Margaret cried. "You should be happy that everything turned out the way it did. Mark was an arrogant and worthless asshole. I didn't like him from the first moment I saw him. I felt that something wasn't right about him. You're very lucky that you left and took Irving away from him in time before things turned out to be more tragic. You're young and beautiful. You're smart, ambitious, and hard-working. You'll be better off without him. You'll reach your goals in life and be successful and happy."

"You're wrong, Margaret. He did so much for Irving and me. Everything that I've ever accomplished was because of him. I'm nothing without him. In fact, I am nothing."

"Who am I speaking to?" Margaret cried in horror. "Is this you, Lisa? You don't sound like yourself. You don't even resemble the Lisa I know. Pull yourself together. Don't you get it? He used you until he broke you. He drained you to the bottom and then he threw you both away without thinking twice."

"He cared about us. He gave Irving a computer and wrote a thousand dollar check for us."

"A computer and a lousy thousand dollars? That's all he gave you? And you think he's generous? That you owe him for the rest of your life?" Margaret yelled out in disbelief. "He put a spell on you. Open your eyes. All he did was throw you out to die. There's no generosity in that. Can't you see it?" She sounded choked with anger. "Forget about him. Finish college, get your degree, a great job, and become incredibly wealthy."

"You don't know what you're saying, Margaret. How am I supposed to pay for my tuition? How will I buy food, pay my bills and clothe Irving? My job will only cover my rent. How are we going to survive?"

"You're a single parent—they'll give you a loan that will cover not only your tuition but housing as well. And I can lend you some money until you get back up on your feet."

"Don't you understand? I'm broke. I'm a loser, a failure. I'll never be able to repay you. I'll never be able to stand up on my own two feet again," Lisa cried in despair.

"My dear, you're breaking my heart. I can feel your pain. I know you're in a very difficult situation. It must be extremely hard for you. But I know you, Lisa. You'll find the strength to get through this. You'll find the courage to make it out. You'll be reborn from your ashes like a phoenix." Margaret laughed through her tears.

Lisa felt a smile spread across her face. Her dear friend Margaret! She must have felt that Lisa was trapped in the dark. She had come to her rescue.

After she hung up the phone, she felt energy flow into her body. Her recent suicidal thoughts now seemed pointless and embarrassing. She couldn't believe that she had come up with such an outrageous, selfish idea. How could she betray her son like that!

She hopped off the bed, took a nice warm shower and changed into some clean clothes. Then she started to unpack the boxes labeled "Kitchen" into the cabinets. She was going to prepare a nice breakfast by the time Irving got up. This morning was going to be special.

CHAPTER THIRTY-THREE

Two months slowly passed by after the divorce. Still, Lisa felt the pain as if it had happened the day before. Every night she tossed and turned in her bed, hopelessly trying to fall asleep, but as soon as she closed her eyes her wandering mind would conjure up images of Mark. She envisioned them dancing together, slowly whirling around to the sounds of music, wrapped in each other's arms. She felt the warmth of Mark's body, the softness of his lips. Her heart was bruised with pain; her despair was unbearable. She missed him. She missed him so much.

She had lost her meaning in life. Every morning she woke up tired and miserable. She no longer had an interest in the world or in the people around her. All she wanted to do was stay in bed and never climb out. She had to learn to live with the pain, and the only way she knew how was to wrap her pain into a dense knot and hide it deep down inside her heart.

She was sure that everybody knew about her situation and felt sorry for her. This realization made her feel even more miserable. An innocent question about how she was doing; a sympathetic glance or gesture directed at her; they all implied pity. Lisa's heart felt even more broken.

She tried to avoid people as much as she could. It was easier to do in college. She only had to listen and write, and could slip out of the class as soon as it finished, practically invisible.

Work, however, was a real challenge to Lisa. She couldn't hide there. She not only had to be visible, she had to have a smile on her face that projected energy and happiness. This was complete torture for her. It took as much energy for her as if she were an Egyptian carrying a brick to the top of a pyramid. The only place that she could receive some sort of relief was in her massage room. She performed the sessions in the dim light of flickering candles, her hands routinely and skillfully moving, but her wandering thoughts floated away to the sounds of ocean splashes and seagull calls.

She visualized Mark, his broad shoulders and strong body. She saw the way he looked at her—compassionately through his designer glasses.

She imagined him cuddling her in his big arms, filling her heart with a sense of serenity and security. The images of them dancing together in each other's arms rolled over and over in her memory. She wanted to stop time and pause these images but the sessions inevitably came to an end and brought Lisa to the cold reality that Mark wasn't there.

Lisa realized she couldn't continue to live like this. This way of life would finally destroy her if she wouldn't change anything about it. She knew that she had to forget Mark. She had to erase everything about him no matter how hard it was. She had to start her life over again. From a blank page, there was no other way around it. She had to do it for her and Irving's sake. She had to do it for both of them.

At home, Lisa seated herself into the chair at her desk. She had to look at her situation from a different angle and find the good points in it. She had a wonderful son, a paying job, and was on track in college. Margaret had been right—she had gotten a loan that would cover her tuition and housing, and Margaret—wonderful Margaret!—had sent her a $5,000 check. She and Irving had a roof over their heads, and food on the table. They lived in a quiet and safe neighborhood where Irving attended a good school. He had made new friends and gotten on the basketball team. Besides losing Mark, their life had not changed dramatically. So far, she had acquired everything they needed to reach a bright future. She just needed to pull herself together and throw Mark out of her mind.

Lisa decided to come up with a constructive plan and write it down. She needed to have it on paper so she'd be able to turn to it when she needed encouragement.

She titled the page *My Plan*; then underlined the title with a red ink and listed the major steps. First, she had to quit smoking and never return to it. Then she had to make her apartment spotless and rearrange all of the furniture. Third, she needed to spend more time with her son and strengthen her bond with him. Fourth, she had to come out from her shell and stop avoiding people. Then she paused, rolling the pen around in between her fingers, and for a moment looked pensively at the space in front of her. Then with a firm hand she wrote in large bold letters – **NO MARK.**

She dropped the pen on the table and an ironic smile curved her lips. *No Mark.* It was easier said than done. How was she supposed to forget him? He owned her mind, her heart, her soul. No matter what she did or where she went she felt his presence at every moment. Lisa bit her lip. She had to do something to free herself of him. She had to block and kill every thought of him right at the root. As soon as his image would pop into her mind, she would concentrate on something else, like multiplying numbers or recalling a poem. This way she could gradually be able to force Mark out of her subconscious for good.

Sorting her thoughts out gave Lisa a burst of energy. She pinned the paper on the wall in front of her desk and smiled. She was determined to stick to her plan no matter what it took.

She made an appointment with a Chinese doctor who advertised a unique method of acupuncture for fighting nicotine addictions. Lisa had five sessions and it was remarkably successful. She didn't have urges to smoke unless she was around someone who was smoking, so she avoided smokers, cigarettes and even talking about smoking. Her senses became sharper and, one day, she walked into her apartment and realized that it was saturated in cigarette smoke. It was an unpleasant surprise to her. She felt sorry that Irving had to breathe this air.

She scrubbed, dusted, and vacuumed until the whole apartment shone with cleanliness. She re-washed all of hers and Irving's clothes and put them in the dryer with a spring scent freshener. She bought and set plants and flowers around their living room. The apartment went through an extreme make-over. Irving noticed the changes in her, which seemed to cheer him up. He offered his helpful hand and while cleaning the house they chatted and joked around a lot like they had in better times.

Their place turned into a fresh, smoke-free environment. They started to spend more time with each other and grew closer. Lisa called her friends, Sonya, Kristina and Sandy. She was afraid that the girls would have a grudge at her since she had avoided them for the past two months. However, they didn't ask any questions. They were delighted to hear from Lisa and wanted to see her again.

Work was less and less of a challenge for Lisa. Her smile became natural and people no longer irritated her. She slowly began healing, feeling rejuvenated and regaining her old spirit.

CHAPTER THIRTY-FOUR

Nevertheless, from time to time Lisa would wake up in the middle of the night with shivers running up and down her spine. Fear would sweep over her from nowhere, like she was the prey hunted by some vicious animal. In a cold sweat, she would sit on her bed shaking from the dreadful horror. Such nights filled her with misery and drained her confidence. She couldn't comprehend how she thought that she had had what it takes to pull everything off. Paralyzed with fear, she had to fight extremely hard to regain control.

At the end of the day, after one such a night, Lisa was laying in her bed mindlessly browsing through her study book. The sudden sound of a phone pierced through the air. Lisa sprang off her bed and rushed to pick it up. Her heart leaped out of her chest as she brought the phone to her ear.

There was a slight cough on the other end of the wire. "Hi, Lisa." Mark's deep voice sounded as clear as if he was right next to her.

She had to hold her chest with her hand to steady her heartbeat. "Hi," she said. She heard him spark his lighter and draw on a cigarette.

"How are you doing? Is everything all right?" He asked.

It took time for her to comprehend the question. No. How could everything be all right? How dare he ask such a question?

"I think we need to talk, Lisa," Mark said crisply.

There was a pause followed by a brief silence. "Talk about what?"

"Lisa, please don't make this harder on me than it already is. Believe me, it took a lot of courage for me to call you. I miss you. I need you and I want to see you," he said, his voice cracking.

Lisa's heart filled with joy. Mark had surrendered to her. He needed her; he couldn't live without her. She was tempted to drag the conversation on to keep him in suspense but everything inside her screamed of happiness. It was hard to control her emotions. She managed to pause. She heard his muscles tighten; the cigarette smoke that he just drew in was stored up inside of him waiting for her response.

"All right," she said. "Where do you want to meet?"

Mark picked her up the following Saturday evening and took her to an exclusive restaurant. They were seated in a quiet corner, surrounded by the flickering light of candles and ambient sounds of music. Just like before, Mark looked at her through his designer glasses. His gaze was so familiar—a combination of masculinity and tenderness. It made her heart melt.

While the food was being prepared, they danced. Everything was exactly as it was in Lisa's dreams. They were whirling around on the hardwood floor wrapped up in each other arms. Lisa leaned into him; his warm body and his masculine scent evoked amazing feelings of belonging and unity.

"I missed you so much, Lisa," Mark whispered in her ear, burning her skin with his breath.

Lisa pressed tightly to his chest; a sigh of relief escaped her mouth. She had thought the same exact thing except she hadn't said it out loud. She missed him; she loved him; she knew she did. She had never stopped loving him, no matter how hard she had tried. The truth was, she could trick her mind but not her heart. Just the sound of his voice, the feel of his touch, was all it took to reawaken her buried feelings.

The dance finished and Mark walked Lisa back to their table. The wine steward poured wine into their glasses. Mark touched his glass to Lisa's.

"To you, Lisa," he said softly.

To us, Lisa thought as she sipped the wine, *to our future.*

Mark reached out for a cigarette pack, opened it and flicked the bottom with his fingertips. Two cigarettes popped out halfway from the pack. Lisa always wondered how Mark did it. She had tried it many times but the cigarettes would never come out. In a strange way, this ability of Mark was very appealing to her.

Mark reached out with his hand to offer Lisa a cigarette from the pack.

"I quit," Lisa said, barely concealing the pride in her voice. Mark's brows flew up as he paused, searching her. His eyes were full of either astonishment or doubt, Lisa couldn't tell.

"Good for you!" he said, managing a smile.

"What did you want to tell me, Mark?" Lisa asked as she sipped her wine.

Mark refilled his glass with wine, took two big gulps and lit up a cigarette.

"Lisa, after you left I felt miserable. I was so depressed; I didn't think I could keep living."

Lisa felt the urge to take a cigarette and inhale the tar-filled smoke. She had to swallow hard to withhold the urge.

"I must have looked so miserable that my friends felt sorry for me. They set me up on blind dates. You wouldn't believe how many beautiful single women are out there. They were calling and jumping all over me. I didn't know that I was such a catch," he said with a laugh.

"Why not? You're a handsome, well-off bachelor now," Lisa said, barely able to refrain from taking a cigarette.

"Lisa," Mark reached out to cover her hand with his; his voice was hoarse.

"That wasn't my point. I don't care about those women. All I care about is you and only you. Night and day I fantasize about you. I walk and see you beside me. I sleep and see you in my dreams; I wake up and hear your voice. At work or at home, alone or with company, I have to grit on my teeth not to call your name." His hand trembled on hers; his designer glasses were foggy.

Mesmerized, Lisa stared at him. He was saying exactly what she felt about him. He had described her dreams and her feelings.

They left the restaurant wrapped in each other's arms. The whole drive to Mark's apartment Lisa sat at the edge of her seat, resting her cheek on Mark's arm. She felt as if they had never separated and that they had always been together. It had all been just a big nightmare; one bad, awful nightmare. Mark still loved her; he had never stopped loving her. They would reunite and leave their wicked past behind.

They started their new future in his bedroom, on their old bed that was fitted with Lisa's favorite linen sheets. Mark's hands were warm and passionate. His body and scent were so familiar and well-known. Lisa's heart was swept in a rush of love that pulsed throughout her veins. Drowned in the hot waves of pleasure and love, she became unaware of time and space.

Afterwards, they lay in each other's arms, both filled with an amazing sense of serenity. Mark lit up a cigarette and passed it to Lisa, as he used to before.

"I quit, remember?" Lisa said, moving her head away from the cigarette.

"Are you sure?" Mark said, smiling and not taking his hand away.

"Yes, I'm sure. Please take it out of my sight. You're challenging me." Lisa laughed.

Mark dragged on the cigarette.

"You've always been so strong and determined, Lisa. That's what I really like about you," he said.

Lisa rolled over and leaned onto his chest. She softly slid her hand up and down his body. The touch brought warmth and tranquility to her.

The phone interrupted their moment.

Mark picked it up and a wide, lusty smile came across his face. He sat up and lowered his legs to the floor.

"I miss you too," he said into the receiver. "Oh, I was just working late." He stole a sidelong look at Lisa and continued to talk on the phone. "No, now isn't a good time. I'm so tired and I need to wake up early in the morning, but I'll call you tomorrow." He made the sound of a kiss as he hung up the phone, a wide, satisfied smile on his face.

Lisa couldn't believe what she had just heard. Blood rushed to her head and furiously pounded at her temples.

"Was that a woman?" Her voice broke as she asked.

Mark looked at her patiently. "What did you think would happen after you left me, Lisa? That I'd become a monk for the rest of my life?" He drew on his cigarette and came to his feet. "Well, the truth is that I'm not a monk and just like any other man, I have my needs."

Lisa felt like she was suffocating; she couldn't breathe; the rage was overwhelming. "You just made love to me. I'm still in your bed and you're setting up a date with another woman!"

Mark looked offended. "I wasn't setting up a date with her. I just said that I'd call her tomorrow and nothing more."

Lisa sprang up from the bed and started to grab her clothes off the floor. Her hands were trembling. She was in such a rush to get dressed that she couldn't manage to get her hands into the right sleeves. In fury, she almost tore her shirt apart as she finally yanked it over her head.

"Come on Lisa!" Mark reached out to put his hand on her shoulder. Disgusted, she jerked away from his hand.

His left brow went up. "It was my old girlfriend, what did you expect me to say to her? Did you want me to be rude to the woman I shared my bed with?" His stare was calm and innocent.

The sudden comprehension struck Lisa. Mark was a sick man, and it wasn't all due to depression. He was crazy. He was mad.

Scowling, she managed to squeeze out through her teeth. "Don't twist things around. You called me and dragged me out to a restaurant. You said that you still loved me and missed me. I thought you wanted all of us to get back together. We made love, and now you're telling me that you didn't know what else to say to that woman while the bed sheets were still warm from our bodies?"

Mark looked at her, stunned. "If you thought that I was going to take you back right on the spot, then you were wrong, Lisa." His gaze looked sympathetic to her naiveté. "Yes, I did miss you; your touch, your voice. I missed your magical aura, which had always energized and invigorated me. I've never met a woman in my life who has had such an effect on me." He paused, and then smiled at her. "There's a definite chemistry and attraction between us. But, don't you think for one moment that it's enough to start a life together again. Look, we already lived together and it didn't work out. Let's not be hasty. Let's take things slow and see how everything unravels."

His reasoning, as always, was clear and logical. Lisa rubbed her temples with her hands. She worried for her sanity.

"You're a piece of work," was all she could say. She had to hurry; she had to run from him before she went mad. "Just take me home," she said. "No, call a cab, just call a damn cab now!" And as he kept standing there, she grabbed the phone, called a cab herself and rushed toward the door. At the door, she paused.

"I don't want to see you again, Mark, ever. I don't want to hear from you or know anything about you for the rest of my life." Her voice was distinct and firm. She meant what she said and she wanted to make sure that it was clear to him.

"Never say never, Lisa. Wait till you desperately need a shoulder to lean on, and then see that there's nobody there for you." There was either a sort of threat, or a last act of desperation in his voice. Lisa couldn't tell.

With a sidelong glance she saw Mark grinning at her, but his face was pale.

Lisa said nothing. She opened the door, then closed it firmly behind her.

CHAPTER THIRTY-FIVE

Lisa whipped open the door to the taxicab and hopped inside. A simple thought filled her mind: Mark was a madman, an evil madman. Everything was crystal clear now. She was bewildered how she could've been so blind around him all this time. He said he missed her aura. Of course he did! He needed to feed off it. He sucked up her energy like a vampire would suck up blood.

Lisa buried her face in her hands. Images of her life with Mark started to roll past in her head. The events she recalled now were revealed under a new light.

Lisa remembered everything about the night when he made her quit her job. Mark asked her not to go to work. He made it crystal clear to her that he didn't think her job was good for her. He stated that he wanted her to quit her job for good. He didn't ask Lisa's opinion but simply made an ultimatum. He played with her mind, threatening to leave. She thought that he was an old-fashioned man who knew what was in the best interest for his woman. She thought that his concerns were about her best interests, when in fact he was only concerned about himself. He wanted her to become dependent upon him. He wanted her to have no rights to fight with him. He planted fear inside her. He wanted her to stay in constant fear, believing that she was nothing without him.

Lisa recalled the long, exhausting evenings that were spent drinking coffee, smoking, and talking. She remembered the long conversations in which he shared his pain and dissatisfaction with life. She would put all of her energy into helping him cope with it. At the end, she would feel worn out but Mark would be happier and stronger. She thought that she was helping him but the truth was that he didn't need her help. He needed her energy and he would do whatever it took to have her release it.

He wanted her to stay in constant fear, believing that she was nothing without him and that she couldn't survive without him. He made her dependent upon him by taking away her job and money, and made her fear the fact that he could leave at any time he wanted. He kept her on a tight leash and when he thought the leash became weak, he divorced her, expecting her to crawl back and never break out of the leash again. He played games with her mind and heart in his sick, twisted way.

Lisa realized that no matter how hard she had tried, their marriage had never had a chance. No marriage had a chance with Mark. He just kept the relationship going until he saw no more use in it and then without any mercy he would throw his victim away.

He had never loved her. He didn't even know what love was. He measured it with the amount of power he could gain from it.

She was his victim. Lisa crossed her legs and looked through the window. Why had he chosen her? What was there about her that assured him that he would be able to manipulate and abuse her? He must have thought from the first moment they met that she was the type of soil that matched his plant. He must have felt that her aura had an endless supply of energy and compassion ready to be released to him.

He had an unexplainable power over her. He was in such darkness that it radiated to her in the form of nightmares and fears. Dreadful goosebumps ran all over Lisa's skin as she thought of what would have happened to Irving if she had left him with Mark. She thanked God for helping her find a way to take Irving with her and break away from Mark's curse.

***

A month later it was May, and Lisa's spring semester was coming to an end. She put all of her will into her studies and completed the semester on the best note possible.

She had only two prerequisites left and decided to take them in the summer. This way she would be able to apply for the physical therapy program right away and, if admitted, would start school in the upcoming fall. Lisa wondered what she should do with Irving so he wouldn't be home alone the whole summer. There wasn't much to think about since they didn't have many choices. All of Irving's friends were going to a camp located in a nearby park. Irving was very excited about the idea. This was the best possible solution for both of them. Lisa signed Irving up for camp and enrolled herself in the summer semester. They had everything planned and figured out.

The summer was beautiful. Tall green trees swayed over the roads, creating cool shade. Colorful flowers bloomed, giving off fresh, rejuvenating scents. It was warm and sunny outside, and inside Lisa felt the same way. Sometimes her fears and nightmares would return, making her wake up in the middle of the night covered in sweat. However, she now knew how to battle them. She understood that this darkness came from Mark, who was calling out to her, and that she should just ignore it. This realization helped her calm down, go back to sleep and wake up in the morning, free from the nightmares.

***

Her life continued on the right path. Lisa did well in school. She was at the top of both of her classes. Her relationships with Sandy, Kristina and Sonya grew stronger. At work, she became acquainted with her clientele and received well-earned appreciation. She was also happy for Irving. He loved his summer camp. He became tan and looked stronger and taller. Every day he brought home exciting stories about field trips, swimming activities, games and competitions. Everything was coming together.

And then Mark called her one night when she was getting ready for bed.

"Do you think about me at all, Lisa?"

"What? Why are you calling me, Mark? What do you want?" Lisa's heart pounded in her chest.

"You have the nerve to ask me that?"

Lisa gasped for air. She felt a rush of blood coming to her face. "You've never asked me how I am, or if I'm alive at all." Mark's voice was filled with authentic indignation.

Lisa was speechless. She couldn't believe what she had just heard. The man who had manipulated her into a jobless, moneyless existence and then divorced her, was now accusing her of being negligent to him. This was outrageous. Lisa couldn't comprehend his way of thinking. It was impossible to even try to understand it and stay sane at the same time.

"Why did you call me? What do you want?" she managed to repeat her questions calmly.

"I want to get together so we can talk."

"There's nothing to talk about, Mark."

"Who do you think you are, Lisa? You think you're going to make it without me? You're wrong; you're nothing without me. Hasn't life taught you anything?" His voice was full of anger. "You'll never pull it off. You're poor. You don't have any money. You're heading straight to the bottom of a pit and you're taking Irving with you. Come back to me, Lisa. You can't survive without me. For once, don't let your pride own you. Let's meet up, Lisa. Let's talk. If not for yourself, then at least do it for Irving."

Her fury was white hot, but at the same time, she knew that he was speaking out of desperation.

"Don't worry about us. We're none of your concern, Mark," she said.

There was a long silence on the other end of the wire, and then he spoke. His voice was weak and could barely be heard. "I can't live without you Lisa. I need you. I'll end my life if you don't come back to me."

191

"I'll never come back to you, Mark; you have to accept that. Take care of yourself. Please never call us again."

She hung up the phone and sat there for a while longer, holding the phone in between her legs and mindlessly staring into space. Then she dialed a number.

"This is Connie," a nice polite voice answered.

Lisa coughed. "Hi Connie, this is Lisa."

After a brief silence, she sensed Connie's lips purse.

"Is there something you want?" Connie asked finally.

The truth was that Lisa didn't know what she wanted. She just knew that she had to make this call. This was the last thing she would do for Mark.

"I just spoke with Mark. He's very depressed. He needs somebody to be around him."

"What does she want?" Lisa heard Jerome's voice in the background. "Tell her that Mark doesn't need her, that it's Irving he misses and needs. He treated him like his own son." Lisa's blood exploded into her temples.

"You should go back to him. This would be best for you and your son. Irving blossomed around Mark. They had a great relationship and you took it away from them," Connie said patiently. Lisa took a long deep breath.

"I'm not going back to him," she said succinctly. "This is not why I called. Mark's depressed and he needs attention. I think you two, as his friends, should know that."

She heard Jerome take the phone from Connie; his voice sounded softer.

"I can't always put a pillow under him if he falls. What is meant to be is meant to be. No one can be held responsible for him." Jerome paused, then asked. "Is there anything else you want to inform me about, Lisa?"

Lisa shook her head. She had said everything she wanted to say. This was the last thing she could do for Mark.

"No. That's it. Goodbye, Jerome." She hung up the phone. Then she turned back under the covers and fell asleep.

Lisa had a dream that night. She was sitting in a moving train looking out the window. It was a gorgeous day outside. The train passed by infinite fields of golden wheat that swayed in a gentle breeze. Colorful wildflowers bloomed alongside the track. Lisa breathed in the invigorating scent of nature.

Then, big heavy clouds appeared in the sky, blocking the sun. Darkness started to fall. The golden wheat gradually turned into grayish, dry grass, which yielded to the hostile wind. Everything moved slowly and seemed unrealistic. It was as if they were carried into a parallel universe.

Suddenly, an oncoming train blocked the panorama. Lisa looked into the cart and could clearly make out faces. One cabin froze right in front of her. A handsome, broad-shouldered man with long wavy hair smiled at her through the window. He looked directly into her eyes. His look emitted warmth and tenderness. It seemed to call out to her. Lisa couldn't take her eyes off him. She felt an incredible urge to stand up and walk over to that man. Charmed, she kept staring at him.

Both of the trains were still frozen. The man in the other train across from her didn't move. He just continued to smile at her. His expression was a mixture of irony and confidence. Lisa understood that she had no other choice but to go to him. This realization sent her body into a cold sweat. She felt there was something wrong about him, that he was some sort of a trap. She didn't know what he was, but she knew that she shouldn't go to him. And yet, her body leaned forward to him. It was pulled by some intangible magnetic force. Lisa gathered all of her strength and resisted the force with all of her might. She stood still. She didn't move.

All of a sudden there was a loud rumble. Everything became pitch black. Lisa's train was now entering a tunnel. The other train was still outside, slowly falling behind. Lisa noticed a dramatic change in the man. His shoulders slumped down, his face turned pale. The man's eyes no longer called out to her.

Her train passed through the tunnel and brought Lisa out into the light. She stuck her head out the window and looked back at the tunnel. The last car of the other train was barely in the light. There was a person sitting on the roof of it facing her. Lisa looked closer and saw that it was the man from the cabin. He was squatting on the end of the train. His long wavy hair was no longer there. He was bald, his nose holding up glasses. His lips were curved with an ironic smile. For a moment, the sun illuminated him and Lisa saw two horns sticking out from his head. Then a shadow covered him and his train gradually faded away.

Lisa woke up and curled her legs on the bed. The dream had seemed so real, and she couldn't stop thinking about it. She was sure that it was Mark sitting on the roof of that train. The horns on his head flashed in her memory. She knew that it was him. He came from there, from the world of darkness, and he had wanted to take her there with him. Lisa stared thoughtfully in the space in front of her. Mark did possess an inexplicable power over her and she had walked a long way into the darkness with him. But Mark had underestimated her. She was able to find the strength and stop at the edge of the cliff. He couldn't make her take the last step. He couldn't defeat her.

***

There was only one brief moment when Lisa saw Mark again. She was buying groceries at the store and bumped into him. Mark was wearing tight blue jeans and a hand-knitted sweater that outlined his muscular body.

"Hi Lisa, you look great," he said, smiling, studying her from head to toe.

"Hi Mark." Lisa smiled back at him. She noticed that he looked very handsome. Mark continued studying her.

Lisa flinched under his direct stare and looked away. "I'm in a great hurry," she mumbled. "I have to buy more things and be at work soon."

Mark didn't say anything. He just silently followed her with his eyes as she walked away. She felt his stare on her back until she went around the corner to another section. She stopped there and took a deep breath. All of her feelings and memories about him were stirred up again in her heart. She was afraid that if she stood next to him for another second, she would fall into his embrace and lean against that knitted sweater just to feel the warmth of his body again, and the strength of his arms. She ran away from him, but the truth was that she was trying to run away from herself to escape her inexplicable, mysterious attraction to him.

Lisa wondered for a long time about the unbelievable power that Mark had had over her. It was a mystery to her how she would ever get Mark out of her heart.

CHAPTER THIRTY-SIX

In the middle of August Lisa received a letter of acceptance from her top-choice Physical Therapy school. She read it while sitting at the table. "Congratulations! You have been accepted into our physical therapy program..." This letter was her well-earned reward. She knew that she was getting closer to her goal.

The physical therapy program started in September. The schedule was very intense. Lisa had to cut her hours at work to just Saturdays and Sundays since her classes were Monday through Friday from 8 a.m. to 5 p.m. Her curriculum included Science, Anatomy labs, practice classes and supervised clinical experience. Lisa studied biomechanics, neuroanatomy, human growth and development, manifestations of disease, examination techniques, and therapeutic procedures. She learned muscular, skeletal and cardiovascular systems both in theory and on a human cadaver. In the practice classes she received hands-on experience by practicing the various physical therapy techniques and equipment on other students. Performing a massage was a part of the physical therapy treatment and everybody turned to her for help since she was a professional massage therapist. The teachers always used her as an example to show others how she performed the massage. Lisa became very popular. Other students liked being in her group. They would practice and gather after school to study together.

The program was extremely demanding. It required a lot of effort and studying. Still, Lisa liked what the program taught her. It inspired her to think about this great profession and how she could, one day, help other people.

Lisa studied day and night, always aiming for her goal. Two years passed, and at last, she graduated, passed the licensure exam and received her physical therapy license. Her hard work had finally paid off.

Lisa invited Sandy, Kristina, and Sonya to a restaurant where she and a few of her close classmates were celebrating. They were seated at a cozy table right across from a pianist, who played exhilarating classical music.

They ate, talked, drank, and laughed. Everything was at its best except that Margaret wasn't there. Lisa missed her. Margaret was her dearest friend. She had played a huge part in Lisa's success and deserved to be there with her. However, Margaret was far away in California and couldn't make it to Chicago. But she had called the day before and said that even though she wasn't going to be there physically she would be there in spirit.

A couple of weeks after the party, Margaret called Lisa again. She announced that there was a great job opportunity for Lisa in one of the largest hospitals in San Diego. All Lisa had to do was send them her resume. She was stunned. Margaret had actually been analyzing the market and had started a job search while Lisa was moving closer to graduation. She couldn't believe that her old friend was serious. Did she expect Lisa to just drop everything and move to California?

Margaret was indeed serious. She came up with a list of benefits that San Diego had over Chicago. She presented statistical and census data. She said that there was a thirty percent greater demand for physical therapy specialists in hospitals and that there were thousands of physical therapy businesses in California. Lisa would never be left without a job there. In addition, San Diego was on the Pacific Ocean where the average year-round temperature was seventy degrees. Margaret asked Lisa to imagine herself and Irving sunbathing near the ocean or in their own backyard pool during any season. Lisa smiled. Margaret knew exactly what to say to win her over. The warm temperature in San Diego was indeed much more appealing to her than the cold and snowy Chicago winters. She also couldn't ignore the fact that San Diego had a higher demand for physical therapists. And living in the same city with her best friend Margaret was a significant factor itself.

The idea that at first seemed ridiculous now became an essential step. The more Lisa thought about it, the more she liked the idea. She spoke to Irving and was surprised by his enthusiasm and excitement about moving to another city. Although he wasn't too happy about leaving his neighborhood and his friends behind, the thought of an adventure in a city by the ocean was irresistible to him. If she had any doubts remaining, Irving cleared them up.

Lisa sent her resume to the hospital Margaret had recommended and was surprised to get an offer within a week. Then she called and told Margaret to expect her in San Diego approximately by the end of June. Margaret was ecstatic. She began searching for an apartment in time for Lisa's arrival and Lisa started preparing for her move. She had to find a new tenant for her apartment, close her bills, take care of Irving's school transfer, make goodbye visits to her friends, and pack. She found that leaving this city was going to be easy. Lisa had no regrets or doubts.

"Please fasten your seat belts," said the flight attendant, interrupting Lisa's dream. She stretched in her seat, fastened her seat belt, and then glanced over to Irving. He was looking out the window, watching the plane descend. Lisa leaned over to look out the window with him. The plane landed with a thump, a squeal of rubber and the roar of reverse-thrusting engines, all of which thoroughly thrilled Irving. In a few minutes the flight attendant announced that passengers could exit the plane.

It was a beautiful, sunny day outside. Lisa spotted Margaret as soon as they walked out of the airport with their luggage. There were lots of hugs full of tears and joy. They were so happy to see each other and Margaret was impatient to bring them to her house. They threw the bags into the trunk of Margaret's red Mustang convertible and headed out of the airport.

They were driving along a road that was covered by patches of shade from beautiful palm trees. The variety of plants and colorful flowers all together looked exotic and magnificent to Lisa's Chicago eye. She enjoyed California's weather and its nature from that first moment.

Margaret made a right turn onto a small, quiet street and soon pulled into her driveway. Lisa stepped out of the car to see a large, white, two-story house surrounded by a beautiful green garden. The place was spectacular. Margaret opened the door and let them inside. They walked into a bright hall that was illuminated by two big skylights. In front of them, all the way across the hall and through the living room was a sliding glass door that led out to the backyard's beautiful pool.

"Can I go swimming in the pool?" Irving asked, full of excitement.

"Sure, Irving. As long as it's fine with your mom." Margaret patted his shoulder.

"Of course it is. I'd also like to see the pool as well," Lisa said, smiling.

"Very well," Margaret said. "Let me show you outside and then I'll go prepare some lemonade."

Margaret grabbed a beach towel from a closet, handed it to Irving, and all of them headed to the pool.

As Lisa stepped out onto the porch, she heard her cell phone ring. She rushed back into the living room where she had put down her purse and pulled out the phone.

"Hi, Lisa. It's Connie."

Lisa's heart lurched with a bad premonition. She felt that something horrible had happened.

"Mark's dead. He died yesterday. He shot himself in the head." Connie's voice trembled. Lisa felt dizzy. She had to lower herself onto the couch.

"I wasn't sure if I should call you or not," Connie continued. "But then I decided that it was my duty to inform you about it. If you think I made a mistake calling you, tell me."

"No, you did the right thing. Thank you for making the call." Lisa said, barely hearing her own voice.

"It was just so horrible. The past couple of days we hadn't heard a thing from Mark. It was very unlike him, he usually called us every day. Jerome tried to reach him on the phone a couple of times but was unsuccessful. Then we became really worried, and yesterday Jerome went over to Mark's place and buzzed his condo. There was no answer. Jerome buzzed and talked to the other neighbors and they decided to call the police. The cops broke into the condo and found Mark laying there with a gun in his right hand. There was blood everywhere...," Connie spoke through her sobs. "Jerome almost went crazy; he couldn't believe what he saw. We're both in shock. We just can't believe Mark did that."

Connie was saying something else but Lisa no longer heard her. She dropped her hand that held the phone and blindly stared in front of her. Margaret walked in with the lemonade and stopped, frozen to the spot in the middle of the living room. She looked frightened.

"Are you okay? Is everything all right?" she asked with concern. Lisa saw Margaret's lips moving but she didn't hear a single word.

Only one thought stayed in her mind. *He let her go. He had finally let her go.*

The End

ABOUT ERIN ASLIN

Erin Aslin grew up in the bustling capital of Kiev, Ukraine, and in 1992, she immigrated with her son, Jerry, to Chicago's North Shore, where she still lives. While she has worked in the corporate world, in Information Technology, her passion has always been in reading and writing. Being on a life-long spiritual search, she has met with spiritual teachers who opened the floodgates to self-recognition that led her to direct experiences of what we call God, the Source of All. Since then her search stopped and her life has never been the same.

With a strong desire to start helping people by applying sacred knowledge she received through revelations and direct experiences, she found her passion in Intuitive Counseling, Quantum Healing Hypnosis, Past Life Regression and other energy modalities, thus empowering her clients to change their lives for the better. Her clairvoyant abilities, clear guidance, and compassionate nature help her to assist her clients in shifting their vibrational energy to a higher frequency; hence, steering their lives in a more positive direction. She offers tools, insights, and support that inspires and leads to personal growth and lasting transformation.

Erin also produces and posts videos on her YouTube channel on the topics of spirituality and awakening, as well as messages to humanity from a Higher Power– either through her channeling or segments from her client sessions.

Through the Clouds is her debut novel. It is a story that she felt was inside her and that she needed to share. She hopes the story of Lisa Trubin inspires and helps many women out there who find themselves in similar situations to break through the "darkness" and emerge with their hearts open to love and life again.